GENESIS

Eilís Barrett

Gill Books

Gill Books
Hume Avenue
Park West
Dublin 12
www.gillbooks.ie

Gill Books is an imprint of M.H. Gill & Co.

9780 7171 7435 5
Designed by www.grahamthew.ie
Typesetting by O'K Graphic Design, Dublin
Edited by Rachel Pierce
Proofread by Emma Dunne
Printed by Clays Ltd, Suffolk

This book is typeset in 11/17 pt Plantin
Section heads in Neutra text bold

The paper used in this book comes from the wood pulp of managed forests. For every tree felled, at least one tree is planted, thereby renewing natural resources.

A CIP catalogue record for this book is available from the British Library.

To Andrew, the calm in the storm.

About the Author

Eilís Barrett is 18 and hails from Galway, on Ireland's west coast, where she shares a home with her mother, three brothers and her dog, Rosie. Passionate about all things literary, she can usually be found reading or writing stories filled with action, adventure and true love. When she's not working on a new story or reading Jane Austen, she plays the piano, on which she is self-taught.

At the age of 15, Eilís signed a two-book deal with Gill Books. She has since spoken at Eason's inaugural Irish YA convention and was honoured by *Irish Tatler* as a Future Maker, one of the young women they believe have the brilliance to shape the next era, as well as being named one of *The Irish Times'* 50 people to watch in 2017. *Genesis* is her second novel and is the sequel to the critically acclaimed *Oasis*. For more information, visit www.eilisbarrett.com.

PART ONE

HELL

1

It's been six months. Six months since I've seen anything outside of this place.

Six months ago – I was in the Celian City, pushing Aaron, the boy I used to love, in front of me, my fingers vice-like around the gun in my pocket, attempting to do the unthinkable.

A night before that – I was awake in the middle of the night, barefoot and cold, but human. So acutely aware of my humanity as I pressed closer to Kole, my fingers in his hair and my heartbeat in my temples and his mouth pressed to mine.

But in the time that separates then from now, humanity has begun to feel a lot less concrete. I press closer to the stone walls of my cell, trying to ignore the blisters on my feet and the bloody, bruised numbness of the rest of my body. In this suffocating space I try to push myself back to a time when I could breathe. When the cold felt less like the slow, methodical thud of death's approach, and being awake didn't mean trying to block out the sound of wailing things beyond the walls of my cell. When I felt my humanity like air in my lungs, like blood in my veins, like thin but tightly held hope.

Because terror used to feel like a knife and a gun and gripping to life with bloodied fingers. Now, it just feels like consciousness.

2

My hands didn't shake enough after I shot him. I stared down at them, and they were covered in blood, which didn't make any sense. I wasn't that close to him. I wasn't that close – I remembered that. But he was right in front of me then, at my feet, and his blood was staining my boots and my fingers and the gun, and my hands were trembling so hard that the gun fell to the floor beside him. But it's not enough. It should have been worse. I should have been shaking so badly that I tore apart. Because that's what it felt like. It felt like I was being torn apart.

I squeezed my eyes shut, tightening my shaking hands into fists, and slipped to the floor beside him. I imagined that if I closed my eyes tightly enough that it would all have been a dream, and I would wake up somewhere far from the Celian City, where the floor wasn't stained with blood.

'Quincy?' a tentative voice asked, and my eyes shot open.

The light was different then, muted, and it threw strange shadows across the face in front of me, but it didn't stop me from recognising him immediately.

'Kole.' He pulled me up by my hands, and I collapsed against him, breathing like a drowning person who had just found the surface.

'It's okay,' he whispered, and he was warmer than anything else in the world. He guided my face towards his own, but the second his lips connected with mine, a shockwave ran through me.

I pulled back, turning around. I knew this place. I'd been here before. The narrow hallway, barely lit by an open door several feet from us. I was barefoot and cold and I was panicking, and he appeared when I needed him, because that's what he always did.

It felt right. All of it felt right, except the fact that I'd felt this before. I'd been here before, in this hall with him before everything unravelled—

'Quincy, stop panicking,' he cooed, drawing me closer, pulling my arms to rest around his neck. 'I can tell when you're panicking.'

My response died in my throat when I saw cold blue eyes staring back at me.

'Aaron?' I wanted to bite the word back. I was going insane. This wasn't happening. I was going insane.

But he didn't get mad. He didn't accuse me of insanity or look at me like I'd lost my mind. He didn't even look confused.

He smiled, and he tilted his head to the side, and his smile wasn't his perfect smile anymore because the blood filling his mouth was leaking out between his teeth and staining them red. It poured down his chin and he started babbling around it, cooing to me in garbled strings of words that made no sense, and I tried to pull away, but I couldn't because my hands were locked around his throat and he wouldn't stop smiling. Why wouldn't he stop smiling at me? Why wouldn't he stop?

I woke up cold. The kind of cold that seeps into your bones and slows your heart, the kind of cold that makes you want to just lie still, fall asleep and never wake up again. But when I finally forced my eyes to open, I was met with complete darkness, and the fear that spiked through me had me crawling onto my hands and knees, pushing myself up so I could stand.

The ground beneath was slick, and I had to reach out and catch myself against the wall so I wouldn't fall. Bending my head back, I tried to look up, but the room was too dark to see the ceiling. I took a shaky step away from the wall, and my footsteps echoed, causing me to go still again.

I took another small step forward, and another and another, until I met the next wall, too quickly. Whatever room they had me in was small, small enough that I could cross it in two or three steps. I slid back onto the floor then, scraping my fingers through my hair as I forced an unsteady breath through my lips.

The longer I sat there, the colder it got, and the colder it got, the closer the walls felt around me, like they were slowly edging in to crush me. My breathing became shallow and I rolled to my knees, pressing my hands against the floor, which was hard and cold and damp, just like the wall.

'It's okay,' I told myself. 'I fixed it. He's safe. They're safe.'

I told myself that was all that mattered. I knew what I was doing when I forced Kole to leave me there in that elevator, knew what that would mean. All that had mattered to me in that moment was knowing that he was safe, and knowing that he would get Sophi out with him.

It was all that had mattered to me then, but in this unfathomable place, shivering and scared, I began to feel it like seeping cold. Achingly familiar, the regret rose up, and it dragged my guilt up with it.

3

I'm hungry. I'm always hungry. It feels like something separate from me, a gnawing, greedy beast within me, screeching and howling for relief.

I shuffle barefoot along gravelly sand, and I order my brain to believe that I can't feel the maddening stinging as grains of sand grate along the wounds on the soles of my feet. I tell myself I can't feel it, will the searing pain away, but it doesn't leave me. It shoots up my legs with each painful step.

I hear a sound to my left and I turn too fast, vision blurring as I reach out towards nothing to steady myself. It's just a buzzard. My vision slowly refocuses and I breathe deeply with relief, even though my stomach turns at the sight of the huge bird picking away at the fresh carcass.

Human carcass. A boy, too young to be in here. Too stupid to stay alive.

I keep moving, tightening my hand on the knife inside my pocket. There's got to be something I can find here. There's no chance of finding food, but maybe something I can trade. A weapon, or a tool, or something that would be valued on the Outside. No one really cares about things like that in here, but sometimes Tao does, if it's good enough.

But the place has been scraped clean. The bodies have been raided, first of goods and then, remembering the buzzard, of flesh. It's been too long since the last shipment of food. Everyone is half-starved and half-mad and fully ready to kill for what they need.

My fingers glide over the knife in my pocket. It's worn and not the sharpest, but it's the most precious thing I have. I don't want to have to trade it, but there's no use in having a knife if you're dead.

I give up. I'm not going to find anything, and I'm not willing to be out here in the middle of the day. During the day, exposed by the light, you're more likely to have your throat slit than find your next meal.

When I return to my cell there's a man standing in the centre of the floor and my stomach curls with fear.

'Get out.' My voice doesn't shake, but my hand does, gripping my knife within my pocket. 'Get out of my room.'

'This ain't your room.' His smile is yellow, his lips cracked and bleeding as they stretch around his teeth. 'This is everyone's room.'

'I said, get out.' I move further inside, past the railings that separate my cell from the rest of the Colosseum, and walk over to my corner. There's a strange blanket and some ratty clothes left on the makeshift bed and I bristle. I pick them up and throw them at him, hitting him square in the chest.

'Get out of here before I skin you alive.' I pull the knife out.

His eyes go wide, showing the bloodshot whites of his eyes.

'I don't want no trouble,' he mumbles.

He did want trouble, I think, as he stumbles out the door, almost tripping over his clothes on the way. But he wanted trouble with the defenceless, not someone with a knife and the will to use it.

This has been happening more and more frequently. It feels like every time I return to my cell, some new idiot is trying to take it. There aren't enough cells in the prison for everyone, so most people end up sleeping in the big communal areas or out in the open, both of which are dangerous. Groups of looters go around during the night, robbing those too stupid or too naive to sleep with one eye open.

I haven't slept deeply since I first arrived here. It's not worth a few hours' sleep to wake up with nothing.

'Hey.'

I turn around as Clarke walks into the room, her eyes snagging on the knife in my hand.

'I'm fine,' I say, putting the knife back into my pocket. All the inmates wear the same thing: a pair of trousers and a tunic made in matching, thin material. It does little to stand up against the rough wear of the Colosseum, but at least the loose fabric conceals the knife.

Clarke ignores what I actually said in favour of whatever it is she's reading off me, as usual.

'What's going on?'

'Nothing. There are just too many people in this damn prison.'

'How many people is a good amount of people for a prison?' she asks, dropping down into the corner and leaning her head against the wall.

'Most of the people out there deserve this place.'

'But not you,' she says, staring at me.

I might get mad if I thought she actually meant it, but I know she doesn't. Besides, she wouldn't be in here if it weren't for me, so I can't help but let it slide.

'When did you leave?' she asks as I move to sit beside her.

'An hour ago.'

'I was here an hour ago.' She turns to look at me. 'You weren't here.'

'Oh.' My heart drops a little. 'It must have been earlier then. The seasons are changing – it's hard to tell the time.'

She keeps looking at me, watching, her eyes analytical as I twitch beneath her steady gaze. She nods, but I can tell she's not convinced.

I know what she's thinking. That this isn't the first time this has happened. That this isn't even the first time this has happened this week. Time is a strange beast within these walls for everyone, but there's a difference between forgetting what time it is and losing time. Suddenly being somewhere and not knowing how you got there.

'Still no sign of the shipment,' she murmurs a few minutes later, moving her focus from me to sharpening her knife with that damned stone she carries around in her pocket.

I can tell that she's trying to take the pressure off me, but still I don't respond. The shipments she's talking about are the deliveries of food into the prison. It's supposed to be every four weeks, but it regularly slips into the fifth or sixth, or even seventh. And since they only give us the bare minimum to begin with, a late shipment leads to starving inmates, and starving inmates leads to irritable, violent inmates.

More violent than usual.

'How much longer?' I ask, not even turning to look at her. I shouldn't be asking at all. It's not the first time I've asked her this week, and I know that she doesn't know, but I can't help asking anyway.

The prison is built much like Oasis itself, with two seemingly impenetrable outer walls wrapping around it, but instead of the beautiful Celian City, we're gifted with the Colosseum, a bowl-like building with two layers of cells, no food and an open centre where inmates wander without any supervision or control. We are the most hated people in Oasis; the ones they want to forget, but not before we suffer. Without Officers there is no one to keep control, and with no one to keep control, we live on the brink of vicious anarchy. They throw us in here and leave us to our own devices, knowing, hoping, we'll tear each other apart. It's like a cage of wild animals left to wreak havoc on each other.

I never would have thought an open cell could be more terrifying than a locked door.

If we were on our own, there would be no chance of getting out. But while I was in the Celian City, with Aaron and Kole and Jay, Clarke was creating a back-up plan. Her pessimism has become the only chance we have of escaping this place.

The past six months stretch out behind me like a series of slightly altered photographs. Nothing much has changed from the first week, and yet the torture of being stuck here feels a little more acute with each passing day. I should be able to stay focused. To stay present. With criminals and murderers surrounding me at all times, I should be able to force myself out of the past. But I can't. All I can think about is what happened and what I'm going to do when I get back out. Find Sophi, Kole, Jay and the others, kill the OP, like I should have done months ago, and rip Oasis apart in the process.

'What was that?' Clarke asks.

'What?'

'That face. You keep making that face.'

'Nothing.' I shake my head, but there's no amount of shaking that can rid my mind of their faces. The OP's, as I stood before him with a gun pointed at his head. Sophi's, as I left her with Nails, a fog of promises hanging in the air between us. And Kole's, a million images folding in on top of each other – the night before we left for Oasis, the night he kissed me in the hall, my last memory of him as we stood in that elevator, the air filled with fear and grief and something else I was too afraid to admit.

'Nothing,' I say again, and it feels like a punch in the gut.

4

Six months ago I chose to step out of an elevator and into the arms of the enemy. There was a fierce calm then, and it was such a tangible thing, such a presence surrounding me, that when I stepped out over a dozen Celian City Officers just stared at me. Suddenly uncertain. They expected me to scream, to thrash and pitch for the door towards some imagined ability to escape the City of Light, but I was never that stupid.

Instead I tightened my grip, on my own gun and on the one I had taken from him, and I gritted my teeth in the resolution that if I was going down, I was bringing as many of them down with me as I could.

I had told Kole – beautiful, naive Kole, still hopeful that we might complete our grand escape – that we'd find each other afterwards, but I wasn't really sure which 'after' I meant. Because at the time, I was naive too. In a different, bloodier way than Kole was, but naive still. I thought I would step out from behind those steel doors and blood would spill, mine along with theirs, and I would die in Oasis, in a hail of bullets and righteous anger.

I imagined myself a hero. I would not do much, but I would die with more of their blood on my hands than they could draw from me. And that would be enough.

But they didn't fight back. They didn't unload their weapons into my chest or drain my blood out on to the pristine floors of the Justice Tower. They pushed me against the too-white walls, disengaged my weapon from my hands with an ease that echoed Kole's skill, and then there was a pinch at my neck and my consciousness slid off me like water sluicing off a roof.

Only two. Afterwards, I couldn't stop thinking about that. I only shot two of them – one in the chest, one in the leg – and then they had me.

I had never imagined it would end so simply.

5

I don't sleep at night. At first, it was because I was too scared to. The prison is already a dangerous place, and when the darkness descends it feels impossible to protect yourself. But after a while you realise that sleeping means being vulnerable. In the Colosseum, being vulnerable means being dead.

I glance down at Clarke. She's still asleep, and has been for four hours. I want to wake her because the sun's coming up and I'm exhausted, but she doesn't usually sleep this long. She probably needs it more than I do.

So instead of waking her I stare at my hands, tapping out rhythms between my fingertips as I wonder how much longer it will take for me to go insane.

Or maybe I'm already insane. It's hard to tell sometimes.

Clarke told me that long ago they used something called Morse code, a form of communication based entirely on various signal combinations with corresponding letters. Sometimes it was flashes of light, sometimes it was clicks. Sometimes it was just tapping.

I imagine that this half-mad habit of tapping my fingertips together is Morse code. Go back and forth between different combinations and pretend someone can understand me. Sometimes I even try to make up meanings behind different combinations, but I never remember them for long.

Nothing exists in here for long.

Is this insanity? Easing a chattering mind with meaningless tics? Or does insanity come after this? How much longer do I have before I'm screaming and clawing at my own skin?

Time doesn't mean anything in here. There's the vague sense we get of time based on the light coming and going, but it's hazy and it recedes the longer you are here. I brush my fingers against the scummy wall beside my head, touching each scratch mark, each miserable attempt at keeping track of how many days have passed since we were put here.

I lean my head back against the wall and try to push the world around me far enough away to catch my breath. I can hear shouts outside, probably another fight breaking out, but it's not unusual enough to draw my attention away. Instead I unfold the escape plan in my head, like a worn map.

It's simple. Nails has a contact within the Officers who operate the Colosseum's security. When the food shipment arrives outside the gates, an alarm will be set off, giving us less than a minute to slip through and into the truck, where we will be given a uniform and an

ID, just enough to get us past security. Somewhere on the outside, someone would find us. Give us food, supplies, a plan.

It's simple. Simple, and maybe almost impossible, but it was the only chance we had.

I don't know what Clarke gave him so that he would help us like this, but she says he agreed easily enough. And yet, here we are. Six months later. We have one opportunity every month, and it's been missed five times.

'Quincy?' Clarke groans, rolling onto her back. 'What the hell are you doing?'

I freeze. I've started thumping the back of my head against the wall, as if it will shake out the doubts clawing their way through my thoughts. I'm anxious. I'm always anxious when delivery day is on the horizon.

'I'm sorry,' I say quietly, squeezing my eyes closed. 'I'm just worried.'

'No, really?' she says.

'You know that it's possible to respond to people with something other than sarcasm, right?'

'Oh no, really? All this time I thought it was the only way.'

I shoot her a withering look, which she ignores, as she slowly sits up beside me.

'I'm awake now,' she huffs after a minute or two, pulling her hair back. 'You can sleep if you need to.'

I need to, that's for sure, but whether I can or not is arguable.

'Do you think he's forgotten?' I ask suddenly. Sometimes when it's dark and the prison is unusually quiet, the things you're most afraid of just slip out, like the world is finally the same colour as the place inside of you that holds your fears, and you can't tell the difference between inside and outside anymore.

'Who's forgotten?' Clarke sounds tired, resigned. She knows the process, the way my mind twists in the dark when I'm exhausted, and though she pretends not to, she already knows what I'm talking about.

'Nails,' I say. 'Do you think he's forgotten that he promised to help?'

'No, Quincy, he hasn't forgotten.'

While fear swells within me, anger is growing in Clarke. She doesn't doubt for a second that Nails remembers his promise. In her mind, every month passed is another betrayal, another month he's forcing us to live in here.

I don't know how to respond, so I let it go. And as with a lot of things in here, we're left with nothing but intangible hope.

Clarke sighs. 'Until it happens, we just have to look out for ourselves. That's all that's left.'

She makes it sound so easy.

6

Tao controls the food distribution within the Colosseum. As much as Victor would like to think he has just as much power in here, he knows that's not true, and so does everyone else.

There are two gangs in here, and Victor and Tao are the leaders. Rivalry between them is intense – for food and for members.

Alliances between the gangs change over time – new members are taken in and die, old members are betrayed and return for revenge – but Victor and Tao remain steady. They earned their place long before Clarke and I arrived, and they hold onto it with tight fists.

Victor is dangerous and vicious, but Tao is cunning. He knows when to play nicely. So once the food is delivered it's split between the two gangs, almost evenly.

Almost. Tao is also smart enough to know that dominance is something that must be constantly reaffirmed within the Colosseum. As long as Tao's dominance goes unquestioned, everything is fine. For the time we've been in here, Victor has accepted that state of affairs. The gangs coexist peacefully enough, considering the situation. People live and die by Tao and Victor's hands every day, but there hasn't been a gang war in years.

Inside the Colosseum, that qualifies as peace.

Once the food is split, there are two ways to get some: you either trade goods or you trade services.

Some jobs – stealing supplies, killing and doing recon on the opposite gang – are well paid and could keep Clarke and me in food for weeks. Others, like teaching a newbie a lesson or even coercing them into a particular gang, doesn't last us until the end of the week.

Of course, there is a third option. Joining one of the gangs comes with benefits – you don't go hungry, you get to sleep in the guarded upper rooms and you're provided with weapons.

But there are downsides as well. The second you sign on, the leaders own you. Loyalty is prized above everything else, and Tao is indiscriminate when it comes to killing people he suspects of being disloyal. Plus you owe a debt, and I'm not interested in owing a debt to anyone, especially not these people.

Gang rules are simple: do what the leader tells you to do, never attack your own gang members and if you try to leave, you die. None of which I can comply with. None of which I can risk even pretending to comply with. I can't get tied down in here. There's no point. All it will do is make it harder to get out, and I already have enough chips stacked against me.

The heat of the sun pelts down onto the sandy earth beneath us, and stragglers wander the common barefoot, begging and yelling in turns. They won't get any sympathy here. I look down at my own bare feet, wishing for a pair of shoes. Those were traded last cycle, when we ran out of food and everyone was too hungry to care about new members or old feuds.

With Clarke beside me, we walk straight through the common and into the west cells, where the less gruesome of the two gang leaders holds his court. We walk in silence until we reach the last flight of stairs. Clarke stops me with a hand on my shoulder.

'Watch it,' she says. By which she means, be careful, be on your guard, be safe. Sometimes things come out of Clarke's mouth rougher than she means them, and sometimes they come out just as rough as she means them.

You learn to tell the difference after a while.

I nod wordlessly, and we continue on. We're met at the door by two surly looking guards, and when they see it's us, they push us roughly into the next room. There we're disarmed and then brought into Tao's room.

Tao's room is a mismatched amalgamation of everything that comes into this prison that he decides is valuable. The Officers don't care what you bring in with you, as long as you can't use it to escape, so people turn up with everything from knives to extra clothes to random knick-knacks.

The photos, though, they're his favourite. One wall of the room is lined with photographs of families, of individuals and couples, children, parents, grandparents – he doesn't care who's in the picture, it seems, he just wants to own them. He demands something of value from every new member of the gang, and for a lot of people that means photographs.

They're rare in the Outer Sector. They're an unnecessary expense, but even if they weren't, what would the Dormants take photos of? The Outer Sector and everyone in it is filthy, depressed and decaying. Few people want reminders of that.

A lot of the pictures are from the Inner Sector. Perfect family photos set before perfect white houses with perfect children in a line. A lot of the time, those photos come from men and women thought to be sympathisers of the rebellion. Otherwise, it's just someone who tried to climb the ladder a little too fast and ended up taking something from someone powerful. Sometimes that means another Oasis Government Official. Sometimes it means the Oasis President himself. Sometimes it means *Oasis*.

'Ladies.' Tao grins, splayed out on a couch made from crates and dirty blankets. 'What can I do for you today?'

'We need food,' Clarke says, trying and failing to curb the growl in her voice.

'We want work,' I correct, cutting a glare at Clarke. She has trouble keeping her mouth shut, but we can't risk her getting us in trouble. Not now. Not when shipment day is so close. 'Is there anything you need dealt with?'

We're not the only people who work for Tao. Even the few people who work outside the gangs all come to Tao. He's less likely to cut your throat than Victor, and he tends to pay better too, so people come to him.

But Tao is smarter than he lets on, and he knows the difference between a scalpel and an axe ... and when he needs one over the other.

And that's where we come in.

He turns his head to the side, watching us. His dark hair hangs down his back in a long ponytail, sweat sticking the flyaway hairs to his tanned forehead.

'I have work,' he says slowly, as if considering every possibility. 'But I do not have payment.'

'And why would we work for you if we weren't getting paid?' I ask, careful to measure my tone as I glance around the room. There are almost a dozen other men here, Tao's closest, and they all watch us with bored expressions. They're leaving Clarke and me out in the middle of the floor as an attempt to intimidate us, but we've been through this too many times to be shaken by their scare tactics.

'Because I can offer you something else.' He nods to himself slowly, and I glance at Clarke.

'Like what?' Clarke asks.

'Blindness can be a blessing, depending on what you're doing.'

For a second I think he's talking about me, but then I realise he's talking about himself. That he would be blind. Blind to what?

Unless he's saying he'll ignore something, in which case—

Oh God.

He knows.

He knows, he knows, he knows.

I don't dare to look over at Clarke in case they see something passing between us, but the screaming in my head is so loud I'm afraid Tao can hear it from across the room.

'What do you need us to do?' I try to sound cool and collected, like I'm still weighing up the deal.

How does he know?

Is he the only one?

We haven't done anything in preparation for the escape, so I don't understand how he possibly could have found out.

Unless he's bluffing. Maybe he knows everyone in here is trying to escape in one way or another, and he's just banking on the fact that I'll get spooked and work for free.

'There's a new one,' he says, staring up at the ceiling. 'And I want him.'

'Who?' Clarke cuts in. I want to look over at her, to gauge her response without giving away my own fear, but I have to trust that she knows what she's doing.

'Noah West,' he says, flipping himself suddenly off the couch and striding towards the photograph wall. He plucks a picture down, strides across the room to drop it into Clarke's hand.

Clarke glances down at the photo, and while I can see her out of the corner of my eye, I don't dare look down as well. We can only risk one of us losing focus at a time.

At the end of the day, whether Tao knows about the escape plan or not doesn't really matter. He has the power to make our lives hell, no matter what. If he's not happy, he'll be more than willing to punish us for it. So the fact that he could be bluffing can't influence our decision, since it doesn't influence our reaction.

Not really. Not in any way that matters.

You can't escape if you're dead.

There's a lull in the air as Clarke weighs up the offer, and I hold my breath as Tao continues to stare at us.

'We'll see what we can do,' Clarke says. 'But we'll need to keep the picture.'

For a moment Tao's eyes twitch. He doesn't like people taking his stuff, especially one of his photographs, but we need it. Eventually he nods.

'Ladies.' He sighs, his mood soured somewhat at the loss of a photo. 'It was a pleasure.'

Clarke simply grunts in response as we leave. We take our weapons and the photo with us, letting the silence speak between us.

7

I could barely tell if I was awake or unconscious, dead or alive. I don't know how long I sat there or whether or not I even stayed awake the whole time. I just knew that they left me like that for long enough that my entire body had gone numb, my hands locked into fists, fingers too cold to unfurl. It was an icebox, and it was freezing me a second at a time.

Then the light came, sudden and blinding and from above me. I blinked up, trying to see anything other than burning light, but before my eyes could adjust something was falling in to land alongside me.

I scrabbled around in the dark for a moment until my frozen hands met the end of a rope, and then I was looking up again, but I still couldn't see anyone.

The rope was thick, with a loop tied in the end. Was I supposed to use it to climb out? Was it a trick? Why would they let me out?

My brain was too numb from cold to even think about anything but getting out as soon as I could, so I caught the rope with both hands and pulled, trying to drag myself up, but I didn't even get a metre off the ground before I slipped straight back, the rope burning my palms on the way down.

I don't know if I would have even been able to do that on a good day, but as it was I was too frozen and exhausted to pull myself along.

The second I let go, however, the rope started pulling back up. I panicked for a second, seeing my chance to get out slipping through my fingers, but then it dropped back down a moment later.

Because I wasn't on the other end. They want me up, whoever 'they' are.

I glanced around frantically, trying to figure out a way to hold on all the way to the top, until I remembered the loop at the end of the rope.

This time when I caught hold of it, I threaded my foot through the loop before I pulled on the rope, signalling for them to pull me up.

I almost fell twice on the way up, but from sheer force of fear, I held on.

Held on right to the top, and then they had what they wanted.

8

We don't say anything. Not until we're in the relative safety of our cell. Safety is a strong word, though. We don't talk until we return to the relative defensibility of our cell.

'Show me,' I say, the minute we're inside.

Clarke stands at the door for a moment, making sure no one has followed us.

'Noah West.' She sighs, slapping the photo into my hand. The picture is of an Officer, not a civilian, with tightly cropped light brown hair and blue eyes. He looks serious in the photo, his blue uniform perfectly fitted to him, his mouth set in a hard line, his posture rigid. But he's young, and there are laugh lines around his eyes.

'Where did Tao even get this?' I ask, flipping it over and checking the back for a date. Most photos that come in here are mementos, pictures of family or loved ones, of happier times. This looks more like a mug shot than a portrait.

'Who knows,' Clarke says, pulling our blankets out of her bag and laying them flat on the floor before lying down, throwing an arm over her face.

'He knows something,' she says.

'I know.' I sit down heavily on the floor.

'But how could he know about the escape? It's not like we broadcast it.'

'What if he's bluffing?' I ask.

'He's not,' she says, shaking her head. 'He has something on us. I just don't know what.'

'So what now? We just work for him for free until we get out? Do you really think he'd actually turn a blind eye to us getting out of here?'

'Probably not.' She's chewing her lip. 'We need to find out what he has on us first. Then we can make a decision on what to do next.'

'Okay,' I say, rolling my knife between my palms. 'Okay, okay, okay. We need to find out who else knows. He's probably told someone, right?'

'I don't know, but it's our only option. There's no way he's going to tell us himself.'

'If he told anyone, it's going to be Hoff,' I mutter. Hoff is Tao's right-hand man, and usually the first one to know of Tao's plans. 'But there's no way Hoff's going to tell us anything.'

'Unless … '

'Unless what?'

'Unless we give him the only thing that Tao can't.'

I stare at her.

'Hoff has a kid,' she says. 'Back in the Outer Sector.'

'So what? We threaten the kid?' I ask, thinking it over. I've crossed more lines than I'd like to admit while I've been in here, but that's one even I can't imagine crossing.

Clarke shakes her head. 'No, no point,' she says. 'It's not like we can find out where she is, and even if we could, Hoff would smash our heads in before he'd roll over on that one.'

'You're right,' I say, but I'm agreeing more out of relief than genuine agreement, even though she is right. Hoff isn't the kind of guy to roll on just a threat alone.

'So we bring him in on the escape,' she says, nodding as if that's the obvious conclusion.

'*What?*' I look up at her, the knife freezing between my fingers.

'Bring Hoff in on the escape. Tell him he'll get to see his kid again. Soon. I'd say he'd give us just about anything if we dangled that in front of him.'

'But that doesn't make any sense. The plan is for the two of us, not for three people. He'll ruin it.'

'No he won't,' Clarke says slowly. 'Because we're not gonna bring him in on the real escape. We're gonna find out what he knows and then send him off on a wild goose chase while we escape.'

I sit back, thinking. It *could* work, but it's extremely dangerous. Lying to Hoff, getting into Tao's business, sneaking behind his back *and* escaping.

But then, it's not like we have any other options.

'So what do we do now?'

'We take care of this West kid, deliver him with a bow tied around him to Tao, and we get to Hoff later. We can't do it while Tao's eyes are on us.'

I guess that's our only choice. Now we just need to figure out where the hell West's been hiding since he got here.

9

It wasn't a well they held me in. Wells are meant for water: this was built for people.

Next came a room. A real one, though it had no windows. Just a chair and a door.

I had tried to make a pathetic attempt to run from them the second they pulled me got out of the icebox pit, which won me a burst lip and a bruised, possibly broken rib and little else.

I didn't try to fight them again when they dragged me into that room and tied me to the chair. They didn't blindfold me, or even attempt to hide their faces, which I guess meant they didn't think that mattered.

Maybe because they didn't expect me to make it out of that room alive.

They left me there, and shortly afterwards someone else came in. I could hear them walking down the corridor outside.

Their steps were slow. Too slow. They were in no rush to get to me, but they weren't hesitant either. They were just calm. Too calm.

The door opening spread light across the floor, and even with the bulb flickering above my head, I wasn't used to the light after all the hours in the pit, and I flinched away from it.

He laughed.

'You're always like this when we take you out.' His voice was deep and warm, but something indefinable about it made terror spear into my gut.

He looked young enough, in his early thirties maybe, broad-shouldered and tall. He looked like a demon wearing a human's skin, and that's how I'll always remember him.

'You're not going to talk?' He smiled, coming to stand in front of me. He lifted my chin with two fingers, forcing me to look into his eyes.

I don't remember what colour his eyes were, except that they looked like they didn't belong to him. They were too bright, too vibrant. He had seen them in someone else's head and had wanted them, and he had taken them. I was sure of it.

'Okay then,' he said, that gentle smile still on his face. 'Whatever you want.'

Without warning, his fist cracked into my jaw, harder than I thought was possible, snapping my head to the side.

I stared down at the blood pooling by the leg of the chair, wondering how much more blood I'd give to this floor.

Time didn't exist in that room. There was only him and me. I was tied down, powerless and pathetic. The only way to resist was in my mind, by journeying far away and out of that place in my head. As he hurt me and asked questions and told me he had everyone I'd ever loved locked up in rooms all along this corridor, I floated off and away, lost in remembered moments. He hated that. Punished it. And I wished so hard I could stay away for good.

10

'I just need to know where he is.' It sounds too much like begging, but it's not like I have anything to bargain with. 'I swear I'll come back to you the second I get paid.'

Gag is the last person I want to come to with this. Small and sinewy, the only reason he survives in here is because nothing turns his stomach. As long as Gag gets what he wants, nothing is too far, nothing is too disgusting. But always for a price, and right now I have nothing to pay him with.

'This kid, he's a ghost, yeah?' Gag gets up off the bed in his cell, coming towards me. I repress the urge to take a step backwards as he comes closer. 'Ghosts are hard to find.'

'Yes, but you can find him.'

'Maybe,' he allows. 'But you know I don't work for free.' He reaches out to touch a bony finger against my shoulder, but I knock his hand away.

'I told you I'll pay you once *I* get paid.'

He laughs a hollow, hacking laugh. 'I didn't last this long doing favours, skinny.' He grins, showing a mouthful of rotten teeth.

I almost laugh. Gag is fond of giving people nicknames, but he looks more skeletal than some corpses I've seen out rotting in the common, so he should keep his mouth shut.

'Fine,' I grunt. 'But you'll regret this.'

He won't, most likely, but I'm angry. He's the fourth source today who's refused to give me anything.

Whether or not Noah West can be found is not the issue. It's whether or not I'll ever find him.

Gag just laughs as I turn on my heel, giving up. Gag has made his position clear, and there's nothing I'm going to say that will change it.

Clarke stays in the cell while I do a preliminary run for information. Smart people tend to try to stay under the radar when they first arrive, at least for a few weeks. A new face is considered fresh meat, but if you keep to the perimeters and stay out of everyone's way, you might be able to buy yourself some time.

It's a good thing for the newbie, but a bad thing for us.

I finally admit defeat and return to the cell, exhausted and sweating.

'Any luck?' Clarke asks, without opening her eyes from where she rests with her back to the wall at the far side of the cell. She does that sometimes, practises footstep recognition so that she'll know who's coming when she's asleep.

Or at least, as close to sleep as Clarke ever seems to get.

'Nothing.' I sigh. 'It's like he doesn't exist.'

'He exists. He's just hiding.'

'I'm starving,' I say, in an attempt to change the subject. I've spent hours looking for this guy. I don't know if I can talk about him anymore.

'Have you asked Illa yet?'

I drop down beside her on the blankets, dropping my head into my hands.

'Not yet.' I try not to sound as exhausted as I feel. Illa isn't exactly the most generous woman, and we're not in a position to trade much. We're not really in a position to trade anything.

'Whatever.' Clarke stands up from her place on the ground. 'I'm going to find something to eat.'

I give her a look. If it was that simple, I wouldn't be starving right now.

'I'll figure it out.' She shrugs. 'If I'm not back in an hour, I'm dead.'

I lie back against the wall and close my eyes for a few minutes. I try to go over the plan to find Noah, get info out of Hoff and get out from under Tao's thumb, but that's not where my mind keeps drifting.

I hope he's with her now.

I imagine Kole and Sophia in a house, somewhere so far from Oasis that they'll never be found. I imagine Jay's there too. I imagine that Mark and Walter are in the background, bickering. I imagine that Kole is reading to Sophi from a book that has nothing to do with Oasis. One of the books that Clarke has told me about, the ones her parents read to her, from before Oasis and the Virus.

I try to pull one of Kole's smiles from memory, but it's never fully right. It's always too fast or too straight. Kole's smiles, as rare as they were, are one of the things that I hold on to. Sometimes it's a blanket keeping me warm on a cold night. Sometimes it's a knife of pure, sharp hope.

I'll see that smile again, I swear to myself. I'll see Sophi's too. I even miss Jay's jack-knife grins. I miss all of them.

I can feel myself drifting dangerously close to sleep, but in the space between wake and sleep the prison melts away, and that's all I really want.

There isn't anything I don't miss from the Base. It's funny how something that felt so desperate and meagre at the time seems like a luxury now. The Base had smiles, as rare as they were. It had laughter sometimes. All there is here is fear and the stench of human desperation. The power that's ugly out there is primal and rancid in here.

I'm almost asleep when I hear it.

Two sets of footsteps and Clarke's voice, not a scream so much as a yell. When I scramble to my feet, she's standing at the door, a man pressing a knife to her throat.

It only takes me a split second to recognise that face.

Noah West.

11

They put me back in the icebox pit, and I was grateful for it. I clung to the walls for hours, expecting them to come back for me, but they didn't.

Eventually I fell asleep, and when I woke up they still hadn't come. The thirst came next, and the hunger, and the freezing cold kept pressing in around me like it wanted something from me, like it wanted me back.

When the rope fell down again, I dragged myself across the floor of the pit and I let them pull me up, and tears burned paths across my torn face the whole way.

But they gave me water and bread, and I didn't refuse it this time. I couldn't.

When they dragged me back into the room, it was payment for what I couldn't live without.

Nothing comes without a price.

12

'*Clarke.*' My heart beats skyrockets as I take in the scene in front of me.

'Don't move,' Noah says, pushing Clarke further into the cell as he comes behind her, careful to keep the knife pressed tightly to her throat. 'And don't reach for any weapon you're hiding.'

I go completely still, reeling, hand halfway to my pocket as I try to piece together what's going on.

'What do you want?' I ask, watching his eyes flit across the room, taking in every detail.

He's restless, his hand readjusting on the knife every few seconds, but there's something about the way he's watching his surroundings that speaks to some kind of experience. His nervous stance doesn't match his cautious but calm expression, and it's throwing me off.

'I've heard you've been looking for me.' He shrugs, as if this is a normal reaction. As if he isn't a hair's breadth from slitting a girl's throat.

'Tao has,' I tell him, keeping my voice calm. 'He has an offer for you.'

'I'm not interested in Tao's offers,' Noah says, and the way he says Tao's name … Something's off. There's something going on here that I don't understand.

'It's easier,' I say, 'to survive in here under Tao's protection.'

'Then why aren't you under Tao's protection?'

'I have my reasons,' I say. 'I can look after myself.'

'Well so can I,' he responds. 'Clearly.'

'I'm sure you can.' I make eye contact with Clarke. She doesn't look scared, just enraged. 'But I don't understand what we've done to make you angry. We're just the messengers.'

'I know Tao works with the Officers,' West spits, his expression souring. 'I don't work with Oasis scum.'

My eyes widen. That's what wasn't adding up.

'You're a rebel,' I say. Not a question: a statement. Noah's expression falters, but only for a moment, before being replaced with a fierce mixture of pride and anger.

'Yes, I am.' His chin rises a fraction. 'What does that mean to you?'

I hold my breath for a beat, two beats, and then I step forward until I'm standing right in front of Clarke. Noah's eyes widen a fraction as he tries to figure out how he's supposed to react to my sudden lack of fear.

'It means we're on the same side,' I say, and between one blink and the next, I catch his wrist and Clarke spins away from him as I twist the knife from his grip, throwing it at the wall behind me.

Clarke wheels around quickly, rage in her eyes. She's so fast, in fact, that he's still staring at me in confusion when she catches him by his collar, pulling him down to her height. She spits her next words with all the venom of a viper.

'Next time you decide to threaten someone, find out who they are before you start making enemies you don't want.'

I get the distinct impression that she's not so much angry at the fact that he just attacked a fellow rebel than that he was stupid enough to attack *her.*

Clarke is not a good enemy to have, and she's certainly not an easy one to shake.

Noah at least has the sense to look scared, until Clarke lets go of his collar and turns on her heel in disgust.

Noah takes a step back when Clarke releases him.

'How do I know that you're telling the truth?' he demands, taking another step involuntarily backwards. 'Are you a Genesis recruit?'

'No,' I say slowly. 'Are you?'

The flash in his eyes is all I need to know, and apparently it's all Clarke needs to know as well.

'You work for Genesis?'

He stares us down, says nothing.

'Genesis isn't the only rebellion, Noah,' I say, trying to keep my tone civil.

'If it were, we'd all be screwed,' Clarke cuts in. 'You're cowards, all of you. Hiding out while everyone dies, when we *know* you have the resources to help. You're not a rebellion, you're a group of idiots who think they can hide from Oasis. You can't.'

'You don't know anything about Genesis,' he growls.

Clearly Clarke hit a nerve, and I'm not in the mood to break up a fist fight.

'And we don't know anything about you, either. So I'd recommend you get out of here before I make you get out.'

'Fine,' he snaps. His eyes touch on the knife behind me, but I step towards him just a fraction, and he turns on his heel.

If he's not willing to stand his ground, he shouldn't go around putting knives to people's throats.

He disappears out into the prison, and I finally breathe a sigh of temporary relief.

'You okay?' I ask Clarke, who's still pacing like a caged tiger.

'Do you think he's lying?' she asks, ignoring my actual question. 'Do you think he's really with Genesis?'

'Who knows? In here, anyone could say anything, and we wouldn't have any way of knowing if it were true or not.'

I slump down onto the floor to watch her pace.

'I don't like him knowing about us,' Clarke mutters.

'Why?'

'We don't know anything about him, or about Genesis for that matter. Whether he's lying or not, he's dangerous.'

'I know. But we still need him if we're going to keep Tao off our backs.'

'You think putting Tao and Noah in the same room is a good idea? Considering what they both know?'

'No, I don't.' I close my eyes, trying to steady my breathing. Everyone here falls into two camps: the criminals and the rebels. Everyone knows which one is better. Tao has ties with the Officers, and he's taken it upon himself to do them the favour of cutting out the rebel scum.

How, in this of all places, Oasis still has power, I have no idea. I just know the rules and how to follow them so as not to get myself killed.

I've been imagining a hundred ways this could play out since we were given this job, but none of them ended up like this. 'But we don't have any other option.'

'There are always options. The option to kill him still stands.'

I glance up at her, to make sure she's serious, but she's not looking at me. 'Clarke,' I growl. 'We're not killing him.'

'Do you think he'd hesitate to kill us?'

'I don't know, but that doesn't mean—'

'Don't be naive.'

'I'm not being naive!' I sit up, and Clarke won't stop pacing. 'You need to calm down.'

'He put a *knife* to my throat!' she yells, stopping dead in her tracks. 'And I don't need to calm down. I need to deal with this. I'm not willing to let him get close enough to Tao to ruin this for us. We're going to have one chance to get out, and he's not going to be the reason we miss it.'

I grit my teeth. There's nothing I can do, not when she's like this. She doesn't get worked up easily, but when she does, God help the poor fool who made the mistake of pissing her off.

13

'Hey,' he said, quiet again, calm again, his voice half-lulled, like he was almost asleep.

He wasn't almost asleep. Beneath feathered lashes his eyes were always too bright. He could keep his excitement a secret in his face, in his posture, in his tone, but his eyes always gave him away.

'You're still not talking to me?'

I hadn't spoken a single word to him. I hadn't spoken a single word since the ones I spoke to Kole in that elevator. I was afraid, afraid that I *would mess up, give something away and he'd use it against me.*

Or worse, that he'd use it against them.

I didn't know where the others were, didn't know where Kole had taken Sophi and the rest of the rebels, didn't know if Jay had got out of there in one piece, but I knew where they had been. I knew where Nails's hideout was, knew where the Base was.

If I gave them away, after all of this, and they got hurt, I couldn't live with myself.

'Okay,' he said, and I was already tensing, every muscle in my body ready for the punch.

But it didn't come.

'Where is he?' he whispered, crouching down in front of me, placing his hands on my knees. 'Tell me where he is and I won't have to hurt you.'

I turned my face away from him. It was the best I could do. The rest of my body was tied to the chair with coarse ropes that dug into my wrists and ankles. They would rub away at the skin until there wasn't any left, just blisters and blood. Then they would drop me back into the icebox, and my wrists would weep and scab, only to have the scabs torn off with more ropes the next time they dragged me back up.

His hands tightened on my knees, his knuckles turning white. He was trying to draw my attention back to him. He could see I was leaving, disappearing into the depths of my mind where I couldn't feel the welted, broken, bleeding mess he had turned my body into a day at a time, an hour at a time, a blow at a time.

'Quincy.' He always said my name like he was disappointed in me. 'Look at me.'

I turned my face away from him again, refusing to look at him, refusing to answer. Refusing to comply.

He didn't like that. The silence he could deal with, for a while. He would play with me, talk soothing circles around me until I barely understood what he was saying. Eventually, when he got tired of that, the pain would come. And it would be fast and brutal or slow and agonising, whichever he thought would best pick me to pieces that day. But at first, at least, he was patient with silence.

But this was a statement of disobedience, a conscious decision to go against what he asked of me.

And he did not like that.

He released his grip on my knees and leant forward, untying the ropes around my ankles. Then he moved around behind me, untying my hands and freeing me from the chair.

'We're going back to the pit,' he said, grabbing the back of my head and forcing me to stand.

His voice sounded wrong, and panic started to rise in the back of my throat. He never brought me back to the pit. He waited until I was barely conscious, when I wasn't any fun anymore because I wasn't reacting anymore, because I couldn't. Then he called in the two other guards, and he left, and they dragged me back.

But it was never him. He was never the one to dump me back inside.

He pushed me out the door, and I didn't fight back. I had learned my lesson already, more than once, that fighting only made it worse. Down the hall and back to the last door, back to the pit.

He shoved me forward, into the room. In the middle of the room was the opening, the gaping hole in the ground that they lowered me back into day after day. I didn't know why, didn't even ask myself why they would leave me down there instead of just locking me in a cell.

He handed me the rope, and I refused to take it, so he tied it around me. There was something about this whole situation, something about the tension in his shoulders that made me know something had changed.

He was losing his patience, and I kept on testing him. I pushed him away, but the rope was already around me. When I made a dash for the door, he just pulled me back, emotionless.

I tried to lash out at him, but I was weak. However long I had spent there, they had spent it breaking me, and it was working. The fight was gone out of me, and it didn't take much for him to stop me.

'Quiet,' he snapped, but he quickly corrected his tone. 'I didn't want to have to do this, but you won't tell me where he's hiding, so you've left me with no choice.'

He dropped me into the pit, and my knees buckled the second they hit the ground. I didn't know how much more I could take. Wouldn't they kill me soon? Wouldn't they give up eventually? They had to give up eventually. They had to.

A few seconds later I felt something ice cold over my head, and I gasped, the shock forcing the breath out of my lungs.

When I looked up, I couldn't see anything, but it didn't take me long to understand what was going on. He was filling the pit with water. He was going to drown me.

14

I slowly slip the strap of my bag over my head as I watch Clarke like a hawk, trying not to wake her. She fell asleep a few hours ago, but I can't tell how deeply she's sleeping. She's not going to do any good by killing him because she's angry, and unless I fix this before she has the chance, that's exactly what she's going to do. Noah's a rebel, and a Genesis rebel at that, and he could help us. Help *me*. Genesis, if they're real, could help me to find Sophi and Kole and the others. Clarke might think I'm stupid for believing Noah even for a moment, but if there's a chance what he's saying is true, I can't afford to let him die.

I creep noiselessly out of the cell and quickly make my way downstairs. The Colosseum seems empty, which is unusual. When I glance down at the common, I realise why.

It rained last night, so there are small floods across the open area, but the floods are stained red. I quickly count the bodies: six in total.

That's more than normal. Whatever fight broke out last night, it can't have been just over supplies or a single inmate with a grudge against one of the others. It makes me uneasy, like a bad omen. People are hungry, and it's making them prone to lashing out.

And when people lash out in the Colosseum, this is the result.

I look away, refocusing on my attention on walking in a straight line. I step over someone leaning back against the wall in the alcoves, unsure of whether they're dead or asleep and not too keen to figure it out.

When I glance up I see Noah ducking around a corner up ahead, and I can't help but smile. I knew this was where he would go.

After months of waiting for Nails to pull through, Clarke's confidence is shaking. Yes, the deliveries only arrive once a month and she knew going into this that it would take time to put the plan in motion, but time is one month. Two months. Three, even.

Six months means something has gone wrong, and from inside the Colosseum, we have no way of knowing what's happened and no way of formulating a new escape plan. Without outside help, there is no way out.

Clarke's cracking under the pressure, just like me.

I watch as Noah ducks into the old Officer dorm at the end of the hall. Most people avoid that room, since it's small and hard to escape in the event of an attack, but Noah's a rebel and an ex-Officer. And he's cocky.

I'm about to turn down the corridor leading to the room he's just disappeared into when I'm stopped dead by a tight grasp on my arm.

I spring away, grappling for my knife, when I realise it's Clarke standing there, glaring at me.

'Clarke,' I breathe. 'You scared me.'

'What are you doing here?' She catches my arm again, pulling me away sideways and out of sight.

'Clarke …' My eyes drift to the door at the end of the hall. If I don't get in there fast, I lose my chance at convincing Noah to help us.

'You came here behind my back,' she says. There's no arguing that it's an accusation, but there is no emotion in her face when she speaks.

'Clarke, I just saw him—'

'You're lying to me,' she snaps. 'I can tell when you're lying, and you're lying right now. You came looking for him.'

I stare at her for a beat. 'I'm going to talk to him.'

'And say what?'

I watch her, chewing on my lip. She swivels away from me, dragging her hands down her face in frustration.

'If Tao finds out that you're a rebel, he's going to turn you over to the Officers and you know it. You're going to get us killed, do you understand that?'

'I'm trying to protect—'

'Protect who? Who the hell matters more than you and me right now?'

'I'm trying to protect Sophi,' I say through gritted teeth. 'If he really is in contact with Genesis, he could help us find her, find Kole and the others. Get a message to them. Maybe even get us out of here.'

'Exactly what do you think Genesis is, Quincy?' she asks, squinting at me. 'They're not superheroes, and they don't know everything.'

'They're still our best chance.'

'No,' she growls. 'Killing him before Tao gets his hands on him is our best chance. He's a ghost right now – if we get to him before anyone finds him, he'll just disappear. No one has to find out. And if we get out, *that's* our best chance of finding Sophia.'

'You don't get to tell me what's best for her.' I step back. I haven't fought with Clarke, not like this, not since we got landed in here together. 'And you know that that's not how Tao works. If Noah doesn't turn up eventually, he's going to hold someone responsible for it. He wants his pound of flesh now, and he'll get it, whether it's from us or from Noah.'

She stares at me too hard and for too long, like she doesn't recognise me.

'I'm not going to say this again,' she says, her voice slow and calm and even and coldly threatening. 'Turn around. Go back to the cell. Let me deal with him.'

I shake my head. 'I'm going to talk to him. Don't try to stop me again.'

I turn around and walk down the hall without looking back. But my hand hesitates on the door handle. What if she's right? What if Noah ends up doing something stupid and gets us killed?

I glance back to where she stood moments before, but she's already gone. It looks like she was never there in the first place.

I pull the door open.

He's setting his knife down on his bed when he hears me come in. He looks shocked, but only for a second.

'What do you want?' he asks, looking me up and down. It's an obvious intimidation tactic, and I don't let it touch me.

I lean against the door, half so as not to be more threatening than I have to be and half because I want him to know I'm not scared of him.

In here, Noah is the least of my worries.

'I have a proposition for you,' I say calmly.

I don't like his energy. He's too skittish, like he's always ready to throw a punch or take off running.

'I don't want anything from you,' he grunts, turning away and rooting through the bag at his feet as if he actually has any interest in the contents whatsoever.

'Yes, you do. You want the same thing that everyone in here wants.'

'And what's that?'

'To not be in here.'

He turns back to me slowly. 'Genesis is getting me out.'

'When?' I demand. I'm hitting the exact same weak point that Clarke and I have at this exact moment. The only difference is I know that it's his weak spot. He doesn't know that it's ours.

'In a week? In a month? Six months?' I ask, pushing, pushing, waiting for him to snap.

His mouth tightens into a thin line, but he doesn't respond. I have him.

'We're getting out of here in three days,' I say, and I sound sure of myself because I have to.

'How?'

'If I told you that, I wouldn't have anything to bargain with.'

He watches me coolly. 'So what is it that you want from me?'

'I want you to join Tao's gang.' I can tell I've taken him by surprise, because he goes still, squinting at me like I've spoken a different language.

'Why?'

'Because Tao wants you, and if I give you to him, he'll owe me one. And I always want Tao to owe me one.'

'But if you're getting out in three days, why do you need anyone to owe you anything?'

I open my mouth to make an excuse, but Noah's eyes narrow in understanding.

'You need Tao to escape,' he says, and I don't correct him. I do need Tao, just not in the way he thinks.

'So what's in it for me?' he says finally.

'You convince Tao that I recruited you, and we'll take you with us.'

'That's too easy,' he says. 'What aren't you telling me?'

I cross my arms, shifting my stance. He's smarter than I thought.

'Tao doesn't just … let people in. You'll have to prove yourself to him.'

'How?' he says.

'I don't know. I work for him, not with him. I never joined for a reason.'

'So you want me to do something you're not willing to do yourself, so that *you* can escape?'

'So that *we* can escape.' I'm getting frustrated with him, and I stand up straight in the doorway. 'Three days, that's all you have to survive, and then you're done. Out. For good.'

His eyes are calculating, and I feel like the lie is painted across my face. I can't guarantee that he'll be out in three days. I can't guarantee that Nails will pull through for us this week, and if he doesn't, Noah is stuck with Tao. But if I don't pull through for Tao now, I won't live long enough to find out if Nails pulls through.

'When would I have to join them?' he asks.

'Do it now,' I say. 'Or there's no deal.'

He looks down, processing what I've told him.

'How am I supposed to trust that you're not lying to me? What if you don't have an escape plan at all? You're not telling me what it is, so I have no way of knowing if you're going to stab me in the back the moment I turn around.'

'You're right,' I say. 'You can't trust me.'

He looks taken aback.

'And you can't trust Genesis to get you out. And you can't trust Tao. And you can't trust that you'll survive this place. It's all risks, Noah. So take the one that could get you out of here in three days, or take the gamble that I'm lying and turn me down. It's not my problem.'

I turn around and take two steps forward.

'Wait.'

I turn slowly and look at him.

'Fine,' he says, looking at me resentfully. I don't blame him. It's a bad position to be in. 'I'll go see Tao in a while.'

I nod, then I walk out of there, wondering all the while what I've put in motion and whether it'll end up being added to my long list of regrets.

15

The water rose up to my waist before I started begging. Hours or days or weeks I'd spent in that hell, I couldn't even tell how long, and I'd never once opened my mouth. They starved me and beat me and nothing more than a groan of pain had ever passed my lips. But as the water rose higher and higher, I scrambled for some way out, some kind of escape before the water swallowed me, and the screams were pulled from my lungs without my consent.

'STOP!' I yelled, and I could barely get it out, my breathing was so fast and so panicked as the water worked its way over my chest.

I didn't realise then, in that moment, that this was why the walls were damp when I first arrived. That this was why they had put me in the icebox in the first place.

So that when they were done with me, they could kill me like this, slow and painful and terrified.

The water was up to my chin, my hands pressed to the wall like I could pull myself up the completely flat surface. My eyes wouldn't stop searching the space, like I'd be able to find a way out if I just focused hard enough.

That's what I'd always done. I'd figured a way out, I'd figured out a way to survive. I'd survived. It's what I did. It's who I was. Since I was seven years old my whole life had been built around surviving, and it was going to be taken from me, here, in some off-grid Oasis hell camp, alone in a drowning pit.

The water came up over my chin, and I arched my back, forcing my face to stay above the surface for a few more seconds.

Then, just when it was almost too late, the rope was let down again and he pulled me up.

I collapsed out the side of the pit, panting for breath, muscles locked with cold, my entire body shaking uncontrollably.

He knelt down beside me and lifted my soaking wet hair from around my face.

'Are you ready?' he said gently, like he was waking me up from a bad dream.

'What … are you talking about?' I panted.

'Just tell me where he is.' He tucked my hair behind my ear, and I couldn't even find the energy to stop him. 'All Johnson wants to know is where his son is. The only son he has left, remember. You can make up for

killing one by giving him back the other. Tell me and I can stop doing this to you.'

I fell onto my side and looked up at him. 'Go to hell,' I whispered.

Before I could catch a breath, he rolled me over and threw me back down, into the cold, into the water.

Back into the pit.

16

When I get back, Clarke is gone. It's not unusual for her to disappear in the middle of the day, but after what happened with Noah earlier, my heart skips a beat with sudden fear.

I look around the room, but her bag isn't in the corner. That means she took it with her, which means she's okay. I try to slow my breathing down as I dump my own bag in the corner.

I wish she was here. After speaking to Noah, even without her consent, I still need her to be here to ease the pain in my chest. There are too many things that could go wrong, too many ways this plan could fall apart in our hands. And plan is a strong word to use. It was a resourceful move on Clarke's side that she thought to put in place a back-up plan at all. The rest of us were so intent on the mission, we never even considered afterwards. It was Clarke alone who had thought ahead, knew that if we did get caught, they'd put us in the Colosseum. Still, it only works if the plan actually goes through. Right now it's hard to feel that we did much other than get ourselves caught and wait for a rescue that might never take place at all. I want to go looking for her, but there's no point. If she doesn't want me to find her, I won't be able to. She's too confusing. I think I know her, but I only know what she's given me. I know little else about her past other than what she told me that night when Sophi woke from a nightmare, the night Clarke told me about her family being killed.

I know that she grew up on the outside. That Oasis didn't create her, but it tainted her. It turned a little girl into a soldier dead-set on finding revenge for her family. I try to imagine that, at seven years old, taking on that responsibility.

When I was seven, I was dumped into a world of fear and cruelty, and I survived because I knew that I was the only thing that mattered out here. But it changed me. It twisted me into something that fights first and thinks later, something that survives first and thinks later.

But that. Her whole family killed by a mysterious city built a hundred miles from her home. I understood, as much as a seven-year-old can, what happened to me as a child. I was branded a Dormant, a dangerous thing, and I became unwanted the second that test turned up positive. I became unlovable. How could anyone love a monster? How could anyone love someone who could rip civilisation apart in a heartbeat? They told me I had the gene that could breed the Virus and that was it, my death sentence. The Virus was the most feared thing in Oasis, and they said it was in me. But Clarke, she didn't do anything wrong, not a thing. She lived peacefully with her family in a village far from Oasis, never harming anyone, and still they ripped her entire life apart. There's no reasoning that can make sense of that.

I don't know how long I sit there, thinking about things I shouldn't be thinking about, but eventually I pick up my bag and turn to leave again. I need to eat, and I'm not going to sit around worrying about Clarke until she returns from wherever it is she disappeared to.

I feel cold as I walk down the steps, shouldering past a group of inmates that have taken up residence on the stairs. One of them grabs my arm, dragging me back up, and I have to quickly steady my feet underneath me to keep my balance. I pull my knife from my pocket in one clean move, holding it towards him and letting out an animalistic growl to serve as a threat. He pushes me away from him roughly and I don't even look back as I continue down the stairs. He didn't really want anything. They usually don't. He just wanted to see if he could frighten me, maybe shake a few supplies out of me before he was done.

I turn towards Victor's side of the Colosseum. I would exhaust every other source of food in any other situation, but it's been over five weeks since the last delivery. No one but Victor and Tao have food supplies anymore.

I'm about to walk up the stairs to Victor's place when I hear a shout over the hundreds of other voices in the common.

'Taylor!' It sounds like a female voice.

I turn around so swiftly I almost collide with one of Victor's heavies as they head up towards his office.

The girl makes eye contact with me and jerks her hand towards Tao's side of the Colosseum. 'Tao wants to see you.'

I stumble forward without even fully realising what I'm doing, blood rushing in my ears as I cross the expansive opening.

What does he want? She doesn't make eye contact with me when I meet her, just turns on her heel and strides quickly towards the upper right cells. Tao doesn't call people to him: people come to him willingly. I don't know why that's suddenly changed, now of all times.

I follow her up the four flights of stairs to Tao's room, my heart pounding so loudly in my chest I'm convinced she'll hear it and take it as a sign of weakness. But she doesn't even glance at me.

I hesitate for a second outside the door, feeling like I'm walking into a sentencing. I want to turn and run, but there's nowhere to go. Whatever he wants from me, it's better to walk in than be dragged in, so I walk.

17

Tao's men force me to give up my knife before I can enter the inner room. It's standard procedure so I comply automatically, but something about it feels different this time.

When I walk into the room, I notice immediately that he isn't sitting down. He's leaning against the small window, looking out across the common with a calculating eye.

I don't say anything. The fact that my knife is gone makes me feel uncomfortable, as it always does, but there's something about this situation that makes me it feel more acutely. I never want my knife more than right before I need it.

'Quincy,' he says, smiling as he turns around to me, leaning his back against the wall. The room is empty. Too empty. Tao always has at least one of his goons around him at all times. 'Quincy Emerson.'

My heart stops. I can feel adrenaline pouring into my system immediately. 'What did you just say?' My voice is a quiet kind of deadly.

He cocks his head, a curious expression on his face. 'That's your name, right? Emerson.' He already knows. The way he cocks his head to the side as he asks me that, I know that he already knows. He's just mocking me at this point, seeing how much fun he can have while I squirm.

I move to take a step towards him, before realising there's nothing I can do. My eyes catch the glint of a weapon at Tao's side, but my hands are empty.

Vulnerable.

Tao laughs at me. 'Don't go getting any ideas,' he says, and there's a crueller note in his voice than usual. 'Did you think I wouldn't figure it out?'

I grit my teeth, my feet stuck in place.

'What do you want?'

'I want to know how you got out,' he says quietly.

'What?'

'You *escaped*,' he says. 'You broke out of Oasis with no help. And then you broke back in again. I need to know *how*. Getting out of here is one thing, but surviving outside, that's another. I want to know how you got beyond the walls.'

'Luck,' I spit, and he catches me by the collar so quickly that I can't even make a sound before he slams me against the wall, knocking the air out of my lungs.

'I know you're planning something.' His face is so close to mine that I can feel his spit hitting me in the face as he hisses at me. 'I *know* you're planning something.'

It's at that moment that I realise he doesn't actually know anything. He is guessing, just like everyone else.

I have to stop myself from smiling.

I reach up, catching the hand gripping my collar, and pull it off. 'Don't touch me.'

I feel a sudden, eerie calm as I look into his eyes and see nothing but panic. Panic and fear and desperation. He doesn't step back immediately, so I catch his hand on the other side of my collar, twisting his wrist out to break the contact. I use his own arm to push him back against the wall, driving my knee into his stomach so that he slams into the wall that was behind me only a moment ago.

He tries to lash out, his fist going to slam into the side of my face, but I duck, grabbing the knife at his waist and pressing it to his throat.

His eyes widen, with rage more than fear.

'Listen,' I growl, 'if you want to get out of this place alive, you won't say a word about this to anyone.'

'Don't threaten me,' he says, his voice hard.

'No,' I say, pressing the knife harder, drawing blood where the blade bites into his skin. The deep satisfaction I feel from seeing the blood well up around the blade makes me uneasy. I want to push it further, see how far I can go, like bleeding Tao dry will somehow make up for a lifetime's worth of my own wounds. 'You don't threaten *me*. And if you come near me again, I swear to God I'll cut your eyes from your head. I recruited Noah West for you. That means we're even. I owe you nothing.'

I take a step back, and he stays very still, his eyes glancing down to the knife in my hand. Convinced I've made my point I walk away, the knife still in my hand, adrenaline still pumping through me at a speed I can barely process.

'Wait,' he says, his voice soft now. 'I can help. We can help each other. You tell me what I need to know and I'll help you. We can get out together. I can get you anything you need. I *own* this place.'

'Well then I guess we're both idiots,' I say, with a small smile. 'Because you don't own anything, and I'm never getting out of this place.'

I grab my knife from the table in the outer room, keeping Tao's held tightly in my fist. Two of his men are sitting at the table, but I'm out before they can stand up. Behind me, I hear Tao shout in frustration and then a loud crash of something being thrown across the room. I speed up as his goons run in to find out what's wrong. I don't stop, I don't slow down, I walk down the steps, out to the common, across the open space, as I try to keep my hands from shaking.

I just need to cross the common, get up the stairs and across the balcony and then I'm safe, I tell myself, like prayer, a mantra, a chant.

I just need to get up the stairs and across the balcony and then I'm safe.

I just need to get across the balcony and then I'm safe.

I slip into my cell, and my knives clatter to the ground around me, and my knees go out from beneath me as I slide to the floor, and I don't feel safe. None of this feels safe. Nothing feels safe.

18

The only thing that saved me was the rope still knotted around my foot. I had just enough time to catch the rope before I hit the water, but not before the back of my skull cracked against the side of the pit.

I felt the blow ring through me as I fell into the water, and I couldn't find the floor beneath me, couldn't figure out how to get my feet under me and find the air above the water. There was just darkness and the icy chill of the water, and I kept kicking out but I couldn't find anything solid.

When I finally pushed myself to the surface I heard the water again, the rushing sound of it pouring in and filling up. It was already up past my chin; I had to stand on my toes and arch my back just to catch a breath. A few more seconds and it would cover my face.

I could probably figure out a way to keep myself above water for a few minutes after that, if I kicked with my legs and clung to the wall for support, but I was exhausted and my muscles were locking from the cold, and I had spat at my only chance to get out.

I pressed my back against the wall, my breathing a series of gasps as the water rose higher, and I closed my eyes and waited for it.

They're safe, I told myself. I promised myself that I had kept them safe, and that it didn't matter what happened to me now.

I couldn't tell if I was sobbing then or just gasping for air. The water was pushing me down and I was fighting to catch a breath above it, but I had done one good thing.

I had lied and cheated and fought my way to survival my whole life, but I had done this one good thing. I had kept them safe, and that had to mean something.

19

I wake up with a start, grappling for my knife, which is laid across my lap, as I search the room for whatever woke me.

It's Clarke, standing in the door, her bag sliding off her shoulder. My breath whooshes out of me all at once, relief sharp in my chest.

'Clarke,' I whisper, getting to my feet. 'Where the hell have you been?'

She pulls her bag off, turns it upside-down and dumps a pile of cans onto the floor.

'*What?*' I'm awake now, fully alert as I pick up a can, and another, and another. There must be a dozen here. 'How the hell …'

'Told you I'd figure something out.' She grins, but the smile is weary and exhausted, and there's an edge to it. I turn around and grab one of the blankets from behind me, spreading it out and gesturing for her to sit down.

She does, practically crumpling into a pile beside me.

'How did you get all of this?' My chest feels tight with nerves, and my eyes keep flicking around her face. Shouldn't there be something? I expected her to come back and yell at me, or not come back at all. But it's like she's pretending nothing happened.

She shrugs, picking up a can and handing it to me, then shuffling through and picking one out for herself. As far as food goes, canned food like this is the epitome of luxury. Sure, it doesn't taste like much other than gelatinous goo, but it'll last months and months without going bad, and in here, that's about as good as it gets. She pulls out a fork and hands it to me.

'Thanks for the rusty fork,' I grumble, but I don't mean a word of it. I'm so excited about getting to eat at all, whatever I'm eating with doesn't matter.

'Shut up,' she grunts, kicking me in the shin and peeling the metal lid from her tin at the same time. 'Mmmm, grey goodness.' She grins, showing me the inside of her can and then the worn label.

'The label says beef stew,' I say, opening my own. 'The contents say vomit.'

I hear her laughing gently. I can barely see her in this light. By the time whatever light the moon projects gets through the bars that sit atop the Colosseum like a roof, there's barely enough to find your way around. And up here, in the shadow of the cells, I can only just make out her outline.

'But seriously,' I say, after a few spoonfuls – I'm starving, but it still takes a conscious effort not to gag as the gloopy mixture slides down my throat – 'how did you get all of this?'

This is a kill pull. You only get this much food out of someone for a pretty high price, and usually that price is taking out someone unpleasant. We try to avoid those kinds of jobs. They're messy and complicated, and tend to get us pulled into gang fights we don't want any part of.

'Quincy,' Clarke says, scraping out the last of her tin, 'I'm tired, and I want to just sleep and pretend today didn't happen. Can we please not talk about food, or Tao, or the escape or anything right now?'

I go quiet.

'Sure.' I say. 'I just wanted to say—'

'Quincy,' she says, and when she looks at me, there is a pleading look in her eyes. 'Don't.'

I chew on my lip, nodding. There's so much to tell her, but it would only set her off again, pacing, her nervous energy ricocheting off the walls. It can wait. I can keep watch and it can wait.

'Okay.' I lean back.

'Thank you,' she mutters, lying back against the wall for another night of half-sleep. Of waking up at the slightest sound. Of never really falling asleep at all, because every time you begin to slip, your body jolts you back awake.

Too dangerous, your mind screams. Not safe.

Never, ever safe.

20

'Today,' I say to Clarke, coming back to our cell to find her propped up against the wall.

She nods. She already knows.

Word's spread across the Colosseum that the shipment is coming in today, and you can feel the desperation in the air. Their desperation is different from ours, though.

I'm about to open my mouth to ask her a question, to ask if she's ready, when the sound of a scream makes me freeze.

The sound of a scream inside the Colosseum is not unusual, but it was the sound beneath the scream that really scared me. Gunshots sounding in the common.

Before I can think about what I'm doing, I've taken off, running at top speed towards the chaos.

There are people running in every direction, and it takes me a moment to even see what's going on as I'm pushed back by the flow of inmates.

A stand-off, in the middle of the common, between Tao's and Victor's men. But there are more of Tao's men on the balcony, shooting into the crowd, and now people are falling, dropping like flies as the air thickens with the screams of the dying and wounded.

I stumble backwards as someone crashes into me, trying to pull my thoughts together. I turn around, but Clarke isn't there, and I'm pushed against bodies too quickly to find any foothold strong enough to push back against the crowd.

This can't be happening. This *cannot* be happening. The gangs don't fight like this. I've never seen a gun inside the Colosseum, not once. For six months, it's been a chess match. Tao's crew steal food. Victor stabs one of Tao's men. Tao takes out one of Victor's in revenge. And back and forth and back and forth for *months*.

But now, as I look around breathlessly, everything is falling apart. Months, years of tit-for-tat warring has finally come to a head, hours before a delivery. Hours before a crack in the security. Hours before a chance at escape.

I glance around, realising I've lost Clarke.

I don't know what I'm supposed to do, but I know that I need to find Clarke, and fast. With the speed that this fight is devolving, we're both going to get caught in the crosshairs if I don't find her and get someplace safe. *Now.*

I resist the urge to pull my knives out as I shoulder my way through the crowd. Fights are breaking out everywhere, snowballing into a prison-wide free-for-all. If I have a knife in my hand, I'll be seen as a threat, and if I'm seen as a threat, there's no way I'll find Clarke before I get myself killed.

Someone drags on my arm and I lash out at them, hitting blindly before ducking into the crowd, praying that the press of bodies will keep me hidden. Bullets are still going off into the centre of the common, but I stay close to the side, along with almost everyone else, my eyes constantly searching for Clarke. I can't see her anywhere. Then it hits me – maybe she didn't follow me as I thought. She must be waiting for me back in the cell.

The stairs are packed with people, unsure of where to go, but I push my way through the crowd as fast as I can. Halfway up I hear a loud keening sound and whip around to see the gates screeching open, releasing a barrage of Officers into the common.

What is going on? my mind screams. This is not how this was supposed to happen. The gangs don't fight like this, and the Officers don't enter the Colosseum like this, and *it's not supposed to happen like this.*

'CLARKE!' I yell, elbowing past the half awe-struck, half terrified crowd in an attempt to get to our cell. I have to force everything else out of my mind. I have to, or I won't be able to breathe. 'CLARKE!'

I push back inside the cell, but it's empty. It's empty.

She's not here.

Where is she?

And then everything goes black.

21

I kick out, trying to scream through the bag over my head as my arms are crushed to my sides by someone behind me. I try to yell Clarke's name, but the rough fabric muffles my voice as I'm dragged backwards. I can feel my ankle hitting against the cell wall as I'm pulled out onto the balcony, but nothing else is getting in the way. I can hear the shouting, but the gunshots have died off, and as much as I thrash around in an attempt to free myself, I don't feel anyone but the person who's caught me. The balcony and stairs, which were packed moments ago, are now seemingly empty.

I'm hoisted up off my feet and the air is knocked from my chest as I'm thrown over a shoulder. Whoever has me momentarily loses their balance as I continue to lash out, and I can feel them almost lose their footing as they make their way down the stairs, before we both fall in a heap. I slip out of their grip and I'm up and running.

But beneath us the common is packed, and I can't see, and I'm dizzy and I don't know where I'm going and within seconds someone catches me around the waist, pressing what feels terrifyingly like the barrel of a gun to my temple as he growls in my ear, 'Try that again and I'll blow your brains out.'

I freeze, and he grabs me by the back of my tunic and pushes me forwards.

The Colosseum has become eerily quiet, and the rest of my senses start playing tricks on me. I think I can feel something brush against my ankles, a voice in my ear, the sound of a gun loading. But then I hear a quiet wailing to my left, someone crying, and my mind immediately bolts to Clarke.

Where is she? What did they do to her? *What is happening?*

Before I know it I'm being pushed forward again, and then someone sweeps my legs from beneath me, and my breath is knocked from my lungs as I'm thrown onto a hard floor. It has a warmth I'd almost forgotten. Wood. I hear footsteps moving away, and it seems like I'm alone now. I wrestle to my feet, yank the bag off my head and blink into the light. When my eyes adjust, I'm looking at a scene of carnage.

The Colosseum looks like a war zone, littered with bodies, the sand stained crimson. I stare at it in disbelief, unable to think past what I'm looking at. But that's when I see Clarke, motionless. A team of Officers, dragging her along the ground, towards a truck. I look around, and I'm in the back of a truck with a bench running down one side. Outside, there are a semicircle of about half-a-dozen trucks, and Clarke is thrown into one directly across from the one I'm standing in.

I don't know what I'm doing, one second I'm still and the next second I'm moving, lunging across the truck bed and out of it and back towards the Colosseum. As if I will be able to reach her, as if I will be able to do anything even if I did reach her. As if there was any chance of making it out alive now.

But my feet hit the ground, and I run, screaming Clarke's name. I get six feet from the truck she's thrown into before something unbelievably hard and heavy cracks against the back of my skull, and then there's nothing at all.

22

I come to slowly, and immediately feel something soft beneath my head. My eyes blink open, but there's something covering my face, so I can't see. When I try to reach up, I can't move my hands, and there's a sharp tug against my wrists.

I go still, trying to piece together what happened. It comes back to me in bursts, flickers of the Colosseum returning like random puzzle pieces.

I pull against the ties around my wrists, testing them. They're tight, and I can already feel where they've cut into the skin around my wrists, but they don't seem to be attached to anything; I can move my arms up and down behind my back, even if I can't separate my hands.

I go still again, trying to listen for any sounds around me. I have to figure out where I am and who else is here before I can try to move. But I can't hear anything. I hold my breath, trying to shut off all my other senses, and eventually I hear talking. It sounds far away and muffled, not near me. Slowly I roll onto my back, ignoring the pain in my wrists. Sitting up, I push myself up off the floor and into a standing position. I sway slightly on my feet, trying to find my balance blindly.

For a second I just stand there. The ground is definitely solid underneath me, and there's no jostling, so I'm not in a truck bed. Maybe they put me in a cell while I was unconscious? But it doesn't smell like the Colosseum. It's different. It hits me like the shock of cold water: *They brought me back. They brought me back. I'm back in the Room, waiting for him. They only took me out to play with me. They brought me back.*

I can't see anything, but I feel the world tipping to the side as panic washes over me. I take a shaky breath, trying to pull myself together.

I don't know anything yet. I could be anywhere. If they had brought me back there, they would have had to bring me back to Oasis. And I couldn't have been unconscious for that long. I couldn't have.

I couldn't.

I can't think. I can't think of anything but the fact that our chance to escape is blown, and that I don't have any idea where Clarke is, or what they plan on doing with us, or how I'm supposed to get out of this, and it all cycles through my head so fast that it's strangling me, rising the bile in the back of my throat as I try again and again to pull out of restraints that have no intention of breaking.

I see flashes of the Officers taking Clarke. *Officers.* Why? Why now? No sign of them for months, then there they are, barging in on top of us in a wave of blue uniforms.

Suddenly there's a screech and a bang. I snap my head around towards the sound, but I can't see anything but the slight glow of the light that can filter through the blindfold.

I try to move away from the door, my throat closing up at the thought of what happens next, what happens after the door opens, the people on the other side and the symphonies of pain they pull out of you—

I fall backwards, my back cracking against the hard ground. The bonds around my legs tripped me, and now I can hear them approaching, and I try to move, push myself away with my legs, but I'm tied up like an animal and someone is dragging me up by my arms and I try to fight back, but I still can't move and I still can't see and I still can't do anything at all.

My feet are placed back on the ground and I almost pitch forward, but I'm caught and steadied. The tightness around my ankles gives way, and I feel something hard pressed at my back. I know it's a gun.

A voice in my ear says, 'Move'.

I stumble forward, and I can feel the cold from the gun seeping through the fabric of my tunic. The chill of the steel focuses my brain, and I force myself to keep walking forward as my mind searches for ways to escape.

There has to be a way out of this. There's a way out of everything.

A second later I can hear other voices, well over a dozen, and a few steps later the sound of engines fills my ears. I stumble again as I realise I must be in some kind of Officer camp. So it must be an Officer behind me, with the muzzle of his gun imprinting on my back.

We must still be Outside, because I can smell the trees around us and feel the breeze, but how far from the Colosseum we've come I can't tell.

The gun at my back keeps pushing me forward silently, and eventually the sounds of motors and voices begin to diminish, and that's when I understand what's happening.

They're going to kill me.

23

I woke up to the sound of a door opening, not closing. Light, however dim, poured out onto the ground in front of my feet, and I blinked rapidly, struggling to adjust.

He stood in front of me, expression blank, and I thought—

I'm supposed to be dead—

And—

Why am I not dead?—

And—

Not again, please not again—

I jerked my hands towards myself instinctively, but as my wild eyes searched the room, I realised I was back again, back to the beginning, back in the room.

'Don't struggle,' he said, same steady, calm voice from across the room, but he didn't move towards me. 'You'll hurt yourself.'

I went still, squeezing my eyes closed and willing myself to wake up. Willing this to be a nightmare.

My eyes flashed open when I felt his fingers on my chin, lifting my face towards him.

'You look tired,' he cooed, turning his head to the side as he looked down at me, and I pulled away, as far as I could get, but he just caught my face again. 'You get to decide when this is over,' he said. 'Just tell me what I want to know, and it'll stop.'

I knew what was coming next. The pain and the screams that came from me but didn't sound like me, and him and his constant soothing voice, making me feel like I was being turned inside out.

The moments where you desperately search for something that makes sense, for gravity and sanity, and all you're met with is horror, the quiet horror of the one gentle thing in your world being the thing that's tearing you apart.

And it came from my mouth without my permission, was wrenched up from some wretched raw part of myself that couldn't understand why he wouldn't stop, why I wouldn't stop him.

'Please,' I pleaded, and my voice sounded even less like myself in that moment than it did when I was screaming, but I still said it again. 'Please,' and again, 'please,' and again 'please'.

'Say it,' he whispered, and his hand was on my face again, cradling it, my blood slick between his palm and my cheek. 'Say it.'

'I'll tell you.' I could barely speak and I wasn't sure then if it was because my mouth was full of blood or because some part of me was still begging me to stop. 'I'll tell you what I know.'

He went quiet, releasing my face, and I forced my eyes to open and look at him. He was smiling again, but it wasn't the smile I had seen before. It wasn't like any expression I'd ever seen him make, lips pulled back over teeth, his mouth open as he rolled his head back.

'It's always my favourite part,' he said in a sing-song whisper. 'Broken, broken, broken.'

When he shook himself out of his blissful stupor, his eyes locked back onto me, and the look in them was irrevocably different. They were like pools of water that had frozen over and turned to ice.

'Did you actually think you knew anything we didn't?' He chuckled. 'You're an idiot.'

My spine straightened – he was like a different person, like I had blinked and he had been replaced.

'But he wanted you broken first.'

I kick out at the floor, trying to find enough energy to push myself up from where I was slumped on the chair.

'First?' The word is wet with blood and fear, and I can't find the floor with my feet.

'This is only the beginning.' He stepped forward, catching me by my hair and pulling my head back. 'Ruined and sent to rot in hell, that's what he wanted for you.'

He, he, he. For a moment I thought he meant Aaron – I couldn't help it. In there I couldn't tell if he was alive or dead, if he had shot me or if I had shot him. Sometimes I thought I saw his face in dark corners and heard his voice echo into the icebox. 'But the OP didn't order you to be sent to hell,' he mused, that vicious smile pulling at his mouth again. 'No,' he said, as he walked back to the door, calling for the men to come and drag me back out of the room.

'Where you're going is much worse.'

24

I want to run, to die running, but I feel paralysed, muscles disobeying, brain racing. I focus on moving my feet, taking each step. I can hear the breeze rustling through trees around us, and I struggle to keep my footing on the uneven ground. He's taking me away, somewhere no one will hear me die. Somewhere no one will find me after.

The voice again: 'Stop.'

I stop. A second later, I hear the gun load, and every muscle in my body tenses.

I'm ready, I scream inside my head, trying to convince myself that it's true. *I'm ready to die.*

A gunshot rings out, and I wait for the pain. For the world to fade from me. For *something*, but everything is exactly the same.

My fingers claw the blindfold from my face, not caring about the consequences. My eyes work to adjust once again. The light filters in through the thick foliage above me, and an Officer stands a few feet away, the gun back in his holster.

He's already turning away. 'Go,' he says over his shoulder.

'Wait.' My heart is beating too fast, so fast that it's making me lightheaded as I try to comprehend what's going on. 'Why didn't you kill me?'

'I'm just doing my job,' he mutters. 'Now go, before they come looking for us. And you better hope you don't get caught, because you're not getting a second chance.'

I don't wait for him to say more. I don't wait for an explanation or for any of this to make sense. I don't wait in case he plans on shooting me in the back as I run, because it doesn't matter. All I see is the escape, the freedom, the chance.

I'm falling, running, tumbling away from him and the Officers and the Colosseum and everything before something changes. Because I can't die. I'm not ready. I want to *be*. Some heroic part of me wishes I was braver than that, but there are deeper, darker parts that refuse to let go.

And right now, those are the only parts of me I can hear.

25

My muscles shake as I pull myself up higher and higher into the tree. It's been hours, I don't know how many, but enough that the sun has set, and I can barely see my hands in front of my face as I climb.

I couldn't keep running, but I couldn't stay down there either. If I dozed off in the middle of nowhere and the Officers found me, I'd be taken back. Back to the Colosseum. Back inside. And I can't do that.

I can't ever go back.

My foot slips against the bark, and my body slams against the trunk of the tree as I desperately grapple for a better handhold. I right myself, my left foot finding a foothold against a smaller branch, and I pull myself higher, my arms shaking as I beg them not to give out for just one more second. I need to hold on for just one more second.

There has to be a reason he let me go. Maybe this was Nails's plan all along? But why didn't he tell Clarke that to begin with? Something could have changed while we were inside, of course, but I don't understand why they would have split us up if that were the case.

My stomach drops at the thought of her, and I wedge my foot between two branches, pushing myself up onto one of the limbs of the tree so I can catch my breath. I want to keep climbing until the ground beneath me blinks out of existence, but there's no point.

I lean my back against the trunk of the tree, pulling my knees up under my chin. I can tell, in a far-off way, that my feet are bleeding, but I can't *feel* it. I don't know if I'm numb from the cold or the shock or the fear or what, but I can't feel anything.

I don't dare to close my eyes in case I fall asleep. I try to focus on my breathing, to steady the heartbeat pounding in my temples.

I press my knuckles to my forehead and try to think.

Think.

What do I do next? I don't even know where I am.

This isn't how this was supposed to go. Nails was supposed to get us out. *Us*, both of us, together. But Nails isn't here and neither is Clarke and that wasn't the plan, this isn't the plan.

That's when I hear it, the crack of a twig beneath someone's foot. I go completely still. The sound doesn't return. I stay silent, listening for the sound to come again, but it never does.

Did I imagine it? I catch a branch above my head, ready to climb higher, out of view, still staying as quiet as I can. Maybe I'm hearing things because I'm afraid.

But then I hear it again, and my eyes shoot to the ground beneath me, where it came from.

And there, wandering between the trees, is Clarke. I nearly fall out of the tree with relief. I climb down in seconds, terrified of losing sight of her, as if she's about to disappear.

The second I'm on the ground, she sees me, whipping around in the half-light.

'Clarke,' I breathe, staring at her. 'You're alive.'

Her eyes bypass me and land on the tree behind me. 'You climbed a *tree*?'

'What?'

'Why the hell did you climb a tree?'

I'm dumbfounded, and for a second my mouth just opens and shuts. Then I stutter out, 'The Officers could have come after me—'

'And giving yourself no escape route was the best you could come up with? You get kind of stupid when you're panicked, you know that, right?' she says, shouldering past me.

I turn around to stare at her, but she's already walking off, so I follow, almost tripping over the broken branches beneath our feet.

'Clarke, I was *worried* about you. They could have killed you!'

'Of course they weren't going to kill me. Nails's plan must have changed. We're out, aren't we?'

'Because *Officers* took us out at *gunpoint!*'

'Yeah, well, we're also alive. When you find an Officer who releases prisoners out of the kindness of his heart, let me know. I wanna meet him.'

'Clarke!' I grab her shoulder, pull her around to face me, suddenly enraged. 'What is your *problem*? We could have been killed. I didn't know how I was ever going to find you, even if they didn't kill you. And now you're here, and we're safe and we're okay, and *that's* all you have to say to me? That I'm *stupid when I'm panicked*?'

'What was I supposed to say?' Her voice is hard and her expression is harder. 'If you're afraid that you're being tracked, putting yourself in a position where there is no escape is not exactly ideal. There's no point telling you that, though, because it's not like you'd listen to me.'

'What's that supposed to mean?'

'It means that you ignored me when I told you not to talk to Noah. It means that no matter what I say, you do what you want, even if it puts both of us in danger.'

'But I thought—' I blink at her rapidly, trying to form a coherent thought. 'You didn't say anything, after I got back, you didn't say anything …'

'Because there's no point.'

'Clarke …' A lump forms in my throat.

'Don't,' she snaps. 'I'll get over it.'

She turns away from me, but I follow her again.

'No.' I step in front of her. 'Wait. I'm sorry. I'm sorry for not listening.'

She sighs a long, deep sigh, staring down at the ground. 'I need to be able to trust you, Quincy. Not just trust that you'll have my back, but that you'll listen to me. We're supposed to be a team. That's the only thing that kept us alive in the Colosseum.'

'I know.' I nod. 'I know that it's the only way we could have survived in there, I know that. But Clarke, we made it through. We're out.'

She nods, her jaw twitching. 'I know. But now we need a plan. Nails was supposed to have supplies for us, have a plan for after we got out. But we don't even know where we are right now.'

'Well, we need to start moving.' I glance around. 'For all we know, they could be following us.'

'We can figure out where we're going later,' she says. 'Right now I just want more space between me and those Officers.'

I nod. She's right. Regardless of how tired we are, the longer we stay still the more chance there is of them finding us.

And that's not an option.

26

We spend the day walking. Clarke doesn't speak, and I don't make her, but I do follow her lead. I don't have the headspace to decide which direction we should be moving in, and she pulled ahead without a word. I'm not complaining. Now that she's here, and she's safe, my mind has fixated on everything else I swore to myself I'd do once I got out.

Find Sophia. Find Jay and Kole. Find the rebels.

I won't be able to breathe properly until I know they're safe. I *haven't* been able to breathe properly since I left them.

We stop when we find water. It's a small stream cutting through a thicker part of the forest, and we almost missed it. Clarke caught the sound of it before we had gone too far, though, and switched directions so we could drink and rest for a minute.

I dip my hands into the water, almost pulling back at the icy temperature. It runs up my arms as I scoop up handfuls of it to drink, but it's more than worth it when I finally sit back on my heels, the burning thirst in my throat finally quenched.

Clarke is leaning back on her hands, staring upwards, where the gaps in the trees show the sky, as if she can find answers there.

'I've gone over it in my head a thousand times,' she murmurs. 'None of it makes sense.'

'None of what?'

'None of it. None of that. Nothing that happened when we escaped.'

My fingers rip at the grass beneath me. I know that. I knew the plan, backwards and forwards and inside-out, and that was as far from the plan as we could get.

'We can't think about that right now.'

'Like hell we can't. The whole reason that the Colosseum is the Colosseum is because the Officers just dump us in there and throw away the keys. Since when do they charge in to halt riots?'

'I don't know.' I pull my knees up, hooking my arms around them as I look at the stream. It's narrow and shallow, no fear of drowning in it, but my mind flashes back to all those months ago. That's how I met Kole. Underwater. Drowning. That's what I feel like right now, that I'm drowning all over again, but when I look around, he's not here. There's no one to pull me out this time.

'What matters is that we're out. We can find Kole and the others and Sophia and—'

Clarke looks away abruptly, making an irritated sound in the back of her throat.

'What?' I ask, halting mid-sentence.

'You're not thinking anything through, as usual.'

'And what's that supposed to mean?'

'Have you thought about whether or not they're even at the Base anymore? It's stupid to assume they would have stayed. How many attacks do you think it was going to take before they finally left?'

'I don't care,' I mutter, gritting my teeth. 'If they're not there, I'll find them.'

'And what if they're still in Oasis? There's no guarantee they even made it out. The last time I saw them they were running for the wall, but the Officers were after them. God knows what happened.'

My heart drops into my stomach. 'If they're still in Oasis, then I'll go back for them.'

Clarke looks away.

'Why are you being like this?' I ask. 'You knew that this was what I was going to do once I got out.'

She looks down at the grass between her feet, the muscle in her jaw twitching. 'It's not what I'm going to do,' she says, under her breath.

'What?'

'I said, it's not what I'm going to do. All I ever wanted was to take down Oasis. You tried to do that, and it got you locked up in the Colosseum. I wasn't going to just leave you there, and I didn't, but that doesn't mean I can follow you around on every wild goose chase you go on. I need to do what I came here to do.'

'But I promised Sophi I'd come back for her and—'

'That's fine,' she says impatiently. 'But I had a brother before all of this. And parents. I had a family. And I can't forget about them. Not for you, or for anyone.'

'What are you talking about?'

'I'll go as far as the Base with you, but after that, I have to figure out what *my* next move is.'

I look away, staring at the water as it moves past us. 'Okay.' I nod. 'We'll go as far as the Base.'

'What Base?'

Clarke and I jump to our feet in an instant, whipping around to face whoever asked that question.

In the middle of the opening, only a few feet from us, stands Noah.

'What Base?' he repeats.

'How the hell are you here?' Clarke says, and instead of taking a step back, she takes one forward.

'I could ask you the same thing,' he counters.

'It's none of your business.'

'Did you see the gangs go at each other?' he asks, ignoring Clarke's sour tone.

'It wasn't exactly avoidable,' I say through gritted teeth. He's acting like we met him while he was out on a morning stroll.

'You know how long they had been holding back?' he asks, looking utterly amused by the whole thing. 'It was too easy to set them off. Once all hell broke loose, I made a break for it. Managed to get past the Officers who were coming in, hid under a truck, then when they were all inside, I just ran for it.' He looks at us like he's expecting a medal. 'I'm thinking Genesis might have had a hand in it some way.'

I'm alert again, thinking. 'Are you going to them now?'

'Of course.'

I look around, as if Genesis will somehow materialise out of thin air. 'Where is it?'

'Not far. I should get there by nightfall.'

I look over at Clarke, and she gives a tiny shrug.

'Bring us with you,' I say.

He looks hesitant for a moment. 'We'll have to let Silas decide if that's a good idea.'

'Who's Silas?' Clarke asks.

Noah grins at us, enjoying the turning of the tables, the knowledge that he has one over on us now. 'You'll have to just find that out for yourself.'

27

The sun is setting when we step into the middle of a small clearing and Noah stops dead.

'We're here,' he says.

I look at the emptiness around us, confused.

'Oh yes,' Clarke says dryly. 'It's wonderful. So majestic. A true rebel HQ.'

Noah rolls his eyes. 'Not this,' he says, gesturing around him. 'That.'

He points at what at first looks like a boulder, but as we get closer I realise there's an opening in the side, just big enough for one person to fit through. Noah ducks his head and disappears into the darkness. I glance at Clarke. 'This feels wrong,' I mutter.

'What, you thought it was going to be a celian palace?' she scoffs. 'If this really is Genesis, they've survived out here for years without Oasis ever finding them. Living in a hole sounds about right to me.'

I chew on my lip for a moment, and Clarke pushes ahead of me.

'If you're not going, then I am.' She follows Noah inside and I only hesitate for a second before following her.

I don't want to go into that darkness, but it's better than standing out here alone.

I reach my hands out on either side of me to steady myself. There's a steep, pitched incline the second you walk inside, ending abruptly against a cold metal wall.

'The entrance,' Noah explains. I can hear the smile in his voice, even though I can't see a thing.

He raps on the huge metal panel as Clarke and I try to find our footing in the narrow passage. A small window opens in the door, and I see a flash of dark eyes before there's a groaning sound as the door heaves open, releasing us into an inner room, lit with stark, white overhead lights.

I blink against the sudden onslaught of light. Noah strides straight in, Clarke follows him, doesn't hesitate. I stand on the threshold, doubt gnawing at my insides. I don't like this. It feels like another cell, another prison, another mistake. I don't like this.

I have to force my feet to move forwards. I take a step, then another, and then I'm over the threshold, inside, and the door closes behind me. There's no turning back now.

PART TWO

LABYRINTH

1

'Noah.' A dark, curly haired man stands in front of us, staring at Noah in awe. 'Where the *hell* have you been?'

'Prison.' Noah grins, slapping him on the back as he pulls him into an embrace. 'Among other things. Wilke, this is—' He freezes, glancing back at us.

Offering our names up to them like a formal greeting seems absurd, so I just stare back at him, watching as he squirms awkwardly for a moment before turning back to face Wilke, who's looking on in confusion.

'These are some people I met while I was inside,' he says, shifting from one foot to the other. 'And this is Wilke. He's our hacker extraordinaire and resident tech head.'

'I prefer tech genius,' Wilke says, raising an eyebrow as he reaches out to shake my hand. He glances at Clarke briefly, but she gives him a look that would kill weaker men and he backs off quickly.

'I need to go find Silas,' Wilke mutters. 'He's going to want to know about this.'

'Indeed I do.' An older man with greying hair comes towards us down the hall. 'But I'm already here.'

He's not particularly tall, standing only a few inches taller than me, but there's something about the way he looks around, the way he holds himself, that exerts control. I'm not the only one who feels it either. Wilke and Noah react immediately, a subtle but obvious shift in the way they stand, moving to hold their hands behind their backs as if they're Officers in a line-up.

'Silas,' he says, introducing himself as he nods to each of us. 'Noah, it's good to have you back. I look forward to hearing all about your adventure.'

'It was productive, I think. More people are thinking and talking about getting out of Oasis. I really think our time is coming.' Noah nods, his excitement evident. I don't know anything about Noah's past, but I can take a wild guess and say that a lot of it happened here. There's something about the way he relaxed the minute he got through the door that speaks to a steady kind of familiarity.

I can't help wondering what that would feel like. To have a place so familiar that you unconsciously respond to it, automatically feeling better, calmer, safer. I wonder if I returned to the house in the Inner Sector, the one with the perfect white walls and perfect garden, where I lived for the first seven years of my life, would it feel like that, after all this time? Or if I returned to the Base – the closest thing to home I've had since I was taken from the Inner Sector? But of course it wouldn't. I learned my lesson a long time ago. There's no such thing as permanent, and there's no such thing as safe. Not really. Without those things, it's not a home. It's just another building you've spent too long inside.

'Wilke, take the girls to eval, will you?' Silas says, startling me out of my reverie.

'Uh, yeah, sure.' Wilke glances around at all of us, as if he's struggling to keep up with the subtext, but I'm more concerned with what Silas just said.

'What?' Clarke and I say at the same time. 'Eval?'

'Come with me.' Wilke flashes us a smile, but I can't help noticing that there's a tinge of nervousness in it, although maybe that's just because Clarke looks like she's going to kill someone with her bare hands. 'I'll explain while we're walking.'

2

'Evaluation,' he says, running his hand through the curly mess of his hair. Clarke won't stop shooting me looks. 'It's standard procedure. Everyone who comes into Genesis gets a standard evaluation.'

'For what?'

'Well, to make sure you're not a spy.' He laughs awkwardly and won't stop messing with his hair. I suppress the urge to slap his hand away from his head and try to focus on building a mental map of the building.

But this place is a maze. He keeps turning down new corridors, and every time he does, it opens us up to more. I try to keep track of the turns we take, so I can find my way back out if I need to, but every time I add a turn, I forget another one.

I'm beginning to feel more than a little claustrophobic, but he keeps pressing on further. It feels like I'm burying myself alive with each step, and I unconsciously start to slow down.

I don't like this. The halls are too narrow and the lights are too artificial. How deep are we underground now anyway? It could be ten feet or ten thousand feet and I wouldn't be able to tell the difference.

'Okay, so basically,' Wilke starts, fixing his shirt as if he's beginning a speech, 'every new person in Genesis is classed as a new recruit.

No one just stays here – it's a rebel base, not just a hideout. We're here to work and make things happen. So we do evals to make sure you're trustworthy and then more extensive ones to figure out your place in the organisation. For most people, that's as a standard recruit, which means they'll help with the upkeep of the bunker and, of course, when the time comes, they'll be frontline soldiers.'

'Wait.' I stop him mid-monologue. 'Genesis is going to fight Oasis? Physically start a war?'

'Yeah!' He grins, glancing back at me.

I've fallen a few steps behind, the narrow hallways tempting me to just turn around and go back up, up and out and outside and somewhere where the air doesn't feel like it's being pumped in through vents. But now I stop dead, staring up at Wilke and his ridiculously excited expression.

'Silas calls it the three-pronged attack: infiltrate, take out Johnson and retake Oasis.'

'And how are you planning on doing that?' My voice sounds more accusatory than I mean it to. I'm being too emotional, and it's making me careless.

He grins widely. 'We know everything about Oasis. We've been watching them for years. We have our ways.' Then his smile falters. 'I shouldn't have told you any of that, should I?'

I glance over at Clarke, confused.

'Okay, don't tell Silas I told you any of that, right? We're not supposed to tell recruits about the plan until *after* evals.'

He stops at the top of a new hallway, spreading his arms wide. 'Pick a room, any room. We're empty at the moment, so you get to have your choice.'

I look along the row of identical rooms. It doesn't matter which one I choose – it's impossible to differentiate between them anyway.

'This one is my favourite.' He points to the second door on the right. 'But I'm biased. That was my eval room.'

'How long will this take, exactly?' I ask, pulling open the door to Wilke's 'favourite' eval room. It's a white-walled cell, cleaner than the ones at the Colosseum definitely, but a cell nonetheless.

'Depends.' He pulls open the door next to mine, gesturing for Clarke to enter. She glares daggers at him as she passes. 'Can take up to three days, depending on your answers.'

'Three days?'

'Maybe not, though. Might be quicker.' Wilke looks down apologetically.

'Just get in,' Clarke grumbles. 'It's not like we have a choice.' I shoot her a questioning glance. 'Listen, we try to leave now, they either shoot us on the way out or we die in the middle of nowhere. We spent six months in the Colosseum. We can take a few days in here.'

I swallow, staring at the cell. It doesn't look like the Colosseum, I realise, as I step slowly inside the small room. I glance up at the ceiling, the single lightbulb hanging from it and the flickering light it sheds across the emptiness.

I look back at the door, watch with a pounding heart as Wilke flashes me another apologetic smile and closes it. I hear a bolt slide across on the outside. Then Wilke's footsteps as he walks away.

I look around me. No, it doesn't look like the Colosseum at all. It looks like my torture room.

3

'Good morning.' As the door is suddenly thrown open, I see Silas standing there, smiling.

I startle from where I'm seated in the corner of the room, huddled against the wall, trying and failing to fall asleep for the past several hours.

'We'll be starting the first phase of your evaluations now.' He steps back out of the cell, leaving the door open, and I get to my feet awkwardly, trying to stretch cramped muscles as I follow him out into the hall.

There are two guards outside my door, dressed in all black and avoiding eye contact, and they follow me three doors down, to a room holding nothing but a table with a chair on either side.

'Is this really necessary?' I ask, gesturing to the guards.

'Standard procedure.' Silas flashes that sickly sweet smile again. 'Not all of our recruits are quite as amiable as you in the beginning.'

I can't help glancing back at Clarke's cell. I have a hard time imagining that she will be particularly amiable.

I step inside the small room and pull out one of the chairs, plonking myself unceremoniously into the seat and staring Silas down until he follows suit.

'So?' My back aches from sleeping against the wall. 'I don't particularly appreciate escaping a high-security government prison just to be thrown into another cell somewhere else. How does this work, and how quickly can we get it done?'

Silas looks amused. 'I'll ask you a few questions. If I'm satisfied with your answers, we'll move on and continue until everything checks out.'

'And what exactly constitutes you being "satisfied" with my answers?' I don't even try to sound civil. I didn't sleep last night; every time I closed my eyes the room morphed around me, turned into the other room, the one inside Oasis.

He opens a folder on the table, picks up a pen and begins writing. I can't see what he's doing from across the table.

'I'll be able to tell if you're lying, and I assure you, it won't be tolerated.'

I sit back in my chair, glowering at him. Clarke said we had no choice, but I'm beginning to question that.

He looks back up at me. 'Tell me your full name.'

'Quincy Emerson.'

'Age?'

'Eighteen.'

'And you were born …?'

'In the Inner Sector.'

'And what were your test results?'

'Positive for the X Gene.'

'Okay, so you were moved to the Outer Sector at what age?'

'Seven. Everyone knows it's seven. You get tested at seven and moved directly once you test positive.' Under the table my fists are clenched so tightly, my hands are starting to shake.

There's a sensation rising up in my chest, like there's something swelling up inside me. I'm not panicking. I'm not. This is ridiculous. There's no reason for me to be panicking.

'Just trying to keep the facts straight, Miss Emerson,' he says calmly.

Miss Emerson. The only other person who ever called me that was Johnson.

'Where did you spend your time in the Outer Sector?'

'The Dorms, like everyone else who is moved out.'

'And I understand that you were removed from the prison commonly known as the Colosseum only days ago, is this correct?'

'Removed?' As if it was that simple. As if it was a transfer. As if I wasn't blindsided by Officers and dumped in the middle of nowhere for reasons I *still* don't understand.

But I'm not recovering from the Colosseum, or trying to track down those Officers, or trying to figure out why I was taken in the first place. No, I'm locked in this room, dragging out the details of information he already knows.

'So what I would like you to do, Miss Emerson,' he says, pausing his note-taking for a moment and placing his pen on the table to look at me, 'is to explain to me the events that took place between when you were placed in the Outer Sector at seven years of age and finding yourself in the most notorious Oasis prison eleven years later.'

I stare at him, but he doesn't blink.

'You want me to explain my entire life to you?'

'No, I just want to know how your situation changed from being just another Dormant girl in the Outer Sector to being an inmate in an extremely violent and dangerous prison.'

'I broke into the Celian City. I tried and failed to kill the Oasis President and killed a few guards in the process.' My voice doesn't tremble when I say that. I look him right in the eye and speak in an even tone, even as a thousand memories cut into me like hailstones.

'That's quite a story,' he says.

'You don't think I did it? Why else would they have put me in the Colosseum?'

'I'm just confused as to how a teenage girl would be capable of pulling off such a stunt alone.'

'I wasn't alone.' This feels dangerous. I cross my arms over my chest.

'Who helped you?'

'Rebels,' I say. 'From the Outside.'

'You see, Miss Emerson, we're the only rebel force I'm currently aware of. So enlighten me as to how you discovered these *rebels*.'

I'm gritting my teeth so hard, I'm worried they're going to shatter. Every word that comes out of his mouth is so laced with condescension, I'm struggling to hold myself back from jumping across the table at him.

'I escaped from Oasis nine months ago.'

'And you met these rebels then?'

I nod.

'And no one escaped with you? When you met these rebels, you were alone?' He looks up from his notes again.

'Why are you asking me that?'

'I'm just trying to get an idea of how you got into the situation that you claimed you got into.'

'No.' I start shaking my head. There's a look in his eye, something like excitement. Like he's hunting something down and he's just about caught it. 'You're looking for something.'

He smiles, a slow, greedy smile, and shivers run up my spine.

'You're right,' he says, dropping his pen onto the table. 'And it's not some*thing*, it's some*one* I'm looking for.

'We know you've been involved with Aaron Johnson.'

My eyes shoot wide at the mention of his name, and I clench my hands into fists under the table, attempting to suppress my reaction.

Just his name. All he said was his name, and my head is swimming.

'And,' Silas goes on, completely unaware of my reaction, 'we know he helped you escape, taking a great risk in doing so. He obviously cares about you, enough to go against his father. And that means you have the power to make him see that working against Oasis is the only way to forge a better future.'

He doesn't have a clue what he's talking about. I'm looking right at him, and he's lying straight to my face without flinching. He doesn't even know that Aaron is dead, but he's parading his name out in front of me, along with unfounded facts, hoping to confuse me into agreeing with him.

I have to work hard to calm my breathing because I feel like laughing out loud.

'So you want me to get Aaron for you?'

Silas nods. 'That is what we want. It would mean access to extremely valuable information that would ensure our eventual attack on Oasis is successful.'

'But Aaron loves his father,' I say, and the words taste bitter in my mouth. 'More than he loves me.'

Silas smiles. 'Oh now, don't undersell yourself. If he was willing to risk helping you escape, he obviously cares about you a great deal. I think you could persuade him to join with you. To join Genesis.'

Because now I'm part of Genesis, apparently. Now that I'm useful. Now that he can get something out of me.

'But if you know everything about Oasis,' I say, almost enjoying myself now, 'then why keep waiting for things that may or may not help? Why not just plan the attack and execute it and trust in your own ability to overthrow them?'

'We just want to ensure a smooth transition,' Silas says.

'What – of power?' I ask, leaning back in my chair.

'That tone of voice isn't necessary, Miss Emerson,' he says calmly. 'You know as well as I do that this is a complicated situation. Changes will have to be made, as well as sacrifices. But having Aaron on our side will minimise the damage. Both to the rebels and to those still living in Oasis. He leans forward and places his hands flat on the table in front of us. 'Help us take down Oasis. Bring us Aaron Johnson.'

4

'What did you tell them?'

'Not much.' Clarke tears a piece of bread and dips it into the stew we were handed a few minutes ago. It's the first hot meal I've had in months, and I can barely believe how amazing it tastes. 'If you hadn't given Silas what he wanted, I doubt they would have let me out at all.'

My eyes flit around the cafeteria as I chew on my own piece of bread. It's packed in here. The room is enormous, with what looks like about three hundred people sitting at tables just like ours, eating a meal just like ours.

I glance up to the ceiling when the overhead lights start to flicker. It doesn't last long, the pale blue wash of light in the room sputters on and off for a few seconds before settling back to normal. No one else seems to notice, but it makes me feel uneasy. I've been avoiding thinking about how deep underground we are. Being locked up, whether in Oasis or in the Colosseum, that's one thing, but this is completely different. It's not right. It's like being buried alive, all the while pretending nothing has changed.

'Hey!' Clarke says, snapping her fingers in front of my face. I look over at her, shaking my head as I try to tune back in to what she's saying to me. 'I asked you a question.'

'I'm sorry.' I rub my hand down my face in frustration. 'What did you ask?'

'What did you tell him that got us out so quickly?' Clarke asks, polishing off the last of her meal.

'I just said I'd help in any way I could. No matter what.'

Clarke looks at me. 'That's it?'

I shrug. 'I think they just want to be sure we're on their side. And I am.'

She shovels another spoonful into her mouth. I've never told Clarke exactly what happened in the Towers that day. She knows some of it, bits and pieces that slipped out over time in the Colosseum. But she didn't ask for specifics, and I couldn't seem to force the words out of my mouth to explain. I thought the right moment would arrive to admit it, but then I found I never wanted to talk about it. And now it's a piece of information that might keep us alive, might get us what we want, so I'm going to hold onto it. Better she doesn't know the truth – for now, at least.

'What did you think of him?' I ask her, refocusing my attention.

'Silas?' she says. 'Not much.'

'I don't trust him,' I say, which doesn't mean a lot, not between me and Clarke. Trust is something you buy with sweat and blood; Clarke knows that as well as I do.

'Neither do I,' she says, nodding her head, as if she's approving my judgement of him. 'There's something intense about him. He's all fired up for a fight, but he's not actually doing anything. I don't understand why not.'

'I don't want to stay in here any longer than we have to,' I tell her. 'I don't like being under his thumb.'

'I hate it more than you do,' she says. 'But you had a plan before we got here. Find Sophia, find the others, fight back against Oasis. If Genesis can help you with that, you might want to slow down before you make any final judgements. It's not like you know where you're going anyway.'

'Yeah,' I murmur. I stir my stew slowly. Somehow I've lost my appetite.

'If you're not gonna eat that, you better give it to me before I slap you,' Clarke says.

I push the bowl towards her.

'Okay, you need to tell me what's wrong with you, because that was just wrong.'

'What was?' I ask, surprised.

'You just gave me your dinner.'

'You asked for it!'

'That doesn't mean you just hand it over!' she yells. Someone a table over looks across at us in irritation, but Clarke just rolls her eyes, pulling the bowl towards her over the metal table.

I see Wilke crossing the room towards us. It takes him a while to find us, though, because every few tables he passes someone stops him to say something. It's such a normal interaction, as if we haven't buried ourselves down here because the rest of the world is trying to kill us.

I guess you have to get used to it eventually.

He makes it to the head of our table and grins down at us. 'Ready?'

'For what?' I ask, glancing around as if someone is going to jump out at us.

'For the tour.' Wilke smiles. 'I asked Silas if I could be the one to show you around.'

Clarke grabs her bowl and stands up from the table.

'I don't need a tour,' she says, walking towards the door and dropping her bowl in the pile of dirty dishes before disappearing into the hall.

Wilke turns to me with a confused expression. 'Did I do something?' he asks, perplexed.

'No.' I stand up from the table myself, grabbing the rest of the dishes. 'That's just Clarke.'

5

'Silas was here in the beginning,' he says, and there's more than a little admiration in his voice as he leads me away from the cafeteria. 'Genesis was only a handful of rebels at that point. We didn't even have the bunker back then.'

'Really?' I say, feigning interest. It's not that what he's saying isn't interesting. I know I should be paying attention, but I can't help feeling uncomfortable that Clarke's disappeared.

'Yeah! We've been here for almost ten years now, but before that we moved around a lot.'

That catches my attention. 'Ten years?'

'Yup. I'm not sure exactly how long Silas has been a part of the rebellion, but Genesis was officially formed nine years ago, in this bunker.'

'They built it?' I ask, looking around. I can't imagine anyone but Oasis building something like this. It's complex and intricate, and everything is still in good shape after all these years. It's closer to an Inner Sector building than anything I ever saw in the Outer Sector.

'No,' Wilke says, and pulls to the side for a moment to let a group of recruits pass us. 'It was here long before us. Long before Oasis, even.'

I blink at him. *Long before Oasis.* I know it's true, that there was a time before Oasis, a time before the Virus. But it feels fake, like a fairytale told to get little kids to go to sleep.

'It must have been some kind of bomb bunker,' he continues, unfazed by my reaction. 'Silas says it's not the only one either, but it's the closest one to Oasis.'

'Close?' I didn't mean for my voice to rise at the end of that word, but it does anyway. How can they be close to Oasis without getting caught?

'Well, relatively speaking. It takes about five days' walking to get to the Wall.'

The tightness in my chest loosens. *Relatively speaking,* I say to myself.

'When you said about the plan ...' I start slowly, unsure of how to phrase my question. 'The one to take down Oasis – is that real? Is Genesis actually going to attack Oasis?'

It's hard to imagine that, after all this time, they would suddenly launch an actual attack.

'Of course.' Wilke looks more serious now. 'That's our job.'

'How long—'

'Have we been planning it? A long time. But it takes a long time to prepare. At first, we were too divided to really build towards anything. There were people who just wanted to see Oasis burn, and other people who didn't want any more destruction.'

'And now?'

'Now most people understand that a rebellion takes sacrifices, but we're not willing to hurt innocents to see Oasis fall. There are evil people in Oasis, but that doesn't mean everyone has to suffer.'

Evil people. I wonder how they make that distinction. It's easy for me to see Johnson as evil, but what about Aaron? That's harder.

And Kole? That's harder still, but he killed people, just like Aaron did, even if he hated every second of it.

And what about me? I killed Aaron, even if it was to protect Kole. And I killed other people, Officers, to keep myself alive, to keep the people I care about alive. Does that make me evil?

I don't know how they're expecting to draw that line, or how they're supposed to do it in the middle of a war.

Wilke is explaining the layout of the bunker, but I'm having trouble concentrating.

'What?' I blink at him. He sounds like he's speaking gibberish.

'It's simple,' he says, turning left. The halls are poorly lit, apparently to conserve energy. I've yet to have anyone explain to me where exactly their energy comes from. If I think about it too much, how complex their systems must be to keep this place running, I get dizzy. 'Four levels. One: the common room, the cafeteria and the sleeping chambers. Two: the work stations, shooting ranges, weapons rooms, all that kind of stuff. Three: where the food is grown and water filtered. Four: the generator. Each level, excluding level four, is split into wings, and each wing has an alphabetical equivalent. So right now we're on level two, wing C.'

'I'm not going to remember that.' It would be hard enough to memorise all the levels and sections and rooms in this labyrinth if I were paying attention to what Wilke was saying, but I'm too busy watching everything move around me to listen to him.

'You only really need to know three places,' Wilke says, taking my sharp tone in his stride. 'Your room, the cafeteria and the exits. Oh, and wherever your work station is, so four places.'

'Work station?'

'You'll be given a job. Probably tomorrow. Everyone is given something to do to help; that's how we've been able to stay off grid for so long. Everyone plays their part in keeping this place running. Don't worry, though, you only have to work a couple of shifts a week, so you'll have loads of time to yourself.'

Wilke has the kind of optimism that makes you exhausted just listening to it.

'This is where I work,' he says, stopping outside a door and grinning. I don't respond, so he pulls the door open and ushers me into a small, dark room. 'The monitors automatically turn off when I'm not working.' I can see him leaning over from the light shining in from the door, and suddenly monitors start lighting up in front of my eyes.

'What exactly do you ... do, here?' I ask slowly, taking a step towards the screens. They seem to be monitoring some kind of code.

'Mostly I'm the one who filters messages between our sources in Oasis and here, but I do other stuff too.'

'Sources?' I ask, cocking an eyebrow. 'Other stuff?'

Wilke grins, and it makes the blue light from the screens cast strange shadows across his face. 'We have recruits stationed across Oasis – it's how we get most of our information. And as far as other stuff—' He pauses like he's going to explain it, but then he just drops into the chair and spins towards the monitors, pulling out a keyboard and typing frantically.

I stand stock still, confused as to what just happened, but a second later he's pulled up a new screen, and he's pointing at it excitedly.

'A while ago, we organised a sort of protest against Oasis. Something safe, no one actually went into Oasis, but it was enough to show them what we are capable of.'

'Which was …?' I'm staring at the screen along with him now, but it doesn't look any different from any of the ones before it.

'We cut off the power to the fences,' he says, and I go still.

'What fences?'

'The ones around the Outer Sector. Knocked them out for several minutes. The idea was to show Oasis how easy it would be for us to break in, if we ever decided to. Or when we decide to, I guess.' He's rambling excitedly now, but my focus is caught up in something else entirely.

'When was this?' I ask.

'Sometime last year, why?'

'Nothing,' I say, shaking my head and swallowing. It couldn't be a coincidence that Wilke knocked off the power to the fences around the same time I escaped from Oasis.

It feels weird, standing in front of him now. I feel like I should thank him, but at the same time I don't want to say anything. As nice as Wilke might seem, he's a direct link to Silas, and I don't want Silas to know anything about me that he doesn't absolutely have to know.

Not until I figure out exactly what it is that he's planning.

6

We pass our evaluations and are assigned jobs in Genesis. I'm placed on dishwasher duty. Clarke is put on the third floor, down where they grow food. Apparently I don't have the 'physical specifications necessary', which is Silas's way of saying I'm too weak for the job. My laughter was humourless when Silas gave us our assignments. The same reason that had me knocked out of Aaron's Officer training programme just got me stuck washing dishes.

I work the morning shift, which means I miss breakfast and eat with the other morning workers after everyone has left.

The kitchen runs parallel to the dining hall, with a wall in between to separate the two. The cafeteria is jam-packed at meal times and deafeningly loud, but at least everyone is sitting down. In the kitchen, as everyone frantically rushes to keep up, it's like an obstacle course just trying to not get knocked over.

I'm positioned at the far end of the kitchen, where several stainless steel sinks are set up, as far from the stoves as I can get.

I'm washing dishes silently, trying to pull my brain from the chaotic noise around me and towards something like calm, but my thoughts run circles around me.

I haven't seen Silas since my evaluation, but I know when I see him next he's going to press me for an answer. I couldn't answer him then. I needed time to think.

I can't give him what he wants, but if I can use it to get something that I want from him first, maybe it's worth lying about.

After my shift is over, I don't know where Clarke is and I don't have anything else to do, so I end up wandering the halls. My initial reaction to this place being a maze was completely correct. Wilke explained it as if I'd grasp it pretty quickly, but I don't imagine I'll ever understand this place.

That begs the question, though, how long will I have to try to memorise it? How long can we stay here? We still have to find

Kole and Sophia and the others. That's my first priority, but what about when we do find them? Should I bring them back here to be interrogated and filed into line?

I get to the second-floor elevators, the ones that lead to the third and fourth levels, but there's no way through. There's a scanner by the entrance, and they're locked against anyone who hasn't been cleared for work down there.

Which Clarke has. I make a mental note to ask her about it later.

The first and second floors have elevators as go-betweens as well, but I can't convince myself to get in, so I take the stairs, a long, laborious, dizzying task that involves a seemingly endless spiral staircase. I tell myself that I already feel claustrophobic this far underground, and that the elevator will just make that worse, but even I know I'm lying to myself.

It's stupid to think that after all that's happened that something like that would bother me, but even passing the elevators makes my head spin with memories of that day.

I'm walking through one of the second-floor wings when a loud screaming sound stops me dead in my tracks. A girl bumps into me from behind, and when she tries to rush around me, I catch her by the arm.

'What the hell is going on?' I have to shout to be heard over the blaring noise filling the bunker.

The passage is already filling with people, everyone looking around, trying to figure out what's happening.

'It's the siren. Someone's breached the perimeter.' She shrugs off my grip and starts running towards the stairs, and it takes me all of two seconds to sprint after her.

I take the steps two at a time, but the flow of people is slowing me down. Half of them going down, running for the bunkers below, half of them racing upwards, with guns strapped into holsters, heading straight for the exit.

I pass the security room, which streams the footage from the outside cameras, and stop when I catch a glimpse of one of the monitors.

There is no Officer blue. In fact, there are only two people out there, stumbling out into the clearing aimlessly, as if they haven't found us at all. A man and a young girl.

That's when I start screaming.

'*STOP!*' I yell, but no one's paying attention. They're too well trained, too well focused. They file in behind the emergency exit, guns loaded and held at the ready, and I keep screaming, but they're not paying any attention to me as the doors screech open, and thirty pairs of feet sprint out of the bunker and up above ground.

'DONT SHOOT!' I'm pushing past, trying to get out ahead of them, but someone's trying to pull me back inside. '*WAIT!*' They fan out, creating a half-circle around the man and the girl, and time is slowing down, images sharpening as I run out and into the outside air again. I sprint straight into the centre of the semicircle and jump in front of the two people, and suddenly there are thirty guns aimed at me, but I don't care. I don't care about anything but the two people behind me.

Jay pushes Sophi behind him as his eyes widen, taking in the sight around him.

'I SAID, *STOP!*' Everything goes completely silent.

Silas steps out, raising a single hand that makes everyone freeze.

'Silas,' I breathe, relief washing over me. 'Tell them to back off. I know these people.'

Silas just stares at me for a moment, as if he is sizing me up in his head. Then with a flick of his wrist, one of the men behind him is at his side.

'Take them in for questioning,' he says calmly, his eyes still locked with mine.

'No,' I whisper, dumbfounded. I turn around to grab Sophi, but she's already been pulled away from Jay and is being marched to the entrance. One of the rebels tries to catch Jay by the arm, but before he can make contact, Jay's pulled a knife on him, catching the man's chin in his hand and pressing the knife to his throat.

The entire group is back on high alert faster than I can make sense of what's happening.

'Touch me again,' Jay whispers, directly into the man's face, 'and I will cut off your hands.'

'Let go of her,' I say, turning to the woman pushing Sophi towards the Base. She pauses, glancing at Silas for guidance, but it only takes me that long to catch her by the back of her shirt and pull her away from Sophi. '*I said, let go of her.*'

I punch the woman in the face and she falls to ground. I turn to grab hold of Sophi, to hug her, to protect her, but she flinches when I move towards her, her face registering only fear.

'Sophi,' I plead. 'It's me. I won't let them hurt you.'

She cowers away from me, into the boulder at the entrance, shrinking from my outstretched arms.

'Emerson!' Silas yells.

I can't hear him. All I can see are guns, bristling around me like bombs set to explode, and I can't believe this is happening. I can't believe they're not listening to me. *Why are they not listening to me?*

'They're innocent!' I shout. Why can't they see that? They've done nothing wrong but they're being treated like criminals.

'If they are, then we won't have any problems.' Silas is beside me, his tone soothing. 'You know the protocol. It's for everyone's safety.'

They've already disarmed Jay, and then they're dragging them both below ground, and I'm standing in the middle of the clearing, completely unable to do anything about it.

7

The clock in the corner of the room says it's 1:00 a.m. They put me in this room last night to 'cool off', and I've been here for almost six hours. Time is harder to handle when you see every minute, every second passing by. I'm starting to miss the time vacuum that was the Colosseum.

I stare at my hands. Stretch out my fingers, watch the muscles contract and expand as I try to figure out what the hell is going on with me. This is ridiculous. It's just an evaluation. They just have to talk to Silas, then I'll see them. I don't have anything to worry about.

But something shaky in my core makes me feel different. I just need to see them for a few minutes, make sure they're okay, and it'll go away. I'll be able to calm down. I swear to myself that if I'm able to see them for five minutes, I'll be able to breathe properly.

I tighten my hands into fists, feel the bite of my nails against my palms, then release, stretching out my fingers until I can feel the slight tug that comes with overextending. Like my skin's too tight.

That's what I feel like right now. Like my skin's too tight, and my lungs don't have enough room to breathe.

I drop my head into my hands, pulling my knees under my chin. I'm losing my mind. Why am I so scared? What's wrong with me that I can't trust that they'll be okay for a few hours without me? They survived the six months I was gone, didn't they?

8

It's cold. My body jolts upright, and I think that I'm back in the pit, but it's not that kind of cold.

I lift my hand in front of my face and it's blurry, and I don't understand. I don't understand what's going on, why everything feels suspended and unreal and why I can't see anything. And then I try to open my mouth, take a breath, and I suck in a lungful of ice water.

Without thinking, I kick my legs out, panic catching me by the throat as I realise that I'm underwater, that I'm drowning.

Maybe I am back in the pit.

I kick out again, trying to force myself into movement, but I can't. I kick and I kick at the water endlessly, and I don't move. But when I look down, my legs aren't moving at all. They're frozen in place, floating uselessly in the freezing water.

When I look up, there's a face in front of me, and I feel the shock, feel the fear burst out from my chest like an explosion, but I don't move.

I'm frozen in place, and the face gets closer, and I can't see who it is or what it is, but the more I open my mouth and try to scream, the more water fills my lungs, and the more pain shatters through my body.

The face flickers in the water and morphs, and it is Aaron and it is Johnson and it is my tormentor in the icebox and it is the face of every Officer I've ever shot all at once and one after another, tearing each other to pieces as they all reach for me at once. And I try to kick out, but my legs still won't work, and I'm frozen in place as the water consumes me.

9

I wake up violently, every muscle in my body tensing as I sit straight up to the sound of someone rapping on the door so hard I can see it shaking the second I open my eyes.

I must have fallen asleep at some point, because when I glance at the clock, it says 6:44 a.m.

The bolt shoots back with force and I jump to my feet. The door is yanked open and my heart is hammering in my chest.

'Let's go,' Clarke growls.

'What's going on?'

'We're getting Jay and Sophi out.'

I have to jog to keep up with her, because she's already marching down the hall.

Straight to Silas's office.

Clarke practically kicks in the door and I see Silas's head jerk up, startled by the sudden intrusion.

'What—?'

'I want to see them,' Clarke practically shouts, and I place my hand on her arm to calm her, but she shakes free.

'Silas.' I try to breathe around my own frustration. 'We need to talk to you about Sophi and Jay—'

'The inmates.' He nods.

I blink.

Inmates.

Inmates?

I guess to him that's all they are. But my mind can barely comprehend the word. I push into the room after Clarke as he settles back into his desk, back in control. I can hear Clarke grinding her teeth beside me. I flash her a look. I don't know what's gotten into her.

'I need to see them,' she says, like she's trying and failing to ask nicely.

'No,' Silas says, without even looking up from the papers strewn across his desk. I can see maps and lists of names. 'There's a reason why the protocol is in place, and I won't change it for you or anyone else.'

'Silas, just five minutes, please.'

'I said no, Miss Emerson, and I mean no. The inmates could be criminals for all we know.'

'They have names,' I say, and I feel something bubbling up inside of me. 'Sophia Morana and Jay—Jay—' I realise with a shock that I don't know what Jay's surname is. That I don't actually know much about Jay at all.

Stop. I know Jay. He saved my life, and he sat on top of a pile of rubble for an hour until I could figure out why the hell I was so scared of Kole, and he stood by me during the raids. I know him. I don't know his past, but that's not him. Jay is himself, not a collection of answers on Silas's evaluation list.

Silas is looking at me now, eyebrows raised in silent question.

I take a deep breath. 'Five minutes,' I ask. 'That's all I want.'

'How am I supposed to know I can trust him? I don't know him,' Silas questions.

'*I* know him.'

'How?'

'I met Jay when I escaped from Oasis. We fought side by side.' I'm trying to keep calm, keep my head, because I can feel Clarke's anger rising by the second, and we can't both blow.

But this feels too familiar. Herding people's loved ones into cells and basing their worth on test results is Oasis's job, and it has no place here, in a resistance movement.

'And?'

'And *what*? I trust him.'

'I'm not in the business of giving in to demands,' he says slowly. 'But you know as well as I do that it's not Jay that I'm interested in.'

I go still. 'What do you want?' My voice is low and my hackles are raised in a way that only happens when you already know what the answer is.

'I'll let you see them if you bring me Aaron Johnson.'

Clarke looks at me immediately, eyes searching my expression.

'That's not a fair trade. Five minutes with Jay for delivering the OP's son? No.'

'Well, how about this, then.' He leans forward, resting his elbows on his desk. 'Show me the rebels. Show me where you went when you escaped. Bring a small team of recruits to your so-called base. If you let me see that, I'll let you see the inmates.'

'There'll be no one there,' Clarke says. 'It's been too long.'

'Well, I'd like to find that out for sure,' Silas says smoothly. 'If the kind of people who can break back into Oasis are still hiding out there, I'd like to meet them, bring them on board with us.'

An image of Kole flicks into my head. If he's not with Sophi, where is he? Could he be there, at the Base, hiding out? My heart beats faster. He could be. It's possible. And it's where I've wanted to get to all along – this is my best chance to get back there and see for myself.

'When?' Clarke demands.

'Tonight.'

'Okay,' I whisper. 'Let me see them, and I'll bring you to the Base.'

10

I didn't think my hands would shake. That's the thought that runs around my head in circles as my hand hovers about the door handle, trembling. I didn't think I would be scared. Not of this. You'd think after a lifetime of Oasis and all the terror that came with it, I would have lost the ability to be afraid. But consistent fear doesn't numb your ability to be afraid: it just skews it. The sight of a gun doesn't scare me anymore, but this girl and the promises I've made to her, that does. Of all of the terrifying things in this world, *that* does. *That* scares me.

I place my hand on the door handle, and it's cold and steel and I grip it tightly and push through into a room that doesn't feel real.

The last time I saw Sophi, we were both in Nails's place in the Outer Sector. I remember kneeling down in front of her in the common room, taking her small hands in mine, promising her I wouldn't come back to her until I had fixed something. I said that I'd be back, and that when I was, things would be better. Safer. For me and for her.

It doesn't feel real that's she's actually here. She looks up at me now, and suddenly two piercingly blue eyes are punching holes in my chest the same shape as that lie.

She blinks slowly, pushing herself to her feet as I take a hesitant step inside the room. She's taller, and for some reason that seems ridiculous to me. Absurd. Absurd that life kept on moving out here while I was in there. That she grew and changed, that her hair is shorter than it was the last time I saw her.

That she looks even more like Beatrice than she did only six months ago.

'Hey, Sophi,' I croak. She's wearing black trousers and a blue T-shirt, probably provided by Genesis. I can hardly process that she's actually here, sitting in front of me. Real. 'It's been a while.'

It was supposed to be a joke, but it turns into a hiccuped half-sob as she continues to blink at me silently.

She doesn't answer, and it makes me nervous. I shift from one foot to the other, my eyes shooting around the room as if I'll find answers in the dusty corners and the concrete walls.

'How have you been?' I ask, leaning back against the door and hiding my hands behind my back.

'Okay.' Her voice is small, and she won't stop glancing between me and the door behind me.

'Yeah?'

'Yeah.'

'You know, when I told you I'd come back for you, I meant that,' I say, my voice catching. I try to breathe around the lump in my throat, to slow my racing heart. Why is this so hard?

She squints, and for a second my heart plummets. I think for a second that it's anger I see on her face, but it's not. It's fear, it's confusion.

'I'm sorry,' she says, rubbing her palms down her trousers nervously. 'But who are you?'

I laugh, but I almost choke on the sound. 'What?' I ask, and now it's my turn to blink rapidly at her. 'I'm Quincy. Don't you remember me?'

Her mouth makes a small 'O' of shock, and she nods a second later. 'I do,' she says, nodding her head. 'I do, I just … I didn't recognise you.'

My eyes immediately drop to myself, scrawny and bruised and worn out. I've seen my reflection once or twice in the mirrors in the Genesis bathrooms, even though I've tried to avoid it. Caught glimpses of my sunken eyes and gaunt face.

I didn't think I'd become unrecognisable, but I must have been wrong.

It makes sense, I tell myself. She only saw me for a few days all those months ago, and amidst all the madness of Nails's hideout. And she's only young, and a lot has happened, and her whole life has been turned upside-down … and I rationalise it in a thousand ways, but my stomach still turns as I try to force a smile onto my face.

'It's okay,' I say. 'I just wanted you to know that I didn't break my promise. I did come back. It just took longer than I meant it to.'

'That's what Kole told me,' she says, 'before he left me.'

My heart is too tight and my ribs are like a vice around my lungs, not permitting me to breathe under the weight of his name.

'Kole said that?'

'He said you'd be back. He said you'd promised to come back and that you never break your promises.'

'Yeah,' I say, and I don't know when I started crying. 'Yeah, it's true.'

She watches me for a long time after that, letting me calm down.

'He promised he'd come back too,' she says quietly, 'and that he'd bring you with him. But you're here, and he's not. Does that mean he's dead?'

'No.' It's out of my mouth before I find a breath or a heartbeat. I look down at the floor as my heart is wrenched open, and I whisper, 'Maybe.'

11

A guard swings open the door, signalling that our time is up. I glance at Sophi, as she stares up at me with those wide blue eyes. Her shorter hair makes her look older.

'I have to go,' I say, standing up from where I was crouched on the ground. My fingers twitch at my sides. I want to hug her or do something that will offer her some kind of comfort. I'd tell her I was going to come back for her soon, but there's no reason she'd believe me, so I keep my mouth shut.

Her eyes flick to the door. 'Are you going to see Jay?' she asks, and when I nod something brightens in her eyes. She doesn't smile, but she looks happier, calmer. Something like jealousy curls in the pit of my stomach, and I feel like a fool. All I want is for her to be safe, I remind myself. That's all I want.

'Jay and I will have to go somewhere for a few days,' I tell her. She looks alarmed. 'Oh no, don't worry,' I say quickly, 'it's just a quick trip. I'm hoping he'll come too. He might not be able. But we'll be back soon.'

Something crosses her face that I can't read, but for some reason it scares me. She looks so haunted. She's thinking things I can't even begin to fathom.

'Quincy?' she says softly as I turn towards the door.

'Yeah?' I whip around.

'Thank you. For making sure I was okay.'

I blink, hard, to stop the emotions that are welling up inside me from overflowing.

'Of course,' I whisper. 'Always.'

I shoot her a weak smile before walking out the door and closing it behind me.

There's a guard in the hall, a tall, sharp-looking woman with her hair tied tightly behind her head. 'He's in the next cell,' she says, gesturing to the next door.

I lay my back against the wall, closing my eyes and trying to remember how to breathe properly. 'Just give me a second.'

'I don't have all day,' she says, and my eyes blink open.

Just five minutes in a room with Sophia and I feel like my heart's been flayed. How quickly am I supposed to turn around and face Jay?

Ignoring the thudding panic in my chest at the idea, I straighten my spine, walk over to the door and tug it open, my eyes on the woman the whole time.

As if she cares if I'm glaring at her or not.

'Jay?' I ask, and my voice sounds steadier than I feel.

He's lying flat on his back on the single bed in the room, staring at the ceiling. The minute he hears my voice he turns his head, glancing over at the door languidly.

'Jay,' I breathe.

I haven't seen him since Aaron betrayed us in the Justice Tower. He looks awful.

It's easier to imagine Sophia not recognising me, somehow, as I look at Jay. His eyes are sunken and his skin is pale and grey. He looks like cloth that's been stretched too thin, like I can see the gaps forming in the fabric of him.

I remember the first time I saw him, underfed and bruised and beaten. Anyone would think that that's what would have taken the life out of him, but then all I saw in his eyes was the vicious need for revenge.

This is different. This is deathly.

'You're not dead,' he says. Not a question. An observation? Whatever it is, he's saying it to the wall, not to me.

'Neither are you,' I say, closing the door behind me. I lean against it, because I don't know what else I'm supposed to do. I don't know what I expected from him.

'Not yet.' He suddenly swings around to sit up, his tattered boots landing on the ground beneath the bed with a thump. 'Although, they took all my weapons, so we'll see how long that will last.'

'They won't hurt you, Jay.'

He cocks his head to the side, and there it is. The flash of anger, like the spark from a flint stone.

'You gone soft already?' He says it casually, like he couldn't care less, but it's an accusation.

'I didn't do anything,' I growl. What the hell is his problem? The only reason he isn't dead right now is because I stopped them from shooting him.

'Exactly,' he sneers, and I've lost him again. His eyes drag along every inch of the room, as if he'll learn something of me – of Genesis – in the cracks in the plaster.

'What's that supposed to mean?'

'You know exactly what it means.' He doesn't look at me.

'I really don't, Jay. I had to fight to see you, hell, I had to fight to stop them from shooting you yesterday, and all you can manage is an accusation and some kind of cryptic—'

'If you're so good at fighting, why the hell didn't you fight when it *mattered*?' he spits, swinging to face me, and it's then that I realise that he's not angry.

He's seething.

'What?' I breathe, suddenly frozen in place.

'The Celian City?' he says, his voice growing too loud for this small room. 'The elevator? Kole *told* me.'

'Told you *what*?' I look around, as if someone will jump up from a corner and explain to me what the hell is going on.

'THAT YOU WOULDN'T *FIGHT*!' He's on his feet, and he doesn't move towards me, but I flinch back anyway.

'What the hell are you talking about?'

'Why did you send him away?' he asks, a manic glint in his eye. 'What were you *thinking*? You don't get to just pull that sacrificial crap. You're not a hero, Quincy, you're a person.' He deflates suddenly, falling back onto the bed, growling in frustration as he drops his head into his hands.

I just stand there, dumbstruck, in the middle of the room.

'You're angry at me for giving you and Kole a chance to escape?'

A laugh gurgles out of him, and when he looks up at me his grey eyes are cold, but beneath that somewhere, it's like watching a child bleed.

'You really don't get it, do you? I'm angry at you for not at least *trying* to give yourself the same chance. You let him leave without you. You let *us* leave without you. You forced us to just abandon you in that hellhole.'

'Jay, I had to. It was the only way—'

There's a rap on the door, and I want to strangle the guard on the other side. 'Time's up!' she shouts.

There's a moment where we both just stare at each other. He looks mostly the same. Dark grey eyes, hair cropped close to his scalp, a thin, sharp mouth. But it's like the image behind the image is distorted. The energy beneath his skin has shifted, leaving him raw and savage underneath.

Vicious Jay I knew. Vulnerable Jay is a completely different story.

'Don't tell them about that day, what I did. I'm getting you out of here but I need you to keep your mouth shut,' I whisper, the life suddenly gone from me. But his lips are tight and his eyes averted, his hands folded between his knees in a concentrated effort to look untouchable.

To look untouched.

I leave the room without another word, because I don't have words. I did what I had to do to keep Sophi safe. To keep Kole safe. To keep *Jay* safe. If he has a problem with that, there's nothing I can do to fix it.

I pass through the halls numbly, not sure where I'm going. Silas is standing at the door of his office, looking pensive.

'Did you find what you wanted?' he asks calmly. There's almost a trace of worry in his tone, but it feels overpowered by pure curiosity.

'Yes,' I say, and keep walking. But I didn't. I found a terrified girl, a girl to whom I promised more than this, and a boy with more knives in his back than he could ever hold in his hands.

That's not what I was looking for. Not even close.

I stumble through the halls until I find an empty room, one of many in this labyrinth of a bunker. I slam the door behind me, placing my forehead against the cold steel of the door and try to catch my breath. I can hear the clatter of plates and yelling and stomping of feet, so I can't be far from the cafeteria.

I move away from the door, leaning against the wall and sliding down until I'm sitting, pulling my knees up to my chest. I wish Kole was here. That's part of the problem to begin with, I know, that he's not here. That I'm afraid he's never going to be here again. But I just need to hear his voice. Just once. I need to tell him everything that's happened. I don't know what he'd say, but whatever it is, I want it more than anything else right now.

I have to find him. I need to find him. Even if it's just to know that he's okay and to hear that voice one more time. Some completely unreasonable part of me thinks that if I could only hear his voice once more, just one more time, then I'd be okay. I'd be able to cope. To keep going. To *breathe*.

But the only way to find him is to force myself up and out of this room. Forget Jay's cold eyes, Sophi's blank face. Find a place between sanity and insanity where I can work long enough to search for something better.

We remember fear differently than we remember everything else. We can think we've forgotten it, convince ourselves that we've moved on, but the simplest things will have it flooding our brains like acid, and it's there all of a sudden, right in front of you, all around you.

What was a distant memory a moment ago now becomes a kind of pseudo-reality.

I heave a deep breath, pressing my face into my hands as I hunch down. I should quieten here in this quiet place.

I'm not in the Colosseum anymore, so I should feel like I'm not in the Colosseum anymore. I should feel better than this, safer than this, something other than this.

And yet, there are more kinds of fear in the world than I thought was possible. A year ago, back in Oasis, I thought there were two kinds of fear. The kind that seeped through into your bones and lived there, and the kind that strangled you from the outside.

The fear of the Virus, the fear that lived and breathed alongside me like a companion I had known since childhood, and the kind of fear that was unfamiliar, sudden. The fear of things that jump out with knives and vicious intentions.

But there are more. There are vastly more than I ever imagined. Fear of what I don't know, fear of what I do know, fear of people and for them. Fear of loss of control, and fear of responsibility. Fear of my past and how easily it could consume me, and fear because my future is a cliff with an indefinite edge.

There are fears that are born into us. Of fire and pain. And there are fears beaten into us, of people and of ourselves. And somehow the former are so much easier to overcome than the latter.

I look up, but he's not there. I know he's not. But I wish he was. I wish he was like you wish for things you know you shouldn't even want, that kind of crippling longing that only fools suffer.

'I miss you.' I whisper it so quietly, I'm not sure I even said it. 'I miss you.'

They feel like empty words. What use is it if I miss him? What does it matter? For all I know he's dead, and I'm here complaining because it hurts that I miss him.

I feel ridiculous, but I feel. I feel it all, and I hate myself for it, and I continue to feel it anyway.

'I just want to talk to you.' I don't know why I'm crying, or when I started, but there are tears spilling down my face even as I try to speak to the ghosts in my head. 'I just ... I need to just talk to you. Just for five minutes. I could ... I could breathe if I could just talk to you for five minutes.'

But I can't talk to him for five minutes, or five seconds, because I'm here alone, and I don't know where he is.

I curl in on myself and I stare emptily into the darkness, and I wish for things that I shouldn't want. And I'm the only one who feels it. I'm the only one who knows that I'm here.

It's strange how confusing that is to me. That no one will ever know that I sat here on this night, in this place, in this moment of time. Sometimes I'm one of many, a part of something bigger, a part of something stronger.

And sometimes I'm just me, the only one. Just that. The only one.

13

The dark curls around us as we trample through the underbrush behind Clarke, who's leading the group. She knows these woods better than anyone, plus we're the only ones who know where the Base is. We don't have time to spare, so we push on into the darkness.

I didn't even want to look at Silas before we left. I had asked for Jay to join us, but he refused. There was no way he was letting Jay out of that room. But he insisted that Noah and two recruits came with us, just to make sure me and Clarke were outnumbered. I don't even bother finding out the names of the other two men. If Silas insists on sending them with us, fine, but that doesn't mean I have to speak to them.

We hike single file, southbound, in heavy silence.

We walk on and on, resting the following morning, moving on again in the afternoon. We've now spent two days like this, and the exhaustion is beginning to show on everyone's faces.

Eventually even I begin to recognise my surroundings. First it's a grouping of trees that looks familiar, then a clearing that I definitely remember.

I stop when I see the building peeking out between the trees, my heart suddenly taking off in my chest.

Noah pushes me on from behind. I stumble forward and try to swallow the panic rising in my throat. I don't know why. Maybe it's the memories attached to this place. Maybe it's just because I don't like being here again, returning here as a different person. But either way, when the first grey wall pushes out beyond the fringe of trees, I feel like I can't breathe.

And that's when I see the bodies.

They are hanging, one by one, from the windows of the upstairs rooms, feet dangling in a last desperate attempt to find solid ground.

'Oh my God.' My voice is a choked whisper. My hand comes to cover my mouth, but I'm stumbling forward, forward and forward and forward towards the house, towards … towards … Walter.

I stop dead. I can't go any closer. I see every detail like it's right in front of my face. Their throats have been slit, blood pouring down their chests, dripping off bare feet.

I turn away, trying to swallow the bile rising in my throat. I trip over something beneath me, the gravel crunching under my knees. One of the recruits turns around to vomit, and my eyes snap up to Clarke. Nothing registers on her face. She just stares upwards, blankly.

Noah stands behind her, eyes wide, and I feel the incongruous need to explain this to him. Name each ashen, bruised face. Explain that these were people, real people. People I cared about.

Walter.

My heart stutters and I jolt to my feet, scanning for Mark. But he's not there. Suddenly I'm trying to remember every single person, run through a mental tally of the lives that were here for them to take. But there are only seven bodies hanging.

I blink, and then I'm running, towards the house, not slowing down.

The door doesn't budge. I can see cracks down the centre of the old wood, but it's not moving. There must be something left against it on the inside that's stopping it from pushing in. I sprint towards the back door, but when I get there, it's sealed shut too.

'AGH!' I scream, throwing my shoulder into the door again and again, uselessly.

'Hey, hey, hey, hey,' Noah says, coming out of nowhere and pulling me backwards. 'Calm down, you're just hurting yourself.'

I don't have words for him right now, so I just ignore him, pushing past and kicking at the door. Eventually he gives in, pushing me back only long enough to throw his own weight into the door. Four times he does that, and then the door swings open with a crack and a clatter.

I barely see the branch they used to block the door, before jumping past it and in to the kitchen, Noah close behind me.

The table has been flipped up against the front door, the same table that Kole and I had tea on at night when fear, fear of *this*, became too much to bear alone.

I take the stairs two at a time, but when I get up there, I don't find a blood bath, like I'd feared.

There is blood. On the walls, at the windows. But there are no more bodies. None but the ones hanging outside.

'NOAH!' I call, my voice a brittle, cracked thing. 'CLARKE! WE NEED TO GET THEM DOWN!'

I don't know how, but I need to get them down. How long have they been up there, just hanging? There's blood dried into their clothes, but their slit throats continue to ooze blood. It can't have been more than a few hours since this happened.

We were too late. We could have helped them, if we'd only been here a few hours earlier, we could have done *something* …

'Quincy,' Noah calls, and there's something wrong. I can tell there's something wrong just with those two syllables.

He's found the others.

I rush downstairs, my heart in my mouth, but I stop cold at the bottom of the stairs.

Noah stands in the middle of the room, a terrified expression on his face, as someone holds a knife to his throat.

'Mark,' I breathe.

'Quincy?' Mark's voice sounds like a shard of shattered glass, sharp and clear and broken.

Broken, broken, broken.

His knife clatters to the ground. He falls after it as Noah steps backwards sharply, towards the door, and when Mark looks back up at me, I almost wish he didn't. Because a broken voice is just a sound, but when I see his eyes, I feel my chest constrict and my knees are cracking against the stone floors as I drop down beside him.

'He's dead, Quincy,' Mark hiccups, tears streaming as he presses his face into my shoulder.

I wrap my arms around him, and I try to withhold my own pain so it won't bleed into his own. He starts speaking rapidly, sentences emerging in fragments around warbling sobs, and I can't understand a word he's saying.

'Mark, I'm so sorry,' I whisper, and I don't know what else I'm supposed do. There's nothing I can do.

'I should have left,' he says. 'When you left, I had a bad feeling. I wanted to get everyone away from this place. I was afraid they might track us back here. But I was scared.'

I don't know what to do. I don't even know what he's saying, but even if I did, how am I supposed to console him now that Walter is gone?

Gone.

Gone.

Gone.

It never feels right. It never feels real that someone can suddenly unbecome, that they are there, for days and weeks and months and years, and then suddenly they are not. Suddenly all the time in the world has slipped through your fingers and there are no more chances, no more moments, no more days or weeks or months or years.

There isn't anything. Suddenly.

'What was I supposed to do? I couldn't bring everyone out there. I couldn't keep everyone safe out there.' A shudder runs through his entire body, as if his body is remembering. 'Oh God,' he sobs. 'Oh God oh God oh God,'

I glance up, and Noah is gone. He must have slipped past at some point, but I didn't hear anything. I didn't hear anything but the inhuman sounds coming out of Mark.

I sit on the floor with Mark until he can breathe again, and it takes longer than it should. He shouldn't have to be dealing with any of this. But this is the world we live in. Family dies on you or turns on you.

I remember, with the faraway shock that comes with pain, that I took someone's brother from them. I took Kole's brother from him. And I had to, I know that, but lying here on the cold stone floor, I can't figure out which is worse: that this world breeds brothers that turn on each other or that brothers can die at all.

14

We take the bodies down. Slowly and sickeningly, we lower them from the windows and lay them out side by side on the ground below.

Mark insists on helping. I asked him not to. I didn't want him to see Walter like this, but he ignored me.

'He's my brother,' he whispered. 'I have to protect him.'

We dig graves all over again, just as we did before, back then. We lay Walter's body in a makeshift grave beside Lacey's makeshift grave, and I can't help but feel that this place is beginning to feel more like a cemetery than a hideout.

At some point, this place was some kind of refuge to me. It had hunger and pain and loss and fear, yes, but compared to what I had seen, and what I would see, it felt like something safer. It offered some kind of rudimentary protection, and the people within it offered something more.

Something like hope.

But Oasis doesn't want hope, not like this. Any hope that springs up independently, alone and unplanned for, is Oasis's enemy. Because the only power Oasis ever had over us was to strip us of hope.

As long as all our images of the future were centred around Oasis as our saviour, everything was fine. Once we found our own hope, Oasis became something different entirely. It took the people we cared about, and it took our sense of safety, and now it's taking this, the sense that this place was once something a little better, a little safer than everything around it.

Because apparently even that was too much to ask for.

Seven people. The sun is dropping low in the sky by the time we've buried them all. Seven bodies in seven heaped graves.

I leave Mark sitting by Walter's grave. I walk away, to give him space, to let him say whatever he needs to say to his brother who can't hear him. I stand against a tree, letting its strength hold me up, because otherwise I would fall down.

'We have to ask him what happened,' Noah says, coming over to stand beside me.

Clarke is searching the perimeter in the hopes of finding evidence of which way the Officers went. At least if they've gone back to Oasis, we don't have to worry about them right now. But the bloodshed was recent enough, which means they could still be prowling.

The fear of ambush never really subsides.

'I know, but not now. He's heartbroken, Noah, we need to give him a chance to process this.'

'When Silas finds out about this, he's not gonna give him a chance,' Noah whispers fiercely. 'It's better that we get the information now.'

I turn to face Noah, forcing him to look away from Mark.

'Silas isn't going anywhere near him, Noah.'

'Quincy, if you try to fight Silas on this, it won't end well. You don't have to put yourself through that.'

'I'm not going through anything.' I wish my voice wasn't shaking. 'Mark's brother was murdered. *That's* going through something. I'll deal with Silas.'

At that moment Clarke returns through the trees. 'A few footprints west, towards Oasis,' she says, holstering her gun. 'We could try to track them, but it won't do any good. They're hours ahead of us. They've done what they came here to do.'

I don't know whether to be disappointed or relieved. I'm glad they're not here, that we don't have to look over our shoulders while we're out here, but I can't pretend I don't want revenge. Simple, violent revenge. Taking down Oasis, pulling apart their machine, that's the ultimate revenge, but right now I just want blood.

15

There's a small group of people who escaped, about a mile from the house. That's what Mark says, after an hour of sitting by Walter's grave. If he wasn't the only one who could show us where they're hiding, I doubt he would have left at all. As it is, he doesn't talk to anyone, walking at least six metres from us at all times, his head down, lost in thought.

'How many people are gonna be in this group?' Noah asks, squinting into the sunlight.

'I don't know, ten? Fifteen?' I try not to dwell on how many people *should* be in the group.

'Silas isn't going to be happy,' Noah murmurs.

'Screw Silas,' Clarke grumbles, kicking a stone with her boot. My head snaps towards her immediately, but she's staring at the ground. 'Just because everyone from Genesis thinks Silas is some kind of hero doesn't mean the rebellion belongs to him. The rebellion's been alive a lot longer than he has, and it'll live a lot longer than him too.'

'Yes,' Noah says, closing his eyes briefly, like he's struggling not to slap Clarke across the back of the head. 'But the bunker belongs to him, and the weapons belong to him, and the supplies belong to him. And without that, the rebellion wouldn't be anything.'

'Ha!' Clarke's dry laugh sounds like a dead thing. 'That's what he wants you to think.'

Noah's mouth tightens into a hard line, and the second she walks away 'to find somewhere where people aren't stupid', he turns to me.

'What exactly is her problem?'

I snort in response. My eyes snap to Mark and guilt curdles in my stomach, but it was unintentional. That's exactly what I said to Lacey about Clarke during my first week at the Base.

'Too much spirit,' I grunt, and he glares at the back of her head as she walks away.

As we continue on in silence, my eyes drift back to Mark, head down, shoulders slumped, pain in every line of him, even from this distance. Clarke's entire family was murdered by Officers when she was a child, and she's still here with too much spirit. I want that for Mark. I want him to find it again, to not let them break it. But there's something about the way he's turning in on himself, as if he's folding slowly in two, that makes me wonder.

People have breaking points. I know that. There's only so much one person can go through. What if this is it for him? What if this was the one thing that could cripple him? And how long until the rest of us go down with him, picked off one at a time, using the things we love against us until we can't take it anymore?

Mark stops suddenly in front of a tree. Once I've caught up with him, I notice a cut in the bark, like someone's dug a knife into it.

'So I wouldn't get lost,' he says, staring at it. I don't know if there's some significance to this, or if it's just because everything hurts him now, but he's staring at the trunk as if he's not sure he can pull in one more lungful of air.

Pain does strange things to people, and I'm sick of seeing exactly what it does up close.

'Come on,' I say, putting my hand on his shoulder. 'We're almost there.' I don't know if we're almost there. I don't know where we are at all, but Mark needs something to snap him back to reality.

A few metres on we break through another tree line and into a clearing, and suddenly we're surrounded by people jumping defensively to their feet.

I take an automatic step back, reaching for my knife, until I start recognising faces. The rebels, or what's left of them, look like they've been through hell and back since I last saw them. They're thin and drawn looking, and when I start focusing on their faces, I see more than one set of cautious eyes bloodshot from crying.

I've seen these people in pain before, but this is different.

The second they see Mark, they relax slightly, but the sight of Noah and the recruits, complete strangers, makes them reach for their weapons.

I stare at them, numb. Eight? That's what we're left with? Eight people?

Then I realise they're still aiming their guns at Noah. I glance sidelong at Mark, but he's not responding. It's like he can't see what's going on in front of his eyes.

'Lower your weapons!' I yell, stepping out in front of our group. These people are too highly strung, wrung out; in an attempt at keeping themselves safe, they're going to end up shooting one of us without even meaning to. 'They're with us.'

One of them steps towards me, his gun still raised at Noah. Noah stands stock still, and he won't put his gun down. It's aimed at the man's chest, and whether it's defensive or not, it's being taken as a threat, and rightly so.

I flip through a mental catalogue of the rebels, and his name comes to me suddenly.

'Jared,' I say, and the name sounds awkward in my mouth. I never spoke to this man when we lived in the Base. I barely even saw him. I wouldn't even know his name if it weren't for Lacey, constantly telling me who was who and who they were and a million other details I didn't care about then but would kill to know right now. 'I trust him, Jared. It's okay.'

'You trust him? How do we know *we* can trust him? How do we know we can trust *you*?'

I can feel my heart beat as I go still, taken off-guard.

'You know me. You know who I am,' I say, but my voice sounds tight and brittle, like I just got the wind knocked out of me.

'You've been gone for months,' a girl says. Sara or Sierra or something like that. 'How do we know they didn't get to you?'

'*Get to me?*' I laugh, a scratchy, humourless laugh. 'They got to me alright. They tortured me and they locked me up in the Colosseum to rot. But they didn't *turn me*, if that's what you're asking. And if they were trying, they were doing a damn terrible job at it.'

She has the good sense to look ashamed, because I'm this close to walking away and letting them take potshots at each other.

'I'll vouch for her.' Mark speaks up, finally, and all eyes turn to him. 'And if she says we can trust Noah, we can trust Noah.'

Jared blinks, and the girl, whatever her name is, nods slowly. Guns slip back into waistbands and under piles of supplies.

Noah slowly lowers his own gun, and for a second we all just stand in the clearing, staring at each other.

'We brought food,' Clarke says, already tired of this interaction. She slams her backpack in between the two groups and drops down beside it. Everyone glances warily around, but only for a second, before hunger takes over and two groups dissolve into one.

o o o

'Eventually, someone is going to have to tell us what happened.' It's Clarke who speaks over the crackle of the fire that we built as we ate. By the looks on everyone's faces, they haven't eaten properly in a long time. They look like animals, fearful and desperate, as they crowd around the fire, and even now there's an air of distrust as we sit together. They've been out here too long and seen too many things to let one meal turn their instincts off, even if they're too starved to turn it down.

Clarke is the only one brave enough to finally break the fearful silence that's blanketed everyone since we arrived. Or maybe she just doesn't care enough to keep up the pretence. Bravery and carelessness can be a thin line with Clarke.

The second the words are out of her mouth, the camp gets even quieter.

'Kole left,' Mark says finally, and I almost jump at the sound. He's not eating, just sitting in front of the fire, arms slung over his knees, staring into the flames. 'Jay left. And then they attacked. Just like before.'

No one says a word. Everyone has stopped eating. 'It was the middle of the night. They must have been waiting. We didn't see them coming. We just heard the screaming.'

He releases a breath, and I already know that the next words out of his mouth are going to be the most painful.

'We ran. I got as many people as I could, and we ran. And I thought ...' his breath hitches '... I thought Walter was with us ... but he wasn't. And I knew. I knew that if he hadn't gotten away with us, he hadn't got away at all. But you can't ... you can't just give up. So I went back. And—' He stops suddenly, like he knows that if he tries to say one more word, it's going to kill him.

So he doesn't, and neither do we. We don't speak. We finish eating, and we stare at the stars, but somehow they feel farther away. And I wonder if humanity can get to a point where it's so cruel, the stars can't bear to look at us anymore.

When everyone has eaten, we sit staring at the fire. There are so many questions I want to ask, but I don't know if Mark can answer them. I don't know if it's even fair to ask. But then Noah quietly says, 'Where did your comrades go? The ones you said left before it began?'

Mark looks over at him. 'I don't know,' he says dully. 'They made their decision. They left, that's all that matters.'

The others look uncomfortable, and you can feel the tension in his words, the stories pressing against the back of his teeth, the memories he refuses to voice.

More happened than he's willing to say, and I'm not going to be the one to force it out of him.

'Kole left first,' Jared says quietly, speaking up where Mark won't. 'We asked him to stay, but he was bullheaded. He insisted he didn't have a choice.'

'Where did he go?' I almost choke on the words as they force themselves out of my mouth.

'He left ages ago,' Mark says. There's a note of something harsh in his voice, like anger, but muted. 'He said he had to help you.' He looks up at me suddenly and there is accusation in his eyes.

My blood runs cold. 'Me?' I whisper. 'He knew where I was?'

Mark shakes his head. 'No. And he didn't seem to have much of a plan. Just said he had to find you and bring you back.'

My fists clench at my sides, and I drop my head to my chest so they can't see my expression. Why the hell would he do that? There was no way he was going to be able to find me, but he still went running back like an idiot. He was always the one telling us to stop being reckless, but it didn't apply to him apparently.

'I should have gone back for him,' Mark whispers suddenly, his voice frayed, pulling me from my thoughts. He drags a hand through his blond hair as he continues to speak, his eyes burning a hole in the ground by his feet. 'The minute I realised he wasn't with us, I should have gone back. Kole went searching for you, and I didn't go back for my own brother.'

'Mark,' I say gently, 'what happened to Walter is not your fault.'

'None of it is your fault,' Clarke says fiercely. 'They kill and they take and they leave you with nothing. It's them. It's not your fault.'

My fingernails dig into the dirt beneath me, and I stare dead-eyed into the fire. I don't have an explanation for why this happened. I can't tell Mark there's a reason his brother died. I'm not sure I want there to be a reason his brother died. I'm not sure there's a reason good enough, and even if there was, I'm not going to tell Mark that this is okay. That this is fair or normal or right. Because it's not. It's not okay, or fair or normal or right, for someone to die like that, and I won't try to convince him that it is.

'We'll find them,' I say. 'And I swear to God we'll make them pay for what they did to him.'

Mark looks me in the eyes for the first time, staring me dead-on with bloodshot eyes, and he nods. A slow, painful nod.

There isn't any reason that Walter died. Not one that makes sense. But there is a consequence, and I promise him that it will be worse for them than it ever was for him.

16

It takes us three days to get back to the bunker. That's a full twenty-four hours longer than it should have taken us, but exhaustion and grief slow us down.

When I begin to recognise my surroundings again and realise we're not far from the bunker, I sigh audibly, causing Noah to glance over at me.

'I need a shower,' I say, kicking a log out of the way in frustration. Then I realise what a waste of energy it was, get angry at myself and kick the very next log I come across. 'Badly.'

'I don't think a shower is the biggest issue you have right now, Quincy.'

I stop myself from sighing again as I glance up at the group a few feet ahead of us. Mark, head down, shoulders slumped, spirit broken, and an entire band of heartbroken, weary fighters, more than done fighting.

Silas isn't going to be happy to see us coming. These aren't rebels, not anymore. They're refugees, and refugees don't make good recruits.

If they're even willing to be recruited.

We haven't discussed anything past the fact that we know where Genesis is and that they have food and showers. It didn't take much convincing after that. Food and shelter and they were sold, and I didn't want to complicate it any further.

Clarke pulls ahead, leading Mark and the others into the cave-like structure that marks the entrance to the bunker. We plunge into the darkness, following the path that will end at the metal door.

Clarke raps her knuckles against the door impatiently, moving from one foot to the other as she waits for the door to open. The small window in the door pulls open, and someone begins opening the door from the inside out.

I glance around, double-checking that everyone's with us, and I'm caught off-guard by the fact that, even in all their grief, I can see the wonder in everyone's eyes. This is Genesis. The stuff of legends.

And, for a lot of people, a source of hope for the success story of someone living on the Outside.

The lights snap on as the heavy metal door opens and we begin to file inside at long last. I make sure everyone goes in ahead of me, including Mark, who's the last to enter in front of me. I'm staring at his slumped shoulders when I see them suddenly straighten, and my eyes jump to where he's staring.

Jay stands in the hallway, frozen. *He must have been cleared while we were gone.* That's all I think. That is my only thought as Jay freezes in the middle of the hall, but then I see fear, and Jay is never afraid.

Never.

And then Mark's fist is connecting with his face.

I spring into motion the second the crack of impact echoes through the hall, but I'm not the only one. Hands grab at both of them as Jay's head flies into the wall beside him, thumping off the concrete before he pushes himself back off it. Mark lands three more shots before we can prise them apart.

Jay doesn't move at all. He doesn't fight back, and he doesn't even act like he's trying to miss Mark's shots.

'*MARK!*' I yell, just as Silas comes down the hall.

'What is happening here?' Silas asks, quietly, calmly, coming to a stop between Jay and Mark as Jay shakes himself free of the hands holding him back, spitting blood onto the floor.

I wish he was shouting. It would be so much less terrifying if he were shouting.

17

Silas turns to me. 'You're back,' he says, his eyes gliding from me to everyone around me. Fourteen people in all, if you count Noah, Clarke and myself and the two men he sent with us.

'Great observation,' I mutter, and immediately regret it. Silas's eyes harden, and he turns from me to Jay and Mark.

'Twelve hours, Mr Michelson. That's all you've been out of eval, and you're already starting fights?'

I expect Jay to have a snappy retort, considering he didn't start anything at all, but he doesn't say a word, just stares at a mark on the wall above Silas's head.

'Very well,' Silas says. He motions to two recruits behind him. 'Take this young man to a holding cell in Control D, and return Mr Michelson to containment please.'

'Silas—' I start, but Silas is already talking to me.

'You,' he points at me, Clarke and Noah, 'follow me.'

I grit my teeth, and for a moment I want to do nothing more than stand my ground, demand an explanation for what he plans on doing with Jay and Mark.

The others are already following him. I waver momentarily in the hallway, glancing back at the door. After being out in the open, returning to this place feels like digging my own grave. The overhead lights flicker, making me feel nervous and twitchy. But when I glance back towards Silas, he's already disappearing around a corner and I have to jog to catch up with them.

Silas leads us down narrow hallways until we reach his office, closing the door behind us and letting us stew as he takes his time walking around to the other side of his desk. He sits down, shuffling a few papers out of his way.

'I expect a full report both of the events of the mission and the events of this morning.'

'Of course.' Noah nods, shifting his weight as he stands with his hands behind his back.

'But before that, I want to hear what happened.'

We all stand stock still for a moment, until he nods impatiently, and Noah starts.

'There were bodies,' he says, immediately grabbing Silas's attention. 'Hanging from the windows. Officers had come and killed them in the middle of the night and hung them up. There was fresh blood. It couldn't have happened more than a few hours before we got there.'

Silas leans back in his chair. 'Tell me, how do you know that it was Officers who attacked them?'

'Because Mark told us,' Clarke says, previously completely silent in the corner of the room.

'And who else would murder seven innocent people out in the middle of nowhere *other* than Officers?' I ask, bewildered.

'So you fully trust that it was Officers who killed these people, then, correct?'

We all nod, although I notice from the corner of my eye that Noah's nod is slow, like he's not sure what the right answer is.

'And the people you brought back with you? I assume these are your rebels, Miss Emerson?'

Your rebels. He says it so patronisingly that I struggle to keep my expression calm as I answer him.

'Yes, they're the rebels I stayed with before the Colosseum.'

'And is their leader among them?' he asks, and I can nearly hear him calculating the worth of each individual.

'No, their leader had already left,' I say.

'Interesting,' Silas says, considering this. 'And they plan on staying?'

'I don't know what they plan,' I say. 'But they need food and shelter long enough to figure that out, so I brought them here. Is that a problem?'

He twitches his head to the side, as if he's thinking about it. 'Not necessarily. We have systems in place to help them acclimate. As long as they stay out of trouble, there won't be a problem. Just make sure there are no more fights.' He gives me a pointed look.

'They're not going to do anything,' Clarke says from behind me, cutting me off before I have a chance to snap back at Silas.

'Great,' he says with a cold smile. 'That's everything I need to know for now, so you're dismissed.'

I turn away, ready to be out of this room and back with the others. I have to talk to Jay and Mark about what happened in the hallway, but from what I've seen of Mark, there's no chance I'll be able to get them in a room together without a fallout.

'Miss Emerson,' Silas says, before I have a chance to leave. 'You stay.'

I stop in the doorway, and Clarke glances back at me, a question in her eyes. I shake my head, telling her to go on, which she does, however reluctantly.

When I turn around, Silas is leaning back in his chair, eyes drilling into me. 'I was hoping the leader would be among them. Kole Johnson.'

So he knows about Kole. I suppose I shouldn't be surprised. I know Silas isn't telling us everything he knows, but still. How could he know about Kole? I say nothing. I don't mind pursuing a fictional Aaron, but there's no way I'm giving him Kole.

'He could be very useful to us,' Silas says, watching me. 'Was there nothing at all? No one knows a thing about where he's disappeared to?'

'No. He left suddenly and told no one where he was going. He has a habit of doing that.'

'Pity,' he says slowly. He rocks forward on his chair. 'No matter. We'll find him.'

Something about the way he says it sounds like a threat, and I can't help but mentally check what weapons I have on me. Colosseum habits are hard ones to break, but Silas isn't going to attack me. That's not what I'm afraid of.

'I expect your reports on my desk in the morning,' he says, and it's as much of a dismissal as anything.

'No,' I say.

'What was that?'

'Take Jay out of containment, now.'

'And why would I do that?'

'Because I did what you asked, and you locked him back up anyway.'

'Yes, you did do what I wanted. And he was taken out of containment, but the same day he got out, he got in a fight. And now you want me to just let him walk away? That doesn't make any sense.'

'That fight wasn't Jay's fault and you know it.'

'I don't, actually, but even if I did, what would you propose that I do? Throw the other boy out? Suspend him from Genesis? Because if it wasn't Jay's fault, then that means you brought someone in here who's capable of unprovoked attacks. I can't have a violent threat walking around the bunker.'

'His name is Mark, and he isn't a threat to anyone,' I grind out, trying to stop myself from slapping him.

Silas opens his mouth to say something else, but just then a young recruit skids to a halt inside the door.

'Silas, quickly,' she pants.

'What?' Silas demands, the note of irritation in his voice overshot by fear.

'It's the City,' the girl says. 'Something's happened in the City.'

18

The Control Room is already filled with people by the time we get down there, all huddled around the monitors with tense shoulders. The air is thick with fear, and without even seeing what they're looking at, my heart is pounding in my chest.

I push my way through the crowd until I'm in front of the screen, and it takes me a moment to make sense of what I'm seeing.

We're watching footage of a girl prostrate on a bed, thrashing violently as if against something that's holding her down. But nothing is touching her.

I push closer to the monitor, watch her face contort as she turns towards the screen, eyes wide open and pure black.

Pure black and bleeding, trails of crimson blood staining her ashen skin.

I can feel my own blood drain from my face, my stomach dropping as the image changes, another bed, another person, another set of black eyes.

'Wh-what's wrong with them?' I ask breathlessly, turning away as the image shifts again, trying to find someone who will answer me. 'What's going on?'

But everyone looks as shaken as I feel, and no one can look away from the monitor long enough to even register I'm asking a question.

That's when I see Silas standing at the back of the crowd, staring at the images over everyone's heads.

'It's the Virus,' he says, and the word ripples through the crowd so quickly that within seconds it's all I can hear, the word buzzing around the room like a swarm of bees. 'It's back.'

'Oh my God,' a girl says, stumbling backwards, tears rolling down her cheeks. 'Oh my God.'

'No,' I say, my head whipping around to everyone around me, the uproar beginning as panic starts to swell. This doesn't make any sense. We're *Cured*.

We were supposed to be Cured. We were supposed to be safe. How is this happening? Unless Johnson lied to me? But that doesn't make any sense. He couldn't have been lying to me – I saw the Cure myself. I saw it with my own eyes.

Wilke says, 'You're all looking at the wrong thing.'

Everyone goes quiet.

'What do you mean?' Silas asks. He is standing at one of the monitors, breathing heavily as he takes in the images.

'Look where they are.' Wilke's voice is so quiet he almost sounds reverent. 'See how nice the clinic is, how well set up? They're not Dormants. They're Pures.'

There is a shocked silence, then the panicked whispering starts up again, sweeping through the room.

I look at the screen again. He's right. These are not Dormants. This isn't the Outer Sector at all. This isn't possible. This isn't happening. This cannot be happening.

19

'What the hell is going on?' Clarke asks, pulling me far enough from the crowd that we can actually hear ourselves think. Everyone spreads outwards once the doors of the Control Room close, but the din of chatter doesn't stop for a moment.

I can tell by the way she says it that it's not that she didn't catch what they were saying. It's that she can't comprehend it.

And I don't blame her.

I glance back towards the doors, behind which Silas is surely starting to put the wheels in motion to deal with this.

Except, how do you deal with this? It's killing *Pures*. They're supposed to be invincible, and now not even Oasis can keep them safe.

'Quincy,' Clarke says, snapping me back to reality. I look back at her, but I can't focus on her properly. I can't stop thinking about what this means. For Oasis and Genesis, and for me. If I could just get into that room, hear what they were saying …

'This isn't the end of the world,' Clarke says, though we both know that's not true. The Virus was the end of the Old World, and it could just as easily be the end of this one. 'It means Oasis is weak. Weak Pures means a weak Oasis – isn't that what we wanted?'

She's right and wrong at the same time. How are we supposed to make a move on Oasis when the Virus is living inside of it? It would be suicide.

I need to get back in that room. If Oasis already had the Cure, like Johnson told me, and the Virus has now returned, that means one of three things: either the Cure never worked, or the Virus has mutated, or it's something else entirely. Something we've never dealt with before.

Even the idea of it makes me feel cold. The idea of the Virus, but not. A new Virus, one we know nothing about.

I don't know how much they know, about the Virus or the Cure or Johnson's plan. It's obvious they know more than they're letting on, but they could ruin our only chance at taking Oasis down if they screw this up because they don't understand what they're dealing with.

'*Quincy.*' Clarke's voice startles me back again, and I shake my head, forcing myself to look at her. 'What's going on in your head? You're not hearing a word that's coming out of my mouth.' I'm about to try to explain that we have to get into the Control Room, when we're interrupted by a guard coming up behind us.

'Excuse me,' he says, in a tone I'm not used to hearing guards use. 'You're going to have to come with me.'

'What?' Clarke and I say at the same time, glancing at each other warily.

'Come with me,' he repeats. Before we have a chance to ask him what he's talking about, or where he's going, or why we should follow him, he's walking away.

He leads us down to the holding cells, and an uncertain fear starts to bubble in my chest.

'Where are you bringing us?' I ask, and my voice sounds shakier than it should.

He doesn't answer, just reaches out and unbolts the door, pushing it open and gesturing for us to go inside.

I don't even get inside the door before I stop breathing.

The only thing holding Mark from the floor is the belt around his neck, suspending him in the air like he's floating, but he's not because his face is gone blue and he's not moving and … he's not moving …

Clarke stumbles back a step, her face draining of blood, and my heart has stopped beating. I swear it's stopped beating and this doesn't make sense, none of it makes sense, and I keep staring at him as if it will start making sense, but it doesn't, all that happens is my vision starts to blur and my head starts to swim and I think I'm going to pass out.

I turn away too quickly, and the whole room tilts, forcing me to catch myself on the wall.

'What happened?' It comes out like a sob.

'We just found him like this,' the guard says, shaking his head, pale-faced and solemn.

'Get him down,' Clarke says suddenly. When no one responds for a few seconds, she turns on us. 'If you won't do it, give me a knife so that I can, but *get him down.*'

Clarke is the one to take him down, with the help of two recruits. When his body is lowered to the ground, there's a dull thud as he falls, and I feel my stomach drop with it. Once he's down my brain goes quiet. There's no peacefulness in it, but the chaos is gone.

It's as if the second I realised he was actually gone, it cut my emotions off.

I leave Clarke with him in the containment room, cradling his head in her lap, and find myself in front of the Control Room, banging loudly against the door. A guard pulls it open, opening his mouth to tell me to leave, but before he has a chance to, I'm slipping under his arm and into the room.

'I need to talk to you.' And I don't recognise my own voice. The guard tries to catch my arm to pull me back out of the room, but Silas raises a hand to stop him.

'Leave her.' He waits for the guard to back off. 'What is it, Miss Emerson?'

The room is full of people, presumably Silas's inner circle, but I don't recognise most of them.

'It's not the Virus,' I say, and suddenly I have everyone's attention.

'Then what is it, Miss Emerson?'

'I don't know. But it's not the Virus.'

'And how do you know that?'

'Because Oasis already has the Cure.'

Several voices break out after that, and it's hard to hear what anyone is saying, other than general outrage that I would suggest something so ludicrous.

'QUIET!' Silas shouts, and everyone drops suddenly into silence again. 'Quincy,' he says, turning his attention to me. 'What proof do you have of this?'

'I saw it with my own eyes. I spoke to Johnson himself. They've been administering the Cure for years.'

'Why wouldn't they release that information to the public, then? Wouldn't it solidify Oasis's power if they finally found the Cure?'

'The citizens' dependence mattered more,' I say, shaking my head. 'And if everyone was Cured, there would be no more Pures and Dormants. Oasis wasn't willing to give up that power.'

This, finally, seems to land on them. This is Oasis's pattern, through and through. Power first, power above everything.

Silas starts blinking rapidly, a plan forming in his head. He looks almost giddy.

'This could be a good thing. If it's not the Virus, that means it's something else. Something Oasis is unfamiliar with. We need to know how much they know about this new disease. Miss Emerson, now more than ever we need to contact Aaron. He can give us insider information—'

'He's dead,' I say, without inflection. I don't know if I'll regret releasing that information later, but right now I don't care. Right now I don't care about anything.

Everyone looks at Silas as he goes still.

'How do you—'

'I shot him,' I say. 'I shot Aaron Johnson months ago, before I was placed in the Colosseum.'

That's the first time I've said it out loud, and somehow my voice doesn't hitch. I don't sound distraught or emotional or even upset.

I just say it, and I don't feel anything.

Silas looks speechless for the first time, and he looks away from me and towards the floor, as if he's trying to piece his plan back together in his head.

'What if she's lying?' a man at the other end of the table asks, and I don't even turn my head to look at them. 'We don't have any actual proof that she saw the Cure or killed Aaron Johnson.'

'What reason would she have to lie?' someone else responds, and there's another gaping silence.

'What if it is still the Virus? What if there was a mistake, and they weren't Cured at all?'

'Then.' Silas takes a deep breath. 'We'll deal with that. Right now our first priority has to be gathering information. We have no way of knowing how to advance if we don't have a full grasp of the circumstances.'

'So what are we supposed to do? What do we know?'

'Not much,' Silas admits. 'With this … change of circumstances,' he says slowly, 'we're left with very little to inform our next move. That's why we need to set up a task force to go into Oasis and gather information on the outbreak.'

The room goes quiet once again.

'It will be dangerous, I know that. Without any knowledge of what this disease is, it's hard to tell how great a risk it is, exposing yourself to that environment. But it's vital information. I have to know what Oasis has discovered about this affliction.' Silas stops talking and just watches us from the top of the table.

'You don't have to decide now,' Silas says. 'We'll make a decision in twenty-four hours, and we will ask for volunteers. We won't send in people against their will. We will ask for volunteers to do this for Genesis, for our future, and then we'll go in there and find out what's going on.'

For now, that's good enough.

20

The hallways are strangely quiet as I walk towards the wing where Sophia is being held. People are standing around in small groups, whispering to each other. I try to ignore it, but I keep catching the words 'Virus', 'Oasis' and 'Cure' as I speed-walk down the halls, my head down.

Right now I just need to see Sophia. After that, I'll deal with everything else. I can't even think about Mark, not right now. It's too much.

I take a sharp turn down the corridor leading to the temporary housing unit and stop in front of the third door down. I go inside, but she's not there.

Maybe I got the wrong door. I turn on my heel and walk back into the hallway, pulling open the next door in the corridor, but she's not there either. I pull open the next door, and the next, but she's not in any of them.

The next room doesn't open at all, and I wonder if she's been put back into the evaluation chambers. My anger starts rising in the back of my throat, until I hear a voice behind me.

'Quincy.' I spin around to see Silas standing in the corridor, arms crossed. He must have followed me. 'She's not there.'

My heart stops.

'I moved her into the communal sleeping wing an hour ago. She's been placed in the bed next to yours.'

My breath shudders out of me, but for a moment I don't even try to move, though every instinct in me tells me to go find her, make sure she's okay, make sure he's telling the truth.

'Why?' I ask. 'Why did you move her?'

Silas regards me for a moment. 'I want you to know that if you go, I'll ensure her safety.'

'You want *me* to go?' I ask. 'Someone you barely know, let alone trust? Why would you want me to do that?'

'Because you're not afraid. And everyone else is afraid.'

'What?' How could I not be afraid? Everything is falling apart, crumbling away.

'Have you ever heard of the concept of the fight-or-flight response? It proposes that our only two responses to danger are either to fight or to run. But there's a third reaction: freezing. Too many people would prefer to play dead than to fight back against Oasis. I need fighters now more than ever.'

I move forward guardedly. 'And?'

'And what?'

'And what else?' I press. 'Jay's a fighter. More so than I am. You could argue that he's unreliable, but you know well that he's not much more unreliable than I am. There are the people who have nothing left to lose, the people who are so loyal to you and Genesis that they'd gladly give their lives, and the freedom-fighters so hell-bent on being in the history books that they'd prefer to die fighting than to live to see a day when they wouldn't have to.' I come to a halt right in front of him. 'Yes, I'm a fighter, but you have no shortage of them. So why are you here, in the hall, paying me favours to join? What's so special about me?'

For a few seconds he just stares at me, but his softened expression slowly melts into a grin, which dissolves into unsettling laughter.

'What's so special about you?' he asks, and he's not even attempting to hide his amusement. 'You killed the OP's son, and you're asking *me* what's special about you?'

I flinch, but he's not done with me yet.

'You were in love with him, weren't you? I can see it on your face, even if I didn't already know. But he got in the way, right? So he had to go.'

My teeth are gritted so tightly I'm afraid I'm going to break my own jaw.

'You have no idea what you're talking about.'

'Maybe not,' he concedes. 'But you're cold, Miss Emerson, and we both know it. Maybe you've convinced your friends of something else, but no normal person is capable of doing what you've done. You're willing to do what's necessary to get what you want, and you know as well as I do that we both want the same thing.'

His expression has lost all the amusement it held moments ago, but it's replaced by a triumphant glint in his eye that makes me want to slap him across the face. It's nothing but smug satisfaction; what he wants is lining up with what I need, and he knows he has me backed into a corner.

Without even bothering to form a retort I push past him, more than ready to see Sophia again and forget about this.

'Quincy?'

I stop but don't turn around.

'I'm sorry about your friend, Mark.' His face is emotionless. He doesn't deserve to talk about Mark, not now. 'We have moved him to the morgue. He will be given a proper burial. I'm sure you want to avenge this tragedy. I'm sure the blood is boiling in your veins with anger. And that's good. That will ensure you are sharp and ready. Remember, doing what I want is for the good of all: it's in everyone's best interest. Especially yours.'

I keep walking.

All I can think is that I need to find Sophi. Silas's words run on a loop inside my head but something in me just keeps saying that if I see her, I'll be okay. If she's safe, I'll be okay.

I hurry to the communal sleeping area and meet Clarke outside the door, just as she's walking out.

I look over her shoulder, trying to catch a glimpse inside the room, desperate to know that Sophi is safe. She gives me a strange look, taking a step back.

'Mark is in the morgue,' she says, her voice flat. 'He'll be buried tomorrow.'

'I know. Silas told me. Where's Sophi?' I ask, pushing past her. 'Is she in here?' I immediately see that she's nowhere in the room and I look back at Clarke, who's stepped back inside. 'Where is she? Silas said he moved her in her, if he was lying, I'll—'

'Someone dropped her off here a few minutes ago, but she left almost immediately.'

'What do you mean left? Where did she go?' I try to move around Clarke to the door again, but she stops me with a hand on my arm.

'One of the recruits brought her to get something to eat at the cafeteria. That's all.'

'I'll go find her.' The need to see her keeps rising up in the back of my throat, and it feels an awful lot like panic.

'Quincy, she's fine. She'll be back in a few minutes.' Clarke looks me dead in the eye. 'What's wrong?'

I take a slightly shaky step back, running my hand through my hair as if it will help me draw my thoughts together.

'I want to go back Inside, but I don't trust Silas. He said he'd look after Sophi if I left, but how can I do that? And how am I supposed to even decide whether or not to go in? I could stay here with Sophi and keep her safe, but then I'd be giving up on Kole. But if I do go in, what happens to Sophi? I can't leave her here without me. I'll have to bring her with me. Silas will never agree to it, but I don't have any other option. I'll sneak her out and then—'

'Quincy,' Clarke snaps at me. 'Stop.'

I'm confused. 'Stop what?'

'Have you even stopped to think how *she* feels?'

'What?'

'Sophi. Have you stopped even for a second to think how insane all of this is to her?'

'Of course I have.'

'Then why are you acting like this? Don't you think she deserves an opinion as well?'

'Clarke, I have to keep her safe.'

'Would you *stop saying that,* please,' Clarke says through gritted teeth, taking a step towards me. 'You're *obsessed* with keeping her safe, and you've never even wondered if that's your responsibility at all.'

'I owe it to her to keep her safe.'

'Why? Because you got her sister killed?'

I lose my breath the second those words leave her mouth.

'How do you know about that?' I whisper, trying to control the urge to take a step back. There's something about someone suddenly saying out loud what you've been worrying about in your head for so long that feels like a nightmare come to life.

'It's not that complicated. You got a girl killed, and it was cutting you up back at the Base. Then suddenly you turn up with some kid and we're all supposed to pretend she belongs to you?'

'She doesn't belong to me.'

'Well, that's the way you're acting. You don't know a thing about her – did you ever think about that? You don't know her, and yet you're acting like you do. You're *not* her replacement sister, Quincy, you're just some girl who turned up out of nowhere and dragged her into this mess.'

I'm completely silent.

'And you did drag her into this mess. I'm not saying the Outer Sector would have been much better, but you're forcing your actions to affect her life by dragging her into this with you. And you have to realise that that means you're affecting a *person's* life. She's not a way to relieve your guilt – she's a person. So maybe the next time you come up with a great scheme to drag her back into Oasis so *you* can keep her safe, you'll stop thinking about *you* and start thinking about her. Regardless of what you might feel, she's the one who has to deal with the consequences, which means she deserves a choice in what happens.'

She stares at me, waiting for a reaction, but I can't move. Every muscle in my body has locked into place, and I can't even blink at her. I just stare, wide-eyed. I feel like she came over and cut me open, like I have to be bleeding somehow because you can't just *feel* like this.

She releases a long sigh and shakes her head, looking at me with disgust written all over her face. Without giving me a chance to figure out how to speak again, she turns and walks out of the room, slamming the door on the way out.

o o o

I lie on top of the blankets on my bed, staring at the boards above my head, waiting for Sophi to come back. When she does, the door creaking open slowly, allowing light from the hall to breach the otherwise dark room, she glances over at my bed, checking.

When she sees me, she nods, and scurries to the other side of the room. Without a word, she gets into bed and turns to face the wall.

Whether she falls asleep or not I can't tell, but as I lie there, the truth of Clarke's words sinks in. Sophi doesn't even know me. My presence doesn't change how safe she feels, doesn't make any of this easier on her.

I want to be near her. *I* want to think I'm keeping her safe. But does it really matter? Not to her. She doesn't need me in the bed beside her, or in the room with her, or in this bunker at all.

I want her to need me more than she actually does.

There's something I have to do. I wait until I hear Sophi's breathing slow down and become steady, then I roll quietly out of bed and silently leave the room. I make my way to where Jay is being held, in the containment unit. There's no one around. I stand outside his door, steeling myself. After a few minutes I slide back the bolt, step inside and close the door noiselessly behind me.

He's not asleep. Just lying flat on his back, one arm behind his head, staring at the ceiling like he's seeing things up there that I can't.

'Jay,' I say. He doesn't move. I go over to the end of his bed and kick it. *'Jay.'*

He closes his eyes, lets his chest rise and fall with one breath, then opens his eyes to look at me.

'What?' The word is harsh, and he swings his feet out over the side of the bed, sitting up and leaning back against the wall as he says it.

'What have you heard?' I ask, refusing to let him intimidate me.

'Shouting,' he says.

'About?'

'I couldn't make it out.' He stretches his arms up over his head, yawning. 'I was napping. They woke me up.'

'Do you think I actually believe that, or are you just amusing yourself?'

'A little of both.' He grins, but it's fake and forced and it looks wrong.

'They think the Virus is back.' I want to surprise him, shock him out of this apathetic act he's putting on. 'People are dying in Oasis.'

He blinks back at me, refusing to react.

'And it's not the Dormants who are becoming Infected, it's the Pures.' My frustration is bleeding into my tone, as much as I want it not to.

But still there's nothing.

'They don't think it's the Virus. The symptoms are wrong.'

'You just said it was the Virus,' he says, and he has the gall to look amused.

'It's complicated,' I snap.

'It can't be that complicated. It's either the Virus or it isn't.'

'It's hard to tell from out here *what's* going on,' I say, as calmly as I can manage. 'We're not even sure Oasis knows what it is. Silas is organising a team to go in and figure out what's going on. They're not forcing anyone to go because it's too dangerous.'

I wait for a response, but I get nothing.

'Tomorrow I'm going to tell him that I'll go with them,' I say.

'What about the girl?'

My chest feels tight. 'She'll stay here. Silas says he'll make sure she's okay.'

'And you trust him?' Jay's eyebrows rise towards his hairline. He looks half-disgusted.

'No,' I snap, and I can feel my frustration rising to the surface. 'I don't trust him. I don't trust anyone here, but it's better than bringing her back to Oasis.'

He watches my face for a few seconds before looking down at the floor, processing this information.

'And why are you telling *me* this?' he asks.

'Because. I want you to come.'

He laughs under his breath. 'So you've decided that you can ask for help now? Why the hell should I help Genesis?'

'I've decided that I can't afford not to. I need you with me in there.'

'And you need to go in there.' It's phrased like a question, but it's not.

I nod.

He stares up at the ceiling, thinking. I can see him inverting, folding in on himself. I think he's gone on me, disappeared into whatever place he goes in his head when he can't deal with everything anymore, but then he speaks up.

'Fine,' he says, one word, and looks me directly in the eye.

'Fine? You'll do it?'

'If you can convince that tyrant to let me out of this damn cell, then fine. We'll go.'

I nod, and it should feel like more of a victory than it does. But I didn't only come tonight to ask him to join the mission.

'There's something else I have to tell you,' I say, and I sit on the floor by his bed before I continue.

This is the hard part.

When I tell him, he doesn't shout or scream. Part of me wants him to. If Mark had died by someone else's hand, maybe he would have, but he just goes quiet and still, and the blood drains from his face.

'It's my fault.'

'Jay, *no*—'

'Don't argue with me,' he says through gritted teeth. 'I'm not saying it so you'll pity me.'

'Jay, it's not true. You couldn't have done anything.' I try to push the emotions away, the same way I've been doing since Mark was taken down, but it's getting progressively harder as the hours pass and reality sets in.

'I could have stayed,' he says.

'You were protecting Sophi.'

'I could have fought harder. Forced him to come with me.'

'He was being stubborn. You told him to come with you and he refused. You couldn't have done anything else.'

There's a heavy silence for a few minutes before he says, once, quietly, in a whisper, 'He blamed me. Before he died, he blamed me. Doesn't that make it my fault?'

'He was hurting.' I want to reach out to him, ground him somehow, but I know he doesn't want me to, so I force my hands to stay at my sides.

Jay doesn't say anything after that. I don't know if it's because he doesn't want to argue with me, or because he doesn't have anything else to say, but I leave him his silence.

At some point I fall asleep, leaning back against the wall, watching him staring at the ceiling, lost.

21

'I'll do it.'

Silas is in the same meeting room we were in after we got the news about the outbreak, talking to one of the generator technicians, but I don't care.

Silas looks up from the table and stares a hole through me. He says something under his breath to the technician, who promptly leaves, without making eye contact with me.

Silas crosses his arms, leaning back against the table. 'What are your conditions?'

I pause. I didn't think he would expect them, but he clearly knows me better than I thought he did.

'I want to choose who I bring with me.'

He looks down at the ground, considering this. 'I'm not sure how much I can trust Jay,' he says finally.

'I'm not sure how much I can trust you,' I fire back, and he smiles at that.

'Fine.' He agrees quicker than I expected. 'But Noah is going as well.'

It's not that I didn't expect this, but I ask him why anyway.

'I don't trust you,' he says, shrugging. 'And I certainly don't trust Jay. But I trust Noah. I need insurance.'

'You have enough insurance already,' I growl. Sophi is his insurance, and he knows that that didn't go over my head. If I don't do what he needs me to, Sophi is his security deposit.

He smiles at me.

'Jay's going. I want him to go, but even if I didn't, he'd insist on going himself. In case you forgot, this operation hinges on more than just you. Take it or leave it.'

'I'll take it, Miss Emerson,' he says slowly, still smiling. 'I'll take it.'

o o o

I'm standing outside the door when they release Jay for the second time.

'I'm getting the royal treatment now, am I?' he asks, stepping aside as the door slides closed.

This time he's on the right side of it.

'Are you hungry?' I ask, ignoring him. 'Do you want to get something to eat?'

'How long do we have until we're leaving?'

'Twelve hours,' I say. 'Or eleven, now, I guess. I don't know. These people don't know what a clock is.'

Jay follows me down the hall, and he laughs half-heartedly. 'Cause we had so many clocks back in the old Base.'

We get our food and eventually find an empty table.

'So what are we even supposed to be doing in there?' Jay asks.

I rub the bridge of my nose. 'We don't know anything about what's going on, not really. We don't know what the disease is that's attacking the Pures or how to control it. We can't rush on in there if we don't know what we're taking on, and we can't fight Oasis if we don't know how well *they* understand it.'

Jay's eyes flit up over my shoulder, and I turn to see Clarke coming towards us. I feel adrenaline shoot through me at the sight of her, and I immediately feel stupid for reacting like that.

Clarke got angry with me; she told me the truth. That's what Clarke does. It's not always nice and it's certainly not always what I want to hear, but it doesn't mean she was wrong.

It does mean I have to face the consequences.

She sits down across from me, beside Jay, who immediately picks up on the strange atmosphere. He nods to Clarke, who nods back in recognition before immediately starting to eat like nothing happened.

I freeze up, unsure of what to say.

'I assume we're going into Oasis with the team,' she says after a few minutes of silence.

I look at her in shock. 'We?' I ask, shifting my feet nervously under the table.

'Well, I assume we're not going to sit here while they go in?'

'Fair assumption,' Jay comments, going back to eating. I suddenly feel like I'm the only one who doesn't understand what's going on.

'All three of us?' I ask slowly. 'Together?' It feels stupid to be this timid, especially around Clarke, but I can't help it. After a blow-out there tends to be fallout. Instead there's just ... nothing. Like nothing happened at all.

'No,' Clarke says, rolling her eyes. 'We're all going to go individually to avoid overcrowding.'

And there it is. The Clarke snap back. She's said her piece, and now she's done, and she moves on.

Like nothing ever happened.

22

Mark is cremated before we leave. We're not allowed to be there while it happens, but they bring us his ashes afterwards. They're placed in an empty room on a table for half an hour, so we can say our goodbyes.

After that, they're moved to a columbarium on the fourth floor. It's supposed to be symbolic, that those who die for Genesis are its foundation, but it makes me feel sick.

Mark had no love for Genesis. He didn't even agree to join them. He killed himself because his brother was dead. And Walter only died because Oasis killed him.

If we had found Genesis sooner, if Genesis had been willing to help, instead of hiding here—

I stop myself from continuing down that thought process. It's not helping; it's just making me more angry. But everything is making me more angry.

For the half an hour we're given with Mark's ashes, the room is full. Clarke and I stay the entire time, and almost every member of the rebels Mark came here with visits.

Jay doesn't come. I think he's afraid, and though I don't want him to regret it later, I'm not going to force him to come.

That's his decision, either way.

Clarke and I sit in the corner of the room, shoulder to shoulder, and we watch people come and go, and we don't speak. We don't need to – we each know what the other is thinking

About Oasis. About the mission. That we can't just keep letting people die and do nothing about it.

Something has to give, and it can't be us anymore.

23

The next day, Sophi's the only one I speak to before we leave. I try to remind myself of what Clarke had told me. That Sophi doesn't belong to me, and that I don't get to try to replace the hole I punched in her life when Bea died.

'I have to go away again, Sophi.'

She looks up from where she's folding clothes on her bed. 'Where?'

'Back to Oasis. I have to help Silas figure out what's going on in there.'

'Oh.' She twists the ends of her sleeves around her fingers. 'Okay.'

'You're gonna stay here, okay? They'll look after you.'

She just nods this time.

'And I'll come back,' I promise her. I can hear Clarke's voice in the back of my head telling me not to be stupid, but I can't help it.

'That's what you said last time.' She looks at me with those piercing blue eyes, and it's not an accusation so much as a statement.

And she's right.

'I know.' I almost smile. 'This time I'll come back sooner.'

'Do you promise?' she asks.

I shake my head. 'No.'

A sound jumps out of her, and for a second I'm so taken off-guard, I don't even know what it is. But then I realise that she's laughing. When she looks up, there's half a smile on her face.

'At least you're not lying anymore,' she says, still in the same light, quiet voice, but it makes me laugh too.

'At least there's that,' I say.

And if there's one good thing, it's that I got to hear her laugh before I left to go back Inside.

PART THREE

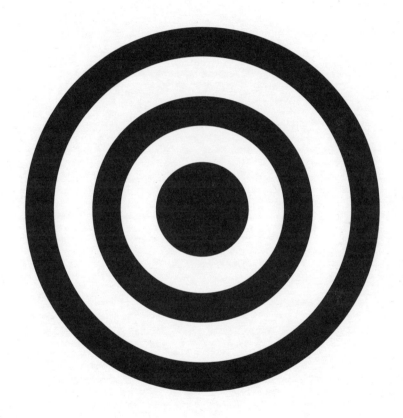

EDEN

1

The trees swallow us whole almost immediately. Though the entrance to Genesis is surrounded by a small clearing, the area around it is densely forested, so we've barely walked ten metres before we can't even see the clearing anymore.

I'm glad of it. A whole life spent in the Outer Sector, smothered by the high dirty buildings and lack of light, has given me an appreciation for this forest. Spending months in the Colosseum and then time buried underground with Genesis has rekindled that appreciation with a vengeance.

I remind myself that I'm not going back forever, but it doesn't do much to calm my nerves. I feel like I'm sentencing myself to death, willingly going back Inside. But I have to. For Walter and Mark, for Kole.

Silas explained the mission a thousand times before we left, and it's ingrained into my head: we'll be transferred to a hospital where they're treating the disease, whatever it is, immediately once we get Inside. After that, our only job is to learn as much as possible about the disease and what's going on inside of Oasis and await further orders.

After that, I don't know. No one will, until we can figure out what's going on.

Clarke comes up behind me. I'm lagging at the back of the group, watching Noah and Jay pull ahead, like they're trying to enforce their authority out here, in the middle of the woods.

'Are you okay?' Clarke says under her breath, her eyes on the boys.

'No,' I say as calmly as I can. 'And I won't be until this is over.'

2

I stare up at the moon. I can barely see it through the trees. It casts shattered light against the ground beneath us, silver bright and glasslike.

I don't know how long it's been since we made camp, but the rest of the day has started to feel detached and far away as my mind wanders in the dark.

No one talked all day. We were walking, keen to cover ground, to make a dent on this goliath of a journey, and the silence was sensible, even if it wasn't comfortable. But after we stopped to eat, the silence became heavier, more obviously forced.

And when Noah finally said it was time to pause for the night, the silence dragged like nails on a blackboard.

This is a different kind of silence. The silence that only comes at night, when people are sleeping. It's almost like I can hear their thoughts even when they don't speak, like I'm picking up on the insufferable buzzing inside their heads and it's echoing the same buzzing in my own head.

And then night comes and washes it clean, and everything is quiet and my mind can ramble around in the empty space their thoughts have left.

However cruel my own thoughts are, at least they are my own.

I hear something move across from me and I nearly have a heart attack.

'What the hell is your problem?' Jay laughs, kicking a stone towards me.

'I thought you were asleep,' I mutter, trying to slow my rapid breathing. 'I thought everyone was asleep.'

He laughs again, but this time there's no humour in it. 'No one sleeps anymore.'

'You should,' I tell him. 'It's going to be a long day tomorrow.'

'You're not exactly sleeping like a baby either,' he throws back, although there's no energy in it. Sleep might evade us, but exhaustion doesn't. It hangs around our necks like a ten-ton weight, pulling down, down, always down.

Silence pools between us for minutes or seconds or hours. Here in the dark, it's harder to feel time slipping through your fingers, even though it's moving at the same pace.

I stare at Jay, and even though I can't see him properly, the same question circles around and around in my head until I feel dizzy. I want to say it, spit it out already, but at the same time, once it's asked, it's answered.

And there's no answer he could give me that would make me feel better.

'Jay,' I whisper, the dam breaking regardless of my logical intentions to keep my mouth shut.

'Yeah,' he says, less of a response and more of an acknowledgement.

'Do you think Kole might still be alive?' I feel the whole world go still as I wait for his response, breath held like he'll have a definitive answer. As if Jay's guess is so much better than mine that it will become a source of closure.

'I don't know,' he says. The moonlight glints off something in his hand, and it takes me a second to realise he's holding a knife, using it to shear the bark from a branch. 'There's no way of knowing for sure.'

'What does your gut tell you?' I ask him, and hate myself for sounding so hopeful, so needy.

He looks over at me. 'My gut says he's alive. I can't imagine this messed-up world without Kole in it. He's tough, Quincy. If there was any way to survive, wherever he is, he'll have taken it.'

'If anything's happened to him, it's because of me,' I say. 'It's my fault.'

'That's not true.' Jay shakes his head, whittling the branch down to a fine point. 'He's lost because he's an idiot, and he throws his life around like it's not important.'

I rub my hands over my face, and the corners of my mouth turn up in a small smile.

'What?' Jay snaps, seeing the look on my face.

'You sound like Kole.'

'What?'

'You sound like Kole talking about you.'

He snorts. 'What he doesn't understand,' he says now, swiping the knife along the branch again, 'is that to throw away your life, you actually have to have a life to throw away.'

It was supposed to be a joke, I can tell, but it comes out with a sour expression and piece of wood flies off into the grass across from us.

'Jay—'

'Don't.' He shakes his head, as if reprimanding himself for saying anything. He takes a breath. 'I need to get some sleep.' He stabs the knife into the earth beside him, turning away from me as he settles down for the night.

But his breathing doesn't even out, and he doesn't sleep.

3

We walk and we walk and we walk, until my feet are blistered and my whole body aches, and then we keep walking. Five days into our hike, we start veering east. Silas explained the route before we left, but it's a lot harder to know for sure now that we're actually out here.

'It's on the south-west side of the wall. Just an entrance, but there will be Officers guarding it. You'd better be prepared.'

After two more hours of walking, I stop dead. The rest of the group pauses. 'Did you hear that?' I ask quietly. There's a low murmuring in the distance, like an engine running.

Noah nods. 'That's probably a vehicle outside the entrance.'

He starts pulling off his backpack, and we follow suit. Our supplies will give us away, and we can't have weapons on us either, so our Officer uniforms and the IDs Silas gave us will have to do. We change quickly, buttoning and belting our Officer uniforms.

Once we've dumped everything incriminating, we continue on, and it's not long until the sounds begin to distinguish themselves from each other. I can hear voices along with the rumbling of the engine, and soon we can see the wall clearly.

My palms start to sweat the second we come up against the tree line. No going back now. I glance over at the others, as if I have to make sure that they're still there. The second we break the tree line we're noticed, and half-a-dozen guns are pointed in our direction. Once they see our uniforms, they lower their guns, but only a fraction.

One of the Officers steps forward. 'ID?' he asks.

Noah steps forward to meet him, reaching his wrist out, but the Officer looks at him strangely.

'These are out of date,' he says, glancing up at us. 'Didn't you get your new IDs?'

'We haven't received ours yet.' Clarke steps up beside Noah. 'Is that going to be a problem?'

The Officer blinks at her for a second, then shakes his head. 'Just go through to registration. They'll process you there.'

My heart is pounding so hard by the time we walk away that it feels like it's going to explode from my chest.

They scan our IDs outside the entrance and check our mission against their list. Silas said he'd get us on that list, using another Genesis informant working inside the Officer force, but when the Officer goes back to check, blood starts rushing in my ears. Someone screwed up a detail, matched a name to the wrong ID. The dates on the doctored list won't be the same as the ones we just gave them.

Something's gone wrong.

I start bracing for an attack. We were stupid not to bring weapons. All that it's done is leave us defenceless …

The gates creak open, and Clarke is pushing me inside ahead of her.

And then we're walking through the gate, just like that. Through the Peace Wall and into Oasis all over again.

4

On the other side there's a gate-house, where our IDs are scanned again before we're escorted inside one of the government buildings and told to wait for pick-up.

I didn't know this place existed in the Outer Sector. It's nothing like the Inner Sector, but the small cluster of buildings in this area stands out against the rest of the OS. They're cleaner, newer, seemingly untouched by the past few decades of denigration every other building in the Outer Sector has faced. It looks wrong out here, like a piece of glass in a sandpit.

I start pacing. My skin feels like there are ants crawling over it. This close to the Officers, anything can happen, regardless of a disguise.

'Why is this taking so long?' I whisper to Clarke.

'It's better than a sewer,' she says sourly. 'Stop complaining.'

I know the plan, and I know Silas has put everything in place for us, but none of this seems right to me. Since when did Oasis let people walk in and out this easily? Sure, we had IDs and uniforms, but this still seems too easy.

Something feels off, and I can't tell if it's adrenaline or paranoia or some kind of sixth sense, but I keep looking over my shoulder as if something is watching us.

The door opens and an Officer comes in, a list in her hand. 'Your transfer is here,' she says.

'Transfer to where?' Noah asks, and the Officer double-checks her list.

'The Justice Tower,' she says. 'That's what my list says. Is that right?'

'What?' My throat feels tight, and I take a step forward. This wasn't the plan. Silas never meant for us to get that close to the OP. How are we supposed to stay undercover right beneath his nose?

'Is there a problem?' the Officer asks.

She's looking at us more closely now, and I realise I have to back down. That I have no other choice. If we start arguing with her, it's just going to draw more attention to us. Attention we can't afford to face.

'Yes,' I say, calmer this time, swallowing. 'That's right.'

She nods slowly, confused by my strange behaviour, but doesn't take her eyes off us as she leads us outside. A transfer van is parked beside the building, and we board along with six other Officers.

Jay stares at me across the van. There's something in that look that gives me chills.

Be ready.

5

The van door slides open, but I'm not blinded by light as I expected. Instead I step out into the relative darkness of some kind of underground drop-off zone. Noah gets out of the van behind me and stretches, somehow managing to seem completely at ease as more Officers line up beside us. Once Jay, Clarke and the other Officers are out, the van roars to life behind us and pulls away. I watch it as it drives through a tunnel at the far side of the zone.

I glance at Jay briefly, making sure he notes the exit too.

A female Officer at the head of the group leads us towards a line of elevators, and we load inside, shoulder to shoulder, my fists tight at my sides. The elevator shakes on the way up, and I rein in the urge to jerk my hands out in both directions to catch myself.

The elevator doors open into a long room lit by fluorescent lights that run the length of it. No windows, though. We must still be underground.

'Ground zero.' A woman steps out from behind us and into the room, walking to the head of our small group. 'This will be your quarters for the remainder of your stay in the Justice Tower. Being assigned here is a privilege and should be treated as one. Standards are high and punishments are brutal, understood?'

'Understood,' the group says. One voice.

'This will serve as your cafeteria. Through that door is your sleeping quarters. You will be issued a rota and a schedule. It will provide all the information you need and will be replaced by a new schedule every week. If you are not on duty, you are here. Understood?'

'Understood.'

'There will be no fighting, no arguments and no talking on duty. Once you leave this room your lips are sealed unless you are asked a question. You will be invisible until you are needed, and when you are needed you will be swift and effective. Understood?'

'Understood.'

'Good. If you break any of these rules, you will be seeing me again. Take it from me – you *never* want to see me again.'

Nervous laughter ripples through the group, which the Officer silences with a glare.

'Take your schedule.' She points at the papers left on the table behind her. 'Learn it, and go get some sleep.'

She walks out of the room without another word, and every single person in the room relaxes visibly the moment the door closes behind her.

I glance at the others before I grab my schedule. My officer name is listed on the head of the paper: Officer Myers. I follow the rest of the group through the doors and into the sleeping quarters.

This room is just as huge. It reminds me of the cafeteria back in Genesis, but instead of tables the room is lined with bunk beds. I glance down at the page in my hand and there's a number – 348 – under *Bunk Number*, so I walk the length of the room searching the bunks for the digits, which are printed on the ends of the beds.

The room is already full of Officers, so I walk the aisle between bunks, dodging them as I search for the right bed. When I find it and lie down, I can barely feel my exhaustion, though I know I'm tired.

But I can hear Silas's words going round and round in my head: 'You'll be transferred to a ward in the Inner Sector. No one will recognise you there; you'll be far enough from the Celian City to stay under the radar.'

I can't panic. I feel it rising up in my chest like it's trying to strangle me, but I can't afford to panic. Within minutes of us arriving the plan is already starting to fall apart, but if I panic I'll lose focus. And if I lose focus we're dead.

6

My body jolts awake at the sound of a siren. At first I'm disorientated, and my heart is pounding in my chest before my feet even hit the ground. When they do, I'm immediately engulfed in a sea of people moving all around, and it takes me only a second to realise what's going on: I'm in the Justice Tower, and that siren signals the beginning of my first day undercover.

I roughly drag my hands down my face, forcing myself to focus before rushing to get ready. I glance around, and everyone is already half-dressed, so I quickly pull my sleep shirt over my head and pull on the blue Officer uniform once again.

It's stupid, but I feel vulnerable changing in front of the other Officers. Some part of me is convinced that this uniform conceals me more than it actually does. Deep down I know that if I'm going to be recognised, then I'll be recognised with or without my uniform.

I'm pulling on my boots as everyone else is lining up by the exits, and I slide into line right as the doors open. The Officers file out quickly, and everyone immediately finds a seat and sits down, filling up the cafeteria in seconds.

I hesitate for a moment, but someone knocks into me from behind, giving me a dirty look for standing in the middle of the floor, so I hastily take a seat at the far end of the room.

There are several monitors placed around the cafeteria that seem to be running an endless loop of Oasis news, but my eyes are dragged to it when I start seeing statistics line the screen, subtitles running along the bottom.

The death toll from the disease is already in the thousands. It's been verified that it's not the Virus, but they don't say anything else, because they don't know anything else.

There are brief shots of the wards, similar to the footage Wilke showed us back in Genesis, but worse. The hospitals are overcrowded, the supplies are running low, no one knows what to do.

I drop my eyes, trying to shovel food down my throat before the day starts. It doesn't taste like anything, but somehow it manages to simultaneously have the consistency of both thick gelatine and wet sand.

There's no diagnosis, no antidote. *It's not the Virus.* That's it, that's all they know. Thousands of people are already dead, and the only information we have is that it's not the Virus.

I can't have been sitting there for more than five minutes before the siren goes off again, and everyone is up and on their feet, filing into the elevators.

I'm pushed by the force of the crowd into one of those elevators, tightly packed into the side as the doors pull closed and we begin going up.

I feel my stomach drop as the sensation of lifting starts, but I refuse to let myself remember the last time I was in one of these things. I refuse.

My schedule listed the second floor as my station, so I get off on the second stop, along with a handful of other Officers. A few of them continue walking down the hall, to wherever they've been assigned, but my station is right here, in front of the elevators.

It's a low-risk, low-security floor. None of the really important meetings takes place here, and the real security exists below and above it, so once I switch out the Officer there before me and he boards the elevator, the hall becomes eerily empty.

For a few minutes, I am tense. Alert. Then minutes bleed into hours, and the walls around me feel like they're moving and blurring and shifting as I stand, and I wait, and I guard in silence.

We're supposed to wait for word from Silas before we make any move, but right now I don't know *how* we're supposed to make a move. There are security cameras at every corner, and if I leave before my replacement arrives, they'll see it.

My back is to the celian wall and the view of the City, my eyes trained on the elevator doors. There are too many memories rising up, so I shut them off altogether.

I can't afford to get overwhelmed. That's what I'm thinking, right before it happens. I can't afford to get overwhelmed.

I hear a *ping*, and the numbers on the elevator start counting down, coming to a stop at *Two*. The doors slide open, and a tall bearded man steps out, followed by a pair of eyes I've seen so many times in dreams and memories that they seem slightly off now that they're actually here, actually staring right at me from just a few feet away.

Kole.

He falters, only for a second, and then he smiles at the man who got out before him, continuing a conversation that obviously began in the elevator.

But my heart is stuttering along like a broken engine, and I passed overwhelmed a hundred miles back, and my lungs don't know how to work when he's in the room and he's just—

He's just walking away.

My brain catches up too slowly, and by the time my eyes follow him, analysing and measuring every step of his walk and every line of his perfectly fitting suit, he's already gone.

My heart restarts like a cluster bomb. Like it stopped beating when I saw him and now it's trying to catch up, and my hands start to shake and my vision does too and the hallway is empty again.

For a second the only thing I can think is: *he's perfect*. There isn't a scratch on him. He's clean shaven, his hair cut and styled, his suit expensive and creaseless and fit to his body like it was made for him.

No split lips. No blooming bruises. No broken bones or torn skin or cuts or burns or any sign of the torture scars that line *my* back in a chaotic army of their own.

The questions after that come one after another, building on each other.

What happened?

Why is he here?

What's going on? Why did he act like I wasn't standing here?

I lean my back against the celian wall and try to force air into my lungs. If anyone caught me like this I'd be reprimanded, but my knees are having trouble holding me up as I stare at the corner he turned and disappeared behind.

I can't afford to be overwhelmed.

7

My shift lasts five more hours. I don't move. I don't fidget or get restless or pace. I just stand and stare at the elevator doors, my body rigid and numb. Once my replacement arrives, I have to board the elevator again and return to ground zero.

I look around the cafeteria, which is bustling with Officers as they come off their shifts, sitting down at meals already set out on the tables.

My mind should be racing, but somehow it's just shut off. Or I am thinking, but it's just so confusing and murky to understand any of it.

I walk across the room, barely able to see the bodies moving around me. One foot in front of the other, one step at a time, each one sounding like a gunshot in my head. Someone pulls me by the arm, and I turn my head, blinking rapidly to try to focus my vision.

It's Noah, staring at me in confusion. He tries to ask me something, but I can't hear him around the rushing in my ears, so I shake him off, leaving him standing in the middle of the cafeteria as I continue to stumble towards the exit.

My lungs don't work anymore, my thoughts feel like light fracturing inside my brain and I have to *think*. I walk into the bathroom, make sure no one is there and stare at myself in the mirror.

I wait for something to click together. Something to start making sense. But all I can see is a vision of Kole walking out of that elevator, over and over and over again on a single, torturous loop.

It doesn't make sense. Nothing's making sense, and I can't slow my heart down for long enough to figure out what's happening. My breathing hasn't even sped up, but I feel like I'm gasping, like I'm drowning in the air around me.

Focus, I think. Pull it together.

I slam my fist into the wall beside the mirror, and I can feel skin and flesh tearing across my knuckles, but it doesn't hurt.

Nothing hurts. I can't *think*.

'Myers!' a gruff voice calls in the next room, and I yank the door open as fast as I can, hiding my bloodied hand behind my back.

'Yes?'

'Let's go. Your assignment.' He nods towards the elevator.

'My next assignment isn't for another twenty minutes—'

'It got changed,' he says. 'Now let's *go*.'

8

He's standing right there, outside the elevator, same black suit, same perfect hair.

Not in my head. Here.

Kole.

He barely looks at me when I step out, just lets his eyes flick in my direction long enough to see that I'm there and then turns on his heel and starts walking in the opposite direction. There's another Officer with us, a tall man with dark ginger hair who follows Kole when he starts walking, and I follow him.

He keeps walking until we pass another elevator, which he stops in front of and boards. I follow him inside along with the other Officer and it begins to drop.

Why is he here?

What's he doing in the Celian City, dressed like an Elite?

We stop on level 60.

We step out of the elevator and follow him as he strides down hallways purposefully. When we come across a reception desk on the sixtieth floor, he stops and orders refreshments sent to the meeting room in 60B.

'Yes, sir.' The attendant nods. 'It will be sent up momentarily.'

'Jameson?' Kole asks, raising two fingers to summon the other Officer without looking around.

'Yes, sir?' The Officer steps forward attentively.

'I want you to make sure everything runs smoothly. The meeting starts in ten minutes and I need it ready by then.'

The Officer's face twitches in confusion, but only for a second. A ludicrous demand, surely, to send a high-level Officer to oversee refreshments, but some things aren't questioned in the Celian City, and apparently the OP's son is one of those things.

The OP's son.

Last year, when Kole told me he was President Johnson's son, I could barely believe him. The entitlement that came so naturally to Aaron was never a part of Kole, so I never really thought about it. Never really *considered* the implications of the relationship.

Until now. And now Kole is treated like a prince among paupers, and he doesn't blink an eye at it, and all I want to know is: where is he gone? This makes no sense to me. I met a boy who was a rebel, who resisted Oasis with every breath in his body, who fought to undo its stranglehold on the population. But that isn't the man who's standing before me now.

This isn't Kole. Not the real Kole. Not *my* Kole.

But what if my Kole was the same as my Aaron? A paper boy built out of lies that tore at the slightest prodding?

What if the Kole I knew never existed at all, not really. What then?

The other Officer leaves to follow his orders, and now it's just Kole and me in the celian halls. Does he even know I'm here, or is he so far gone he won't recognise even me? It's just as I'm thinking this that I see Kole swerve suddenly, catching my arm as he pushes a door open and pulls us both inside.

My senses catch fire, and I start processing every detail of the room like a switch has been turned on in my brain. I see light fragment across the room, glance up to find a chandelier above us. The walls are a warm cream colour, with dark oak floorboards and cream furniture. Books are stacked on the table beside the sofa farthest from the door, four of them, all big tomes except one – it's small, thin, maybe a notebook. There is a second door at the far end of the room, smaller than the one we walked through, the same dark wood of the floors. Too small to be an exit – probably a closet.

And then he's hugging me. He smells so clean, like soap. His suit is perfectly pressed, and he doesn't smell like he used to – of wood and homemade soap, the outdoors. It's like they've washed all the Outside out of him.

And I can't stop myself. I don't know what's going on or who he is now, and yet I can't stop myself. I wrap my hands around his waist, and he presses his face into my neck, and he is warm. So, so warm. Like he was the night before we left Nails's place, when I hugged him that first time and it felt like a stolen luxury and an absolute necessity at the same time. Warm like he was when he kissed me in the hallway the day before we broke into the Celian City, and everything changed. Warm like he was in that cold elevator, when he held me one last time before he disappeared through the roof and out of my life. Until now.

'You're alive,' he whispers, and he pushes me back just far enough to look at me, his hand brushing over my shoulders, down my arms, checking to see that I'm still intact, still okay, still alive. Then he pulls me close again. 'You're alive. You're here.'

I nod into his shoulder, then he pushes me back again, looking me all over. His eyes snag on my cut knuckles, and his mouth twists with worry.

'What happened?' He lifts my hand, inspecting the injury, but I pull my hand away.

'You're *here.*' I barely manage to get the words out, I'm so overwhelmed by this. 'Why are you *here*?'

He tries to take my hand again, but I push him back. I keep him at arm's length, and I wish there weren't two Koles in my head, one a series of unfolding memories, stolen moments and quiet consolation, the boy I knew on the Outside.

The boy I thought I knew.

The other one, he looks too much like Aaron. Pressed and perfect and suited and scented and standing in front of me now, all the real sucked out of him and replaced by the stench of Oasis. And maybe it's the sudden lack of the Kole I knew that makes the sob that escapes me sound quite so much like I'm drowning.

'You're alive,' he whispers, his palm pressed to his forehead as if he actually can't believe I'm in front of him, like I'm a mirage. He's breathless. Relieved. Shocked.

'You're *here*,' I whisper. Breathless. Pained. Confused. 'Why?'

'We don't have much time,' he says, finally coming back to his senses. He glances around the room, at the door and then back at me. He takes two long strides towards me and places a hand either side of my face, making pointed eye contact. 'You need to get out of here. Now.'

I shake him off, and he looks bewildered.

'What *happened* to you?' I whisper, and I hate myself for the way my hand drops to my gun. Just checking, just making sure it's there. But the fear is real, like a presence, and the movement doesn't go unseen by Kole, who takes an automatic step back.

'Quincy, it's complicated …'

'What does that mean? *Why are you here?*'

'It means a lot's happened in six months,' he snaps, and I can't help my eyes flying around the room, finding the most defensible position. Then I stop myself. *This is Kole!* my mind screams.

And there they are again. Two images, layered on top of each other, flickering. A Kole I can trust, and one I cannot.

He presses his palms into his eyes. He sighs. 'I'm sorry. I want to tell you everything, but I just don't have time. I can explain, but right now we need to get you out.'

'I'm not leaving.' I shake my head. 'I can't.'

'What does *that* mean?'

I clench my jaw, trying to hold a million emotions under the surface. But I can see him watching me. He was always too good at knowing what I was actually feeling.

'I can't tell you,' I whisper. I want to tell him. I want to tell him everything. I want to tell him about the Colosseum and escaping and Genesis and Mark. But I can't. I can't trust him with that kind of information. Not now.

'Why?' He already knows. The look on his face tells me that. But the pain in his voice tells me something else, making the two images in my head flicker.

I *want* to trust him.

'Quincy,' he pleads. 'What's going on? Tell me, please.'

'I can't tell you anything.' I step backwards again, cementing my decision. 'I can't tell whose side you're on right now.'

Kole's eyes widen in confusion and then shock and then something akin to horror, but before he can say anything the door slides open.

Noah.

His eyes widen. Not in shock, but in terrified confusion.

'Sir,' he murmurs, saluting Kole. But his eyes quickly fall back on me, trying to communicate something to me without saying anything out loud.

In case the OP's son overhears, I realise, my blood running cold.

'I was having Officer Myers do a security analysis in here,' Kole says smoothly. 'There's an event to be held here next week, and I wasn't sure how many Officers to order. What do you think, Officer Phillips?'

'I'm sure no more than a double round would be necessary, Sir,' Noah answers calmly, regaining his composure.

'Of course,' Kole says. He then walks past us and out the door, into the hallway, continuing to his destination. We trail behind him, escorting him to his meeting upstairs as if nothing happened.

Kole doesn't look at me. Not even for a second. If he can fool people this easily on the Inside, was he fooling us on the Outside? At the meeting room, Noah and I take over from the Officers previously standing guard outside the door, and I try to keep my focus on the wall across from us, my thoughts like a thunderstorm inside my head.

Noah coughs once, and I glance over at him long enough to see him give me a pointed look, as if to say he'll need an explanation later. I nod as I turn back to face the wall across from us.

He'll get an explanation, that's for sure. I just don't know if he'll like it when he does.

9

Our schedule goes on until late that night. The meeting that Kole attends lasts almost five hours, and when they finally exit the meeting room, Kole doesn't even glance in my direction. Two unfamiliar Officers slip into place behind him and he turns away immediately, walking in long strides down the hall until he disappears.

I haven't seen or heard anything from the OP since we got here, and it's beginning to make me nervous. Being this close to him, not only inside Oasis, not only inside the Inner Sector, but inside the Celian City itself, inside the Towers – it's the most dangerous place in the world right now.

But at least if I had seen something of him, or knew where he was, that would be better than this. Looking over my shoulder and waiting for him to appear out of nowhere.

The most disturbing part of all is that Kole seems to be filling in for his father while he's not here.

Kole's father. I try to make it sound normal in my head. I try to make it make sense, but it doesn't. It never will. There is no logical way to bridge the gap between him and the Oasis President.

Kole endured so much in here. If I didn't already know that from his reaction to this place when we broke in, I couldn't avoid seeing the look in his eyes today, like the walls themselves were a threat.

But how does that reaction connect with him choosing to be in here? Did he choose? Did he re-enter his old life willingly?

It doesn't make any sense.

'Myers,' Noah says, and it takes me a second to remember that he's talking to me. That here, my entire life has been reduced down to a precarious, life-threatening secret. 'Let's go.'

We spend another three hours following one of the OP's advisors from meeting to meeting. By the time we're dismissed at the end of the night, I can barely see. I follow Noah downstairs to the Officers' Quarters.

I eat mindlessly, shovelling food into my mouth as my mind repeats everything Kole said to me on a loop, as if I'd find some clue to what's going on in the couple of sentences we were able to share before Noah came in.

We drop our trays off at the end of the queue, and before I can gather my bearings, Noah is grabbing my arm and towing me into the sleeping quarters. Most of the Officers are still in the cafeteria, so it's almost empty.

'What the *hell* was going on earlier?' he asks, turning on me.

Immediately my paranoia sets in and I pull away, frantically looking around the room. 'Keep your voice down,' I hiss.

'If you don't start explaining yourself, I'm contacting Silas and having you pulled off the mission.'

'Don't threaten me.'

'Just tell me what the hell was going *on.*'

I go still for a second. He's acting like he doesn't know anything about my past or about my relationship with Kole. Which means Silas is hiding things, not just from me, but from Noah.

From his own people.

'I know him.' I pull him back behind a bunkbed in the hopes of obscuring us from suspicion. 'I know Kole.'

'You *know* Kole Johnson?'

'From the Outside, yes.'

Noah just blinks at me, as if he is completely incapable of processing what is coming out of my mouth.

'You already know I was on the Outside before the Colosseum.'

'But with *Kole Johnson*?'

I grit my teeth, staring at the floor as I try to regain control over my temper. This is already hard enough – seeing him here, hearing his voice, talking to him – without Noah interrogating me about how I know him.

'Yes, Kole Johnson. He saved my life.' And there it is. I'm defending him already.

'The same Kole Johnson who assassinated over thirty rebel forces inside of Oasis? The same Kole Johnson who *murdered* dozens of innocent people on Oasis's order? *That* Kole Johnson?'

'You don't know anything about him, Noah.' *And neither do I.*

'I know that he was a notorious assassin. I know that Genesis is terrified of him. That *everyone* is afraid of him, because he doesn't care who he kills.'

'He *left* that!' I say, raising my voice and immediately regretting it. When I calm down, I try to start again. 'He left that. He left Oasis. He left that life.'

'Obviously not!' Noah says, pointing towards the doors as if Kole is standing there, watching us. 'If he's changed so much, why is he here now? Why is he inside Oasis, inside the Celian City, *inside the Founding Towers*? He looks like he's one of them, acts like he's one of them, was *born* to be one of them – how much more proof do you need, Quincy? I can't believe you didn't tell Silas this before we left.

You're putting all of us in danger. He could kill us while we sleep,' he says, looking wildly towards his own bunk. 'He could do anything to us. You've jeopardised *everything*.'

I drop down onto the bed, putting my face in my hands. 'I don't know anything anymore. I thought I knew him, but I don't have an explanation for this. Unless … unless he's undercover too.'

'Why? Why would he go undercover? And as what? For whom?'

'He's on our side. Or at least, he used to be. Or he still is.' I try to suppress a growl of frustration. 'I don't know. I'm trying to figure out what's going on. But he escaped Oasis, just like everyone else. I don't know what would make him risk going back to his father.'

Noah seems to calm slightly at my own admission of doubt. He sits down beside me on the bed.

'What if he got sick of being hunted?' Noah asks. 'What if he really did come back to Oasis?'

I try not to let that idea knock the wind out of me, but it's hard to stop it. It's as if we get a choice – death or corruption. But I don't want either for Kole. Even now, when fear and doubt breed panic inside of me, my memories of him before are stronger, and I can't help hoping.

'If he's renegade,' I say slowly, 'then I can't protect him. If he betrayed us, then I *won't* protect him.'

Noah nods, placing a hand on my shoulder. 'It's hard,' he says, 'doubting someone you trusted. But you're doing the right thing. For all our sakes.'

All I can do is nod back as I attempt to swallow the guilt souring in my mouth as the rest of the Officers begin trickling into the room.

10

The next night we each have to report back to Silas, as agreed. Which means sneaking out of the Officers' Quarters and finding someplace where the cameras can't see us. Noah has the phone hidden between his mattress and the bed, so I have to meet him in the underground drop-zone at 2.00 a.m. No earlier, no later.

The last few hours of my shift blur together, the light from outside the celian walls slowly slipping away the only way I can keep track of time. For the most part, I don't see a single soul. The second floor is usually completely empty. That's why it makes no sense that Kole passed through here the other day.

When I finally get back to the Officers' Quarters and lie down in my bunk, it's hard not to slip off to sleep. Exhaustion makes my eyelids heavy, my arms and legs weighted in the bed as I wait. At least the room has clocks, twelve in total, and one is close enough for me to see from my bed.

I watch the seconds tick by, and they feel at once too fast and too slow. I just want to sleep. I just want this to be over. But at 1:50 a.m., when I hear Noah get up and slip out the door, I roll out of bed and creep across the floor, praying all the while that no one will hear me.

I slide the door open slowly and creep through into the cafeteria, where Noah stands by the door. My heart is too loud in my head, like a drum inside my skull. I can feel a headache coming on as Noah reaches for the emergency exit door.

'Wait,' I whisper, belatedly. 'The emergency exits are alarmed.'

'We're not idiots.' He grunts, nodding towards the corners of the room. 'The cameras go on a loop during the night, so they can't see us, and the alarms on the exits we need have been disengaged.'

'How?' I follow Noah, pulling the door closed behind me. The stairs leading down to the drop-zone are wide, so that a large group can get out quickly, but they're unlit, so I keep tight to the wall. I try not to think what would happen if I slipped and fell down these steps.

'Jay,' Noah answers from ahead of me. I can't see him, but I can hear him even as he whispers. The rest of the building is completely silent.

My heart twists strangely. I haven't seen him since we first arrived in Oasis. I haven't seen Clarke either. They were stationed somewhere else, and even though it's only been two days, in here it feels like forever.

Noah pulls me to the left at the bottom of the stairs, down to a corner, behind a wall. Someone steps out, and I almost have a heart attack.

Jay grins, and Clarke stabs him in the ribs with her elbow.

'How are you holdin' up, kid?' he asks, and something feels right again, after so much time of nothing but wrong.

'Everyone wants to kill us,' I grunt.

'So, same?' He grins, razor-tipped smile cutting across his face. It falls off unevenly, though, and for a second I see the cracks. His vision is unfocused, distracted. Being here must be taking a toll on him.

Noah steps past me, pulling the phone from inside his uniform, and I look away from Jay.

'We need to hurry up.' Noah presses a button on top of the phone, and it buzzes before blinking to life. A second later, 2.00 a.m. on the dot, a call comes through, and he answers it.

Silas and Wilke stand in the control room, Silas's hands on his hips as he stares upwards. Wilke grins when he sees us.

'Noah,' Silas says urgently. 'Is it safe to talk?' His eyes land on each one of us individually. It was him who insisted on having all of us meet every few days to keep tabs on everything that was going on, and he's not subtle as he checks to see if we've obeyed the order.

'For now.' Noah glances around the room. 'Safe' is a serious exaggeration, huddled in the corner of a drop-off under the Celian City.

'Well, we better be quick then. What are the updates?'

'They have us positioned in the Towers,' I say, grabbing everyone's attention. 'Something went wrong with the transfer.'

Silas's eyebrows knit together. 'You weren't supposed to be that close to the OP. What happened?'

'Once we were inside the Wall, we were transferred straight to the Towers,' Noah cuts in. 'Quincy and I have been stationed in the Justice Tower.' He glances over at Clarke and Jay.

'They put us in the Peace Tower,' Clarke says. 'But they keep transferring Jay out during the day.'

I snap to attention. 'Where?'

'Guarding hospitals in the Inner Sector. They don't seem to have an antidote, but the medical centres are packed, and people are fighting to get care.'

It's hard for me to picture that – an Oasis institution breaking down under pressure.

Silas looks pensive, and Wilke is looking around, worry evident on his face.

'I'll deal with it,' Silas says after a few moments of silence. 'Give me a few days. Are there any other updates? What have you learned since you arrived?'

'You were right about it only being the Pures who are being infected with the disease,' Noah says, switching gears immediately.

'We already knew that, Noah.' Silas's tone is cold. 'What else?'

Noah twitches. 'Nothing, not yet.'

'And the others? Have they found anything?'

Noah shakes his head. 'They don't seem to be reacting. There's no talk of an antidote since the first broadcast. People keep being admitted to hospitals, but nothing is happening.'

'We don't need an antidote,' Silas says. 'The plan has changed.'

'What?' Noah sounds taken aback.

'Oasis hasn't been this weak since it was first built. This is our only chance to take control.'

'But Silas,' Noah starts. 'People are dying—'

'Pures!' Silas says. 'Pures are dying. That works to our advantage. Once Johnson is taken from power, we'll figure out a way to curb the deaths.'

'That's *disgusting*.' I pull the phone from Noah's hand. 'You can't be serious. That's *exactly* what Johnson would do.'

'Sometimes you have to use the enemy's tactics against them.'

'And lose thousands of lives in the process? Is that how you want to start a new world? With death?'

'It's going to start with death either way,' Silas says. 'But this way we'll actually be able to take control. Don't forget what's on the line here, Miss Emerson. Everyone has people to protect.'

'The only person I see you protecting is yourself.'

I push the phone into Noah's hands. I can't look at Silas's face for one more second. I walk off, fuming, my heart racing as I listen to Noah pick up the conversation and begin planning with Silas, as if he didn't just tell us he was willing to sacrifice thousands of lives just to regain control of Oasis.

I hear footsteps coming up behind me, and Jay's hand falls on my shoulder. I whip around on him, my hand raised threateningly. He catches my wrist and steps towards me.

'*Don't,*' he says. 'I'm not the enemy.'

I shake myself free of him, my breathing heavy. 'Did you hear what he said? Did you *hear it?*'

'Pull yourself together,' he snaps. 'You're not going to be any use to anyone if you're losing it every time something bad happens. You're not going to be any use to Sophi *or* the citizens.'

I fist my hands, digging my fingernails into my palms as I try to regain control of my breathing.

'I'm okay.' I breathe, shaking my head. 'I'm okay, I'm okay.'

'We'll deal with it,' he says. 'I promise.'

'Okay.' I nod my head. I believe him. 'But I'm not letting people die so that Silas can slide his way into Johnson's place.'

Jay nods, then takes a step backwards. He understands. It's not just in my head then, what Silas is doing. There's something toxic about him, something greedy in his eyes. It might not just be Johnson we have to worry about now.

11

Silas wants Noah to report back to him every forty-eight hours, but apparently doesn't need us all there for every communication because it's too dangerous. Because we caused trouble, pushed back against him, and Noah wouldn't. That, apparently, warrants us being cut out of the contact entirely.

He also wants us to do a sweep of each floor of the Justice Tower. It's supposed to give us a better idea of what we're facing, but it's nothing but a distraction. Noah obliges but gets caught on the thirtieth floor and barely skates by on an excuse of confusion.

I don't even leave my post.

When Noah finally finds me, it's our last meal of the day, and he slams his tray down in front of me.

'Stop avoiding me,' he says. He's angry, but it doesn't matter. Why should it? If he can't stand up to Silas, he doesn't deserve my respect. 'Where have you been?'

'It doesn't matter,' I say quietly, staring down at my food.

'You ditched me!' he says, trying to keep his voice down. 'That mission was for the both of us.'

'It wasn't a mission, it was a wild goose chase.'

'And what's that supposed to mean?'

'Are you really that blind?' I sit up straight, looking directly at him. 'Do you actually think he doesn't know the layout of the Towers?'

'We have to be patient—'

'No,' I growl. '*You* can do whatever you want, but I'm done being patient. He's lost sight of what we came here to do, and now he's just wasting our time. He's running us around in circles to throw us off.'

'Why would he do that?' Noah genuinely sounds confused. He's in so deep he can't even see what's right in front of him.

'He's protecting someone. Himself, or …'

'Or who?' Noah's voice drops to a deadly whisper.

'Or Johnson.'

'Why would he be defending *Johnson?* Quincy, Silas is on our side. He wants to take Johnson down just as much as we do.'

'Does he, Noah?' I stand up from the table, taking my dishes with me. 'Does he want to take him down, or does he want to *be* him? Because that line is blurring a lot more than I'm comfortable with.'

Noah drags his hand through his hair. 'He's spent *years* fighting for a rebellion. *Years* creating a force strong enough to overthrow Oasis.'

'Building a rebellion and building an army look very similar in the beginning.'

'You've never heard him speak about the rebellion. You weren't there when no one believed it was possible. You weren't there when it *was* impossible.'

'And neither were you, Noah. He's made you think you owe him something. He's made you think he's someone he's not.'

Noah is turning red in the face, every muscle in his body taut with frustration and anger. 'I'm not an idiot, Quincy, even if you think I am. I know who he is.'

'I don't think you're an idiot.' I glance behind us and shift my feet beneath me. There's a guard in the corner who's noticed us, and it makes me feel skittish. 'And I'm not saying I know what's going on. But I can't trust him like you do.'

'Well if you don't want me to report you and have you removed from this mission, you'd better learn to,' he says, his voice deadly.

I shake my head at him, throw one last glance over my shoulder at the guard and walk off to dump my tray.

A hundred thoughts run through my head, about Noah and Silas and Genesis and Oasis and Kole, and everything all at once, and a roaring begins in my ears.

I wait until I'm at my guard-post to drop my head to my chest, struggling to think clearly. How can I sound so sure when I open my mouth and feel so confused inside my own head?

I'm saying one thing, and thinking another, but the feeling is the same. That bone-deep ache of wrongness. Something's off, and even if I don't know what it is, I can't ignore it.

I don't trust my mind, but I trust my gut.

12

I wake up to the sound of loud talking in the next room. For a second I'm confused, I think I'm somewhere else, I think I'm in the Dorms, or at the Base, but then I start awake, and the room is grey. Celian City, Justice Tower, Officers' Quarters. Day 7.

I jump out of bed and head in the direction of the noise. In the cafeteria, my eyes immediately snap over to the crowd huddled around a broadcast screen in the corner of the room, at least fifty Officers talking loudly around it.

I push my way to the front, and when I finally see what's going on, it takes me a second to realise what it is I'm looking at.

Streets. Grey and filthy, with rubble in piles and garbage in heaps on street corners.

The Outer Sector.

The image changes. People, their faces obscured by dark masks, rioting in the streets.

The image changes again. A fire setting a building ablaze, people screaming on the streets.

The image changes again. A dozen masked people smashing in the windows of an Officer vehicle.

The image changes again. Another, smaller group ganging up on a small Officer unit.

I can barely believe what I'm seeing in front of me. This is it. This is the beginning.

13

We barely have time to catch our breath before the room is flooded with more Officers. The double doors open and a line of men and women in blue uniforms start filing inside, forming a line against the far wall.

Their uniforms are the same as ours, but I don't recognise any of them. As much as I've avoided spending time with the other Officers, we sleep in the same room and eat all our meals together, and you can't help becoming familiar with their faces.

But I've never seen these people before. They must be sourced from other locations, because everyone seems uncomfortable with their presence. I glance around me, trying to figure out what's going on, but a second later the doors open again, and this time it's not just another Officer.

It's Kole Johnson, flanked by a set of guards.

Everyone falls into line immediately, and I have to force myself to focus on standing straight and keeping the correct amount of distance between me and the Officer beside me so I won't flinch as he comes to stand in front of the room.

I force myself not to look away from him as his eyes glide across us. He fits in so well here, so calm and poised, confidence rolling off him in waves. Whether he was the OP's son or not, he'd have control over this room.

And I wonder how this side of him never came out at the Base. With the rebels, he was thrust into leadership, and he hated it. Or at least I thought he did – he played at hating it, maybe. He looks so comfortable now that it's hard for me to even pull up the memories of him from before.

The two Officers who came in behind him step up to his side. Kole raises his hand and points at one of the Officers. He flicks his fingers back, gesturing for the Officer to step forward, which he does. The two Officers flanking him step forward as well and guide the chosen Officer to stand off to the left, his gaze shifting nervously over the Officers still left in line.

Kole points at another Officer, and another, his eyes never stopping their slow glide across the crowd, analysing each one of us and taking his pick. For what, I don't know, but the Officers he's lined up at his left seem to know just as little as I do.

He points at me, gesturing for me to come forward, and it takes me several long seconds to force my legs to disobey my instincts and to take slow steps forward. I'm led into line with the others, and Kole doesn't give me a second glance.

There are over a dozen of us in line before Kole finally nods, signalling that he's done. He whispers orders to one of his Officers and then walks back out, followed by the troop he brought with him, but leaving behind one of his two guards.

We're left standing at the head of the room, unsure of what to do or where to move. Everyone's too afraid to open their mouths and ask what just happened, so we stand stock still until the Officer dismisses the rest of the group to continue on schedule.

Then he comes to stand in front of us. He looks us up and down for only a moment, as if he's analysing us for himself, before shaking his head and telling us to get moving.

Get moving seems to mean *get into the elevators*, because that's what all of the other Officers do. And I fall into line after them, because I don't have any other option.

Whatever Kole is dragging us into, it doesn't seem to be up for discussion.

An Officer I do recognise stops me before I can board the elevator to the loading bank, catching me by the arm as I pass her by. I have to stop myself from jerking away from her, but her grip is too tight to be broken so easily anyway.

'I don't know what kind of bloody hell you're about to wreak out there,' she says, her lips pulling taut over her teeth in something closer to a snarl than a smile, 'but I envy you. Not all of us get the chance to put the Dormants in their place quite so ... violently.' She's practically drooling at the idea, and my stomach roils as she nods to me before releasing my arm.

Once we're down in the landing bay, we're split into two vans and loaded up to go out immediately. They're not waiting around for this to get any worse than it already is, but I want to freeze time for a second, just to catch my breath.

I don't know what I'm doing or what I'm expected to do. I can't kill Dormants; I won't kill them for protesting. I refuse to. But how can I disobey direct orders without drawing attention to myself?

Why did Kole drag me onto this mission in the first place? My blood runs cold at the idea that maybe he chose me for exactly that – to draw attention to me, to get me killed.

Just as I think this, Kole leaps into the van along with us, and the door slides closed after him, signalling for the driver to go. We shift around awkwardly to make room for him, and he takes a seat across from me, his elbows resting on his knees as he leans forward, gun slung between his legs. He doesn't look up at me once, doesn't glance up from where his eyes are drilling into the bottom of the truck bed, but everyone is staring at him.

He's like a myth to them – I can see it in tthe way they look at him. He was built up to be a legend, and then he died and came back to life, which could only burnish his reputation.

I have to force myself to not lash out, but I'm angry. Angry with them, for revering this Kole. They might be afraid of him, but they love him as well. Love this form of him. Armed and ready to kill.

I don't want to see this. Whether he's turned sides or not, I never wanted to see him like this. Them getting to see this version of him robs me of my version of him, the one who would die before he'd do this.

The van jerks to a halt, and Kole's eyes shoot up, catching mine. I glance away as the van starts moving again, passing through the Sector Wall and into the Outer Sector.

The van pulls up and the doors open, and we all get out and form yet another line at the side of the vehicle. We're at some kind of checkpoint between the Outer Sector and the Sector Wall, and we're far from the only Officers here. There are troops everywhere, some lined up in units and some stationed at the entry, but everyone looks restless.

'What's that sound?' an Officer behind me asks as Kole talks to one of the commanding Officers. I attune my hearing to the sounds around me, of engines and talking and van doors opening and closing, and, somewhere farther off in the distance, wailing.

At first I think it's just an alarm, but it's not clear enough to be an alarm. It's a whole cacophony of sounds, a symphony rising out of the Outer Sector, fire and screaming and sirens. A shudder runs down my spine, and no one answers the Officer. Everyone begins to look pale as whatever vicious images they'd dreamt up of what was going to happen today crumble under the seething reality of what we're about to face.

Kole appears out of nowhere in front of us. Either that or I was so distracted by my own thoughts I didn't hear him approach. I can't afford to be this unfocused. Not now, not out here.

'There seems to be a change in the situation,' he says, addressing us directly for the first time since all of this started. 'I'm going to need you all to stay here until we can gather more information.'

I can see the change in everyone's demeanour; the second those words leave his mouth, everyone's shoulders drop in relief.

'Officer Myers, I'll have you and Officer Janko escort me,' he says, but before I can respond he's already giving orders to Janko, sending him in the opposite direction before turning around and walking towards one of the buildings inside the barricades.

Whispers break out within the squad and my heart starts racing as I jog to catch up with him. I don't know what he's trying to do, drawing this much attention to me, but it's going to get me killed.

He walks inside the building, and I follow him. They have set up a makeshift base in one of the rooms; the tables have been pushed against the walls and there are maps spread out across it. Other than that, though, the room is empty.

'Take these,' Kole says, thrusting a pile of clothes into my hands.

'What? Why?'

'You can't go out into the Outer Sector dressed like that,' he says, pointing down at my uniform.

I'm dressed like an Officer. It's hard to even remember that. In the Towers, I feel like I stand out, like it's obvious I'm not what I'm pretending to be, but it's not as obvious as I think. And if the Dormants see me now, as an Officer, I won't make it out of here alive.

He sees my hesitation and pauses for a second, releasing a sigh. 'If you come with me, I'll answer any questions you have,' he says, much gentler than anything he's said to me today. 'I'll explain everything, but first I have to *show* you.'

My reluctance to comply falters. I want to know, but more importantly I *need* to know. If he's really going to answer my questions, then his answers could be the difference between life or death.

Between Clarke's life and death. Between Jay's.

I nod, and he looks relieved, pointing me to a door that leads into another room. Whatever this building was used for before this, it's been in disrepair for a long time. There's no furniture, and all the windows are boarded up, piles of dust and debris building in the corners of the bare floors.

The air is different here, in the Outer Sector, than in the Celian City. Murkier and thicker. In the buildings like this one, abandoned for years, the unmistakable smell of concrete dust fills every room. It takes all of a minute for my lungs to feel coated in the stuff.

This used to be what every place I knew smelled like. There's something disturbingly soothing about it.

I strip off the Officer uniform, and relief washes over me as I pull on the set of clothes Kole gave me. They're a little big, and I have to roll the trousers up at the ankle, but I feel like me again.

I didn't realise I had stopped.

I walk back into the room, back to Kole. We're both dressed all in black, but it looks different on him than it looks on me. Whether he knows it or not, he's still going to stand out. Kole is lean, but he's not scrawny or pale or worn-out looking. It's obvious he hasn't faced the kind of abuse the Dormants take as a natural part of life, and they're going to see that the second they set eyes on him.

Kole grabs two safety vests from the table. 'Put that on.'

'But you just said—' I cut myself off before I can continue, clamping the words down and gritting my teeth. 'Aren't we supposed to be dressing like Dormants? They don't typically walk around with armour on.'

'Yes, but I'm not having you getting shot either,' he mutters. He still won't make eye contact with me, and I don't know why I'm getting so frustrated with him.

Him being quiet makes everything simpler for me. Makes battling the two different versions of him in my head easier. But I think some part of me wants him to speak, to explain himself.

I want to trust him. Whether I actually do or not is a different story.

I pull the vest over my head and strap it in against my sides, grateful for the secure weight of it the second it's on.

He disappears into another room, returning with two jackets, big enough to mostly mask the safety vests underneath. I have to jog to catch up with him as he disappears out of the building and back out into the clearing. But instead of crossing directly over and towards the first exit, he keeps walking along the perimeter of the Sector Wall.

'Where are you going?' I ask, falling into step beside him.

'The riots have got worse,' he says. 'If we go through there,' he points back towards the first entrance the Officers must have built when they first arrived, 'there's no way we'll make it. We need to slip out where they won't notice us. If they realise we're with Oasis, we're as good as dead.'

I have to stop myself from laughing at the idea. That I could end up dead not because of Oasis, but because I was assumed to be *with* them.

We keep walking until we reach the end of the barricades, a few hundred metres from where we entered through the Sector Wall. I can't see how they won't see us exiting from here if there are as many people on the other side as it sounds like there are.

'Zip up,' Kole says, nodding to my jacket. 'Their focus is the front entrance, but when I say go, I want you to keep your head down and just run, okay?'

'Okay.' I nod, swallowing. I don't know why I feel so panicked all of a sudden.

He lifts the wooden frame off the fence, takes a key out and unlocks the padlock on the gate.

'On three,' he says, making pointed eye contact with me before he places both hands on the latch that opens the fence. 'One. Two. Three!'

14

The buildings in the Outer Sector are built tightly together, so I run straight towards the first alley I see, away from the main streets and the throng of rioters overtaking them. I don't let myself look at them, or back to see if Kole is following me. I slip between two buildings and continue running, far enough that the sound of the riots is less of a deafening roar and more of a loud clamouring.

I can hear Kole catching up with me as I slow down. We've run straight into an old factory sector, most of which was abandoned years ago. Even now, the buildings that are still in use seem to be emptied for the riots.

'Come on,' Kole says, pulling us to the right so we can loop back around. 'I don't want it to get us killed, but I need to show you what's going on.'

When we finally start getting closer and I can hear the sounds of the riot growing louder, Kole pulls me down another street and then into one of the buildings.

'What are you doing?' I hiss, but he's already across the room. A second later and he's walking up the stairs, taking them two at a time and disappearing onto the second floor.

The building seems to be abandoned, but I don't understand how he would have known that. Either he's spent time out here before, or he's randomly bounding through the Outer Sector with enough confidence that it looks like he knows what he's doing.

I run to catch up with him, but the next floor is empty, other than another set of stairs across the room. He's not even checking to see if I've bothered to follow him.

But I do. Up thirteen flights of stairs, only able to tell that he's still in the same room as me because I can hear his footsteps as he continues to climb. Eventually there are no more staircases, and the Outer Sector opens out below us from on top of the roof he's led me to. I climb out onto the roof, and I can see him standing at the edge, looking out across the buildings, but even when I get my bearings, I don't move. I don't want to. I heard the riots, saw some stragglers in my periphery as I ran through the buildings, but I don't want to see it.

The riots mean something. More than Kole realises, I think. It means something is changing

When I finally cross the expanse to stand by Kole, he pulls me down to a crouch beside him, so we won't be seen by onlookers on the ground.

'It's a mess,' he mutters, without looking at me. From here we can see the barricades, and around it are more Dormants in one place than I've seen in my whole life.

When I first started my job at the power plant, years ago, I thought that the crowd of workers assembled on the ground floor was enormous. It was too many people to see in one place at one time.

That was a thousand people. This has got to be thirty times that.

The crowd is centred around the main entrance to the Inner Sector, right outside the barricades that were built to keep them out, but they spill into all the surrounding streets. From this distance, they look less like people and more like ants, thousands and thousands of them pushing and shoving and vying for a chance to get at the barricades, get to the Officers within them.

Get to the Inner Sector.

'It won't last long,' Kole says, still partly to himself, as he runs his hands across his face. 'Those barricades weren't built to withstand this kind of rebellion.'

Rebellion. He's right. That's exactly what this is. I just never thought the whole Outer Sector would be able to do something like this. Revolt all at once, and with so much aggression. Something has snapped within them, and I have a feeling they're not planning on backing down any time soon.

'Finally,' I whisper, under my breath, and that is meant for myself, but he hears it anyway.

'They're destroying everything.'

'They're fighting back.'

'As far as Oasis is concerned, that's the same thing.'

'What about you? Is that what this is to you now? Just an inconvenience?' I turn to face him, and it's only then that I realise how windy it is up here, away from the ground. I feel suddenly unstable so close to the edge, and I stand up, taking a shaky step backwards.

Kole's eyes follow me as I do so, but he doesn't move. 'If they wanted to do something about the Virus, they wouldn't just be rioting.'

'What would they be doing? They're Dormants, Kole. They've been cut off from everything. They have no resources, no voice.'

'And you think that setting things on fire and screaming is the way to get a voice?'

'No,' I growl at him, my frustration growing. 'It's not, but it's getting Johnson's attention. You wouldn't be out here if it wasn't. Which means that they've accomplished more in the past few days than they have in the past century.'

'And what next?' he asks, standing up, moving towards me. 'Johnson pulls out the big guns and wipes out the whole population? That's what you want?'

'The Dormants are the only ones not getting sick! That's not exactly going to look good. He doesn't even have an excuse to kill them anymore.'

'You think he cares about that? He's angry. Angry that the Pures are getting sick, angry that he's not in control, angry that *his* life is in danger all of a sudden. And now the Dormants are making a scene. He's going to be out for blood, and if he catches you, you're going to be his first target.'

'Wait.' I stop his rant by holding out a hand in front of me. 'This is what this is about?'

'It's about keeping everyone safe—'

'If you cared about people being safe, you wouldn't have gone back to Johnson!'

'It was my only choice!' he yells, turning around to me suddenly, his back facing the crowds for the first time. 'I was able to see when it was time, and now I need you to do the same thing. Go, Quincy. You don't need to be here anymore.'

'Why do you want me gone so badly? Are you hiding something? Is that what's going on? You don't want me to see what you're doing now that you're back working for Oasis?'

'*Goddammit, Quincy!*' he growls, and my mouth snaps shut. He drags his hand through his hair, pulling in a deep breath. The next time he speaks, his tone is calmer and his voice is quieter, but there's still tension in his words. 'Can't you believe that I just don't want to see him hurt you? Can't you understand that?'

I look down at the ground, swallowing painfully. Something in me says I should say yes. Says that I do believe that. But I shouldn't. It's stupid to believe it, and even more stupid to say it out loud.

The problem with Kole is that when he says things like that and looks at me like he's looking at me right now, I can't tell if I don't trust him, or if I'm just pretending I don't to protect myself.

That way, when he betrays me, I won't have to admit to myself that I didn't expect it.

'You're already out. All you have to do is go – just don't come back, and you'll be safe,' he says, and there's something about his expression, some hopefulness in his eyes that makes my stomach drop.

He really thinks I'm going to agree. He thinks I'd leave, now of all times, after I've seen what's happening.

This was his plan all along, to show me what was going on out here. He thought it would drive me away.

'Kole—' I start, but he cuts me off.

'No, listen. I'll deal with everything else. I'll make sure you get out okay and that no one asks questions until you're long gone. And I'll get the others out too, you know I will. But he knows you, he's *targeted* you. If he finds you in here, I won't be able to protect you from him. But I can protect you now, if you'll just go.'

'After I've seen this?' I ask, genuinely bewildered. 'Kole, the Dormants have spent their whole lives letting Oasis walk all over them. *I've* spent most of *my* life doing the same! They're finally fighting back and you want me to go *now*?'

'Quincy, this is a war. Wars have casualties—'

'And *soldiers*,' I say. 'Someone has to stay behind, that's how this works.'

'But it doesn't have to be you.'

'Don't you get it? It *does* have to be me. I deserve a chance to fix this, to at least try to fix the world we're in. I've run away from Oasis before, Kole, and it just made everything worse. I won't do it again.'

'Why do you always have to be so stubborn?'

'I'm not doing this to make you happy: I'm doing it because it's the right thing.'

'No, it's the reckless thing.'

'It's what needs to be done. Just because it's dangerous doesn't mean it's reckless, they're not the same thing.'

'You don't always have to walk straight into the gunfire, Quincy,' he says, and he sounds like he's in pain.

'And you don't always have to try to protect everyone.'

Kole turns away from me, walking around in a circle as he drags his hand through his hair, trying to figure out a solution. I don't understand why he can't see that this is the solution. It's the only solution that matters, the only one that guarantees our safety.

'Oasis took enough from me,' I say, kicking at the concrete roof beneath us with the toe of my boot. 'I deserve a chance to take something from it in return.'

'And what if that's not what happens? What if you get shot down at the first sign of insubordination and that's it, you've wasted your life?'

'I tried to change something: it's not a waste of a life to try to change something.'

He grits his teeth, staring at me. 'What if I told you I'm not okay with you dying?'

'I would say that it's not your place to care whether I die or not. It's not your job to protect me. You don't have any right to anymore.'

'Why not?' he asks. 'Because I'm back in the Towers? I can't protect you anymore because I gave up that right when I came back, right?' He sounds bitter and angry and too many un-Kole things, but it's not like I can tell him he's wrong.

But the boundaries between what is definitively Kole and what is definitively un-Kole are indistinct to me now. I know that he told me he hated killing people, but I don't know if that was ever the truth. And even if it was, I can't see how, in that moment between kill or be killed, if the fact that his heart doesn't pause and his finger does not hesitate over the trigger is not somehow viciously appealing. At the end of the day, in this world where we live or we die based on our ability to make the choice of life and death for others, Kole is the one most likely to survive. He is a killer, and in memory he may despise the thought of it, but when keeping his heart beating comes down to killing someone else, the thing he has inarguably mastered, how is there no splintered pleasure in that?

'Yes,' I say, and my voice sounds cold even to me.

15

Not another word passes between us after that. We stare out at the Outer Sector for a few more seconds before we can't look at it anymore, and then Kole and I both turn at the exact same moment and head for the exit.

We climb back down the stairs and back out onto the streets.

It makes more sense to me now, how empty everything feels. How could it not when the entire population is focused on one thing? I pay more attention this time as we loop back around to the empty buildings.

Once the riots started, the Officers must have fled, because I haven't seen a single one since we've been out here. Either that or they're already dead. I push that thought to the back of my mind, my throat tight as I step around piles of scrap and debris.

We walk the entire way back around again, staying as far away from the crowds as possible and making that last sprint for the safety of the barricades twice as fast as we did before.

The exit is hidden where the fence is pushed directly against a brick wall, and the exit is on the other side. You would have to loop back a whole block and go through a separate alley to get anywhere near it. Otherwise, it's impossible to tell it's even there.

But it won't take them long. It won't take them long to find every crack in security and use it against the Officers. That is, if they don't break down the barricades themselves first.

Once back Inside, Kole makes sure that the exit is secured before striding across the expanse and disappearing into the building.

I barely have time to change into my Officer uniform again before he's back, and we're ordered to load into the van alongside him. Most of us are just glad to be getting to leave, to go back to the Towers and as far from this madness as we can get, but not everyone gets to return. Twenty Officers are chosen to stay behind, to help defend the stronghold until the next course of action is decided. This time, I'm not one of them.

The trip back to the Towers is silent. Only Kole and I actually went into the Outer Sector and saw it with our own eyes, but everyone looks equally shaken. From the very beginning, Officers are trained to think of us as lesser. We're the Dormants, a threat and a nuisance, and it's expected of us to live our lives apologetically for that. But there is nothing apologetic about the riots. It's infecting the Outer Sector with a whole new feeling, a whole new level of threat. Apathy is giving way to determination, finally, and it's the only way we're going to change anything.

I don't look at Kole on the journey. The more I talk to him, the more confused and frustrated and angry I get. And the more I look at him, the more I can't help talking to him because I have so many questions still, so I fix both problems at once and face away from him for the entire trip back to the Justice Tower.

When we pull up in the drop-zone, the van door opens and two Officers are waiting for Kole, who disappears into the elevator without looking back. Soon he'll talk to Johnson. Talk to him about the riots. And as much as I swear to myself that I don't care, the idea of that conversation makes me shudder.

As little as I really know about Johnson, I know he hates to lose, and I know he'll count this as a loss. Worse even, it's a loss for him and a win for the Outer Sector, for the Dormants. Because they are too many and too strong, and Kole is going to urge him to pull back their forces. Retreating doesn't fit well with the image Johnson is trying to portray, and it's going to be taken out on Kole.

Once Kole is gone, we load into the elevators ourselves, me and the four Officers returning. It's getting dark and everyone on my usual shift is in bed when we return to our quarters.

We're instructed to get some rest, that our normal schedules will start again in the morning. I fall into bed, my body exhausted but my mind racing. I try to go over everything that happened in my head, can't help replaying everything Kole said. If I had agreed with him, I wouldn't be here right now. Back in the centre of Oasis, back where it's most dangerous. But I can't leave, and I know that. I have to finish what I started, whatever that means.

I can't even tell what I'm doing now. The only compass I have left is Oasis. As long as I'm working against them, fighting against them, I have to be doing the right thing.

I fall asleep quickly, with that thought in my head. All we have left is that one thought, that one concept, gripped between white-knuckled hands like the last drop of water in a desert.

Resist.

16

The next morning I'm eating breakfast alone in the cafeteria, and it's the last thing I want to be doing. I want to be doing *something*, but I can feel Noah's eyes on the back of my head. He's determined not to let me go off on my own and do anything. If I try something, Noah will sacrifice me for the 'greater good', I've no doubt about it.

There has to be a way I can go back without him finding out. Noah's shifts are aligned to mine this week so that we eat and sleep at the same times, which means that I can't be gone more than a few hours before he'll know something's up.

And that doesn't even take into account how difficult it will be to slip out during my shift hours. At night there's a gap for sleeping when no one cares where I am, but every minute is accounted for during the day, so I can't just disappear. Doing nothing is killing me. I'm supposed to have Genesis behind me, and that was supposed to make it easier. Instead they've backed me against a wall and I'm under more security now than I was before I ever escaped.

The double doors at the far side of the room are pushed open suddenly and the Officer who first did our orientation walks into the room, followed by two guards on either side of her. The room falls silent immediately, like everyone is holding their breath to make way for whatever she's about to say.

'Officers,' she says, coming to stand at the head of the room. Every head is turned in her direction; you could hear a pin drop in the silence. 'I have an announcement to make regarding the Oasis President, Leroy Johnson.'

A low murmur ripples around and everyone seems to straighten a little, as if he's already in the room. I have to force myself to hear the rest of the announcement over the rushing sound in my ears:

Johnson's here.

Johnson's here.

Johnson's here.

'There is going to be a gathering of Officials tonight,' she continues, and the murmurs resurface but are quickly quietened by a sharp look. 'This will be a celebration of Oasis. We are facing difficult times with our customary bravery, intelligence and fair-mindedness, and the OP wishes to applaud these qualities. The gathering will be held in the Peace Tower, this evening at eight o'clock, and most of you will be required to attend as security detail for VIPs. It is of utmost importance to the OP that the evening progresses smoothly, so if you are chosen to attend, please ensure this.'

It doesn't take a genius to realise that this has nothing to do with celebrating Oasis and everything to do with presenting a certain image to the population. An image of OP as the caring leader who will lead his people to greatness. An image to show that Johnson is still in control. That Oasis is still in control. That it cannot be defeated. Of course, if that were really the case, the Oasis elite wouldn't need an Officer by their side just to attend a party. 'Orientation will start in two hours. Until then, go about your tasks as normal.'

With that final statement we're dismissed and the clock marks the end of our break, so everyone gets to their feet in unison. I try to move forward, act normal, but my knee knocks into the table beside me. I'm already distracted. I'm already out of focus.

Because today could be the day it finally all falls apart.

17

The notice is posted on the wall of the mess hall, dozens of names listed evenly in black type. I'm not the only one trying to see if their name is listed, but I think I'm the only one whose heart drops into their stomach when they see it.

Officer Myers.

I catch Noah's name, a few unfamiliar names below my own, before I'm pushed out of the way, stumbling to stand off to the side. As I stand there, trying not to look as shocked as I feel, I see Clarke pushing out of the crowd. I haven't seen her in days now – always on opposite schedules. But when she looks at me, it only takes a second for her to realise I saw my name.

'You'll be okay,' she says. It's the first thing out of her mouth. 'You'll be fine. Just keep your head down.'

We both know it's a lie, but I nod anyway. She's not listed, and even if she was, she wouldn't be in danger. Johnson doesn't know her. He knows me.

And when he sees me, everything's going to blow up in our faces.

18

Those of us who have been listed for the event gather in one of the huge meeting rooms for orientation, during which we're each assigned to a different Official. Some Officials are assigned multiple Officers; some are assigned just one. Some aren't assigned any. In the Celian City, your rank defines how safe you get to be.

I'm assigned on a single duty, so I won't be working with another Officer. I'm assigned to a barrister named Daniel Ring, shown an image on a screen of the man and lined up by the door.

As the guests begin to file in, Officers break off from the lines, silently tailing whoever they've been assigned to for the rest of the night.

It takes all of my concentration to remember the face of the barrister and to scan each incoming guest to find him, because all I can think about is how close I am to being caught. I don't even have to slip up. I don't have to make a mistake. I don't have to do anything wrong.

I'm going to spend hours in a room with the OP. The last time we were in a room together, I was pointing a gun at his head. That was right before I shot his son. The idea of being sent back to the icebox nearly makes me turn and run, but I can't. There's no way out.

I'm startled from my thoughts as I see the barrister arriving, his mouth set in a hard line as he exits the elevator and makes his way towards the entrance. As smoothly as I can, I break from line as he passes me, following him in through the doors, aided by the staff set at each side to welcome the guests.

And then I'm in a dream. Or at least that's what it feels like.

The room is enormous, bigger than any other room I've seen inside the Towers. The walls are pale gold, with one wall, the celian one, facing the city, completely transparent so you can see the night sky from all the way up here.

I gasp, avoiding a waiter who I almost collide with in my distraction. The barrister has gotten several feet ahead of me, and I have to force myself to refocus on following him.

Once I do, I can barely recognise him. He's still relatively short, burly, with a well-groomed greying beard and dark, beady eyes. But whereas a moment ago, coming up the corridor, he looked harsh, he now looks warm. The moment he walked through the door a smile was plastered across his face as he began to greet people.

He seems to know everyone in the room.

My eyes drift towards the far wall where tables are set out with enough food and drink to sustain a whole village. There are only two hundred guests coming tonight, we were told, but that quantity of food couldn't be consumed by a small army.

The room seems to get more and more full as the barrister winds through the crowd tirelessly, seemingly set on greeting every single Official in the room. Everything is timed to perfection, a new Official walking through the door with just enough time left after the guest before them so that they can make a grand entrance of their own.

My eyes scan endlessly, waiting for Johnson to appear, for him to see me, for everything to fall apart. I tell myself that my endless watchfulness will just look like I'm being scrupulous, but it feels like a banner of guilt across my forehead.

The barrister stops for a moment by one of the tables laid out with food and starts up a conversation with a woman in a red dress. He greets her as Senator Lynn, and her smile is almost as bright as the diamonds around her neck.

Back in the Colosseum, we saw people like this every now and again, although more of them in the last weeks I was there. The wealthy politicians who got too greedy for Johnson's liking, or who started asking questions where they shouldn't, and ended up being left to rot in the Colosseum. Sometimes they'd come in just like this, dressed and pressed and powdered, so obviously strange, different, alien from the environment they'd suddenly been landed into.

Tao's goons had the most fun with those types, the ones who couldn't keep up with what was going on around them, let alone survive. Tao was the only one with any interest in their fineries, their pearls and diamonds and watches; anything else that was found on them belonged to whoever fought hardest for them.

I can't help looking at Senator Lynn and wondering how she'd fare in there with those lowlifes. How long her chin would stay that high when she realised her political manipulation would get her nowhere in a dog-pit.

But then she catches me staring at her and glares at me, offended that I'd have the gall to even look at her, so I'm forced to avert my gaze back to the party. That's when I see the doors open and staff scurrying towards them. My heart sinks. Johnson walks in, with Kole on his heels, and I feel the air being sucked out of the room.

Everyone's attention is immediately drawn to where they just entered, and I can practically feel the room tense. Because everyone wants something, and Johnson's the one who has everything.

I resist the urge to sprint for the exit, digging my fingernails into my wrist behind my back as I force my feet to stay planted beneath me. The barrister is going to want to talk to Johnson, and where he goes, I go. And then I'll have to stand before the OP once again.

You don't forget the face of the girl who killed your son.

Johnson starts greeting people, smiling on them like a benevolent king come to oversee the peasants, and they smile forced smiles back at him. I realise with a kind of faraway shock that they hate him. That everyone in this room hates him, and that he knows it. And that he doesn't care.

This is just how things work in the Celian City. Everyone's standing in this huge room, wearing beautiful clothes, the tables over-flowing with wonderful food, and everyone is hungry for more – more money, more respect, more power.

They're like rats, scrabbling over each other for food, and I can't tell if I want to laugh or vomit.

They're supposed to be happy. This is the *Celian City*, the utopia, the paradise. They're supposed to be living perfect lives in perfect happiness, but they're *desperate*, and it makes me want to scream.

I always thought that we lived like animals in the Outer Sector so that the Pures could live like kings, so they would live in perfect bliss, but they're *still not happy*. They're also desperate, just for different things.

I'm dragged from my own internal chaos when the barrister excuses himself from Senator Lynn to go and greet Johnson, and my heart starts pounding in my chest.

I feel like the room is closing in on top of me, and I'd try to think of a way to get out of this but I can't even think past the haze of terror clouding my mind.

My eyes snap around the room, to the exits, but knowing where they are isn't going to do me any good. If I leave the barrister I'll cause a scene, and in the end Johnson will find me either way.

The barrister is stopped by a man in a blue tie, some veteran Officer, and we pause halfway across the room for a few moments. The security is so high in here that there's almost as many Officers as Officials. Maybe, just maybe, I'll melt into the sea of blue and Johnson won't register me. Maybe.

'Excuse me.' A voice speaks from just behind me, and I almost jump as I turn around, my hand going instinctively to my gun as the barrister turns with me. But when I look up, the voice isn't coming from Johnson, it's coming from Kole.

'I hate to be of inconvenience, Barrister Ring, but if I could borrow your security for just a moment? I need to step out and my father insists I don't leave alone.' Kole smiles warmly, eyes wide with innocence, but there's an undercurrent of forcefulness in his tone.

The barrister splutters an agreement, muttering so many different courtesies I can barely understand him. He's too taken off-guard and star-struck to even realise what a ridiculous request it is to make, considering Kole has at least two Officers on his tail at all times.

But Kole has already turned and started walking quickly through the crowds of people, smiling and nodding at Officials as he passes, but never stopping as he heads towards the exit. The exit on the other side of the room, far from Johnson.

We get out into the hall after what feels like forever, but Kole doesn't let me stop until we're at the elevators, pulling me through the halls until we've gotten in and he's closed the doors, pressing a button on the panel that freezes the elevator in place.

'How—?' I stare at the button blankly, remembering the floors getting terrifyingly lower and lower that day all those months ago.

'The building isn't on security alert.' He sighs, sounding older than he is.

I press my back into the wall of the elevator, forcing myself to breathe once I realise that I have a reprieve, however short it may be. When I open my eyes Kole has his hands over his face, looking like he's about to fray himself into nothing.

'Kole,' I say, and it's not supposed to sound that affected.

'Please,' he whispers, finally looking up. '*Please.*'

I shift uncomfortably, and I don't know if my heart is getting a chance to slow down, locked in here with him.

'Please what?'

'Please, *go*,' he says. 'Just go. Get out of here. Go back to the Outer Sector or get out of Oasis entirely or go anywhere, anywhere that isn't here, with him.'

'I already told you I can't do that.'

'I know, and you told me you can't tell me why, because you don't trust me,' he says. 'But what good is it for you to stay here if you get caught? He nearly caught you tonight. You were *this close* to him.'

'I know,' I mutter, dragging my hands down my face. 'I know that. But I can't just leave.'

'Why?'

'Because I *can't*!' I snap. 'I can't, and I won't tell you why, so you need to stop asking questions I can't answer.'

He watches me for a second, like he's trying to figure out who I am.

'If you go, I'll figure everything else out. I'll figure out an excuse for you disappearing, no one will come looking for you—'

'Kole!'

'What?!' he says, and it's like he finally can't take it anymore. 'I need you *gone*. You're going to get yourself killed, and I can't do anything about it other than get you as far from here as possible, and you're not even letting me do that! I'm going insane.'

He looks at me pleadingly, and there's a tugging, pulling, burning sensation in my chest, and I want to listen to him, but I still don't know if he's telling me the whole truth.

I want to do something to take that terrified expression off his face, but I can't.

'Kole,' I say, and my voice is quiet more for his sake than mine, because I feel like he's going to come apart in front of me if I don't. 'Just go back upstairs, and forget about this. Please. Thank you for getting me out of there, but you don't need to do that anymore. You belong up there with them, not down here with me.' At this point,

I don't even know what I'm saying. I don't know if I'm saying it because I truly believe that, or because I know that down here is dangerous. Down here is where people get hurt and where people die, and I just don't want him here if it means he's in danger.

'I just want to protect you,' he says. 'I want to make sure you're safe. But I can't do that if you don't even trust me not to betray you.'

'You're right,' I say, and I can't swallow the lump in my throat as I step around him, pushing the button to restart the elevator. 'You can't.'

I refuse to look at him the rest of the ride down, but I can feel his eyes burning into me the entire time.

The doors finally open, and the cafeteria is empty. With so much guard duty tonight, everyone is occupied.

'I'll make sure no one realises you're gone,' Kole says, and his voice sounds dead. I nod, stepping off the elevator and turning back around to look at him one more time before the doors close.

'Thank you,' I say quietly, and I don't know if he even hears me before the doors close, but either way he doesn't respond.

19

I wake up, my heart racing in my chest, and immediately feel that something is wrong. Very, very wrong. I am up and out of bed before I even know what I plan on doing, but that's when I hear a loud bang in the bathroom and rush inside to find Jay laying on the bathroom floor, face down.

I'm on my knees, rolling him over, every moment shattering into the next too fast and too slow as I take in the deathly white of his skin, his eyes rolled back in his head.

Please please please please please please please don't be dead please don't be dead you can't die you can't die I can't let you die.

My hands are shaking so badly that it takes me a full minute to find a pulse, slow and weak and there and not gone and still alive.

'Jay.' My heart is in a single syllable, and my voice doesn't sound like my own. 'Jay, please wake up. Please wake up please wake up.'

I pull his head into my lap, and a second later his body jerks, his eyes rolling around in his head a moment before they finally settle, straight ahead. His body starts shaking, and he reaches for my hand, squeezing tightly.

'You're okay,' I whisper. 'It's okay, you're okay. You're okay.'

I know I'm not talking to him. He can't even hear me. But it feels like a prayer and an order at once.

He comes back to me several minutes later, blinking and blinking and blinking like he just woke up.

'Quincy?' he croaks. 'What happened?'

'I don't know.' My voice sounds like it's about to break, and I'm trying so hard not to sound like that. 'I think you collapsed.'

He blinks up at the ceiling and just breathes for a moment. 'I'm dying, aren't I?' he whispers.

'No,' I shake my head vehemently. 'No you're not. You're *fine*.'

He tries to laugh, but it cuts off as he groans, his hands shaking as a wave of pain flows over him. I don't know what's wrong. I don't know what's happening. I don't know what I'm supposed to *do*.

'I think ... I think I can sit up.'

I nod slowly, helping to prop him up against the door, and he closes his eyes for a moment. His breathing is still off, uneven and strange, even as some colour begins to come back to his cheeks.

'You shouldn't be here,' he whispers, after a few minutes of silence.

'Why the hell not?'

His eyes blink open, and he looks exhausted. 'I don't want to infect you.'

For a second I don't understand what he's saying. For a second I blink. For a second I breathe and I stare at him, and I try to work out why he would say that.

When I do, I have to stop myself from falling backwards.

'No,' I growl. 'You're fine.'

'Loss of focus,' he whispers. 'Loss of stamina. Loss of balance—'

'Jay, stop.'

'Weakness. Dizzy spells. Vomiting. Loss of consciousness.'

'Jay, stop.'

'How long until the rest?' he asks. 'The vomiting blood. The hallucinations. The hysteria.'

'How do you even *know* those are the symptoms?'

I feel sick. I feel ill. I feel a terror that I've never experienced in my entire life. Because I have seen people die. I have seen people that I don't know die, and I have seen people that I barely know die. I've seen people I have cared about die.

I have never watched someone I love die.

'They have them printed at the hospital where I've been working,' he says, a half-smile on his face.

My stomach drops. 'How long?' I whisper. 'How long have you known?'

'I've known,' he whispers, leaning his head back against the door, 'since the day Silas told us we weren't to search for the antidote.'

I am shaking all over, terror and anger boiling together. 'You're going to be okay,' I say, fiercely. 'I'm going to find the antidote. You're going to be okay.'

'I believe you,' he says, and smiles a too soft smile. 'I feel stronger now. We better get out of here before someone comes in.'

'Are you sure you're okay to stand?'

'It comes and goes,' he says, shaking his head, and I help him to stand slowly. He seems so much better now that it's hard to imagine that I could have thought he was dead. But there's an obvious subtext. It comes and goes—

For now.

He walks on his own back to his bunk, and he swears he's okay, but those same two words linger in the air after I have gone back to my own bed, to lie and stare at the boards above me for four hours until I have to get up again.

For now. He's okay, for now. And for now is not good enough for me.

20

I drag my thumbnail against the inside of my first finger beneath the dining-room table, trying to subdue the restlessness rising up in my chest.

I need to get back to that facility. Jay needs … I'm not even sure what he needs, but we have to find out what will help him. And every second that ticks by, every menial task that the order and regulation of the Justice Tower forces me into, is like a knife being drawn across my nerves.

My nail goes back and forth across my finger as I stare down at the food on my plate, trying to work up the will to eat some of it. It looks strange, me sitting here and not eating in a room full of hungry Officers.

It looks strange. I stand out. I need to not stand out.

But I can't eat. I can't eat. Not while Jay is sick. Not while I'm failing to do anything to help him.

I waited all morning trying to spot him, but he didn't turn up at breakfast. I've yet to see a trace of him. He must have changed schedules, been put on a different rota from mine.

I'm like a zombie all through my second shift, staring blankly into space and completely ignoring the Officer beside me, unable to focus on anything going on around me.

I keep seeing Jay on the floor, keep seeing his pale face, his eyes rolled back. I can't stop imagining what would have happened if he hadn't woken up. Can't stop thinking about how long I have left to fix this before he doesn't.

Clarke sits down across from me during lunch in the Officer canteen.

'What's wrong?'

'Jay.' I didn't mean to say it, not like that. I'm not sure if I meant to say it at all.

'What?'

'He's been infected. He's dying.'

'*What?*' I can hear the panic in her voice, even if her expression doesn't betray it.

'I'm going to fix it,' I say, and I don't know how I sound so much surer than I feel.

'How?'

'I have a plan.'

o o o

I don't fall asleep that night. I can't. Once everyone else has fallen asleep, I push the blankets off my body, slowly creep to the door.

This doesn't make any sense. I already know that it doesn't. My plan involves breaking into the room where I first found the Cure, in the hopes that that's where they're also working on the antidote.

Flaw 1: Once I'm out of the Officers' Quarters, there will be cameras everywhere.

Flaw 2: I have no idea which room to go to, even if I get past the security.

Flaw 3: Even if everything else works out, the antidote might not be there. Because it might not exist at all.

Even knowing all of this, I can't stop myself. Even after Clarke told me it was idiotic, I can't stop myself.

I have to do *something*.

I slip through into the cafeteria, careful to shut the door quietly behind me, when I hear an all too familiar voice.

'Quincy.'

I freeze, my heart stopping momentarily in my chest as I close my eyes, slowly releasing my hold on the door handle.

When I turn around, Kole is standing in the middle of the cafeteria, staring at me.

He walks across the room until he's right in front of me, close enough that I can see his face.

First instinct: reach out, hand shaking, touch the side of his face, turn it to the side so I can see better. Broken lip, a torn cheek, bruised jaw. My heart twists.

Second instinct: pull back, put two, three feet between us. *Can't trust, don't trust, won't trust.* I feel off-kilter, and the look on his face makes my head hurt.

The world feels like it's imploding on top of itself, like reality is an illusion, and it won't slow down long enough for me to hold on to it.

'What happened?' I ask, and my voice sounds all wrong. Too hurt, too pained.

'Nothing. I'm fine.'

'Who did this to you?' He wants me to back off; his eyes are begging me to leave it be. But I can't. Something protective is roaring in my chest, and whether I should be feeling that or not, I have to at least know *who* did this to him.

'There are consequences to disappearing in the middle of important events,' he says quietly, evenly, and the tone isn't his own. It's parroted back, like an echo of someone else's voice.

His father's voice.

'Go back,' I whisper. 'Please. Just turn around. Just leave me alone.'

I realise with a numb kind of shock that I'm more afraid *for* him than I am *of* him. As my eyes hone in on the details of every scrape and bruise on his face, my heart feels too tight, tighter than it should for someone I so desperately want not to care about.

I want him to turn around so that he'll be safe, or saf*er* at the very least. Because I don't want him to hurt any more than he already has, and I certainly don't want it to be on my hands if he does.

'I can't,' he says. 'Clarke told me what you're doing.'

'What?' For a second I just go still, my brain struggling to deal with what he just said. 'She *told* you?'

'She's trying to keep you alive,' he says, harsher than I expected. 'I know what you're trying to do, and it's going to get you killed.'

'How much did she tell you?' I whisper, and I can hear the sense of betrayal in my voice. I can't believe she did this, behind my back.

'Enough.' He shifts his stance, eyes scanning the room quickly every few seconds. 'If you want to help Jay, I can try to help you do that, but you'll have to come with me.'

'Where?' I knew it was a long shot, going back to where I found the Cure last year, but it was the closest thing to a lead I had.

'Not here,' he says. 'Not in the Celian City. I can bring you, but we need to go now.' He hasn't met my eyes again, but I can't tell if it's because he's lying to me or because he's nervous.

The Justice Tower has eyes, and we both know that.

I want to trust him. I want to trust him so badly. There's a voice screaming in my head that I'm being an idiot not to, but I can't just ignore how easily he could have betrayed us.

'Fine,' I whisper.

It doesn't matter if I trust him or not. I need him.

21

Kole leads me back to the drop-zone, out of the Justice Towers and the Celian City, and we don't say a word to each other the whole time. My breath creates puffs of fog as I follow him through the Inner Sector.

At one point I hear someone coming, and without thinking I step back into the shadows between two buildings, straight into Kole. He reaches out to steady me, pushing me back another step as an Officer passes.

There were never Officers here before. The Inner Sector works like clockwork, has worked like clockwork for so long that no one questions the system. You wake up and you go to school and work and you come home and you eat and you perform the activities you're assigned and then you go to bed.

And once the doors lock for curfew, no one steps outside. And still, there is no one on these streets: even with the riots in the Outer Sector, with a disease ravaging the Inner Sector, the streets here are silent, obedient.

But Oasis knows. It knows that this means something has changed. That the unyielding trust that was placed in its hands is beginning to shake. If Oasis can't protect the Pures like they were promised, what else is Oasis lying about?

So things have changed. Even in this quiet way, things have changed.

The citizens don't trust Oasis, so Oasis doesn't trust the citizens. Streets that used to be completely dead all night have Officers, however few, patrolling. Watching. Monitoring.

Kole releases a shaky breath from behind me as the Officer moves on, and I swallow, pushing away and back on and forward, and as long as I keep moving and don't think and keep my focus, everything will be okay. I'm fine, I'm fine, I'm *fine* …

We stop in the alley by a long white building that has the anonymous, blank look of a research facility.

'Are you okay?' I ask, unintentionally. It's like a programme built into my system that I can't delete. But I can't talk like that or think like that. Not until I know if I can trust him.

'Yeah.' He nods, his eyes flitting around the building, deconstructing, analysing, planning. 'Just follow my lead.' He turns back, taking a different route towards the building, so we come out at a different, closer angle. He reaches back, as if to take my hand, and then pulls his hand back towards himself sharply. I glance up at his profile, lit by the light of the building, before he sprints the short distance between the shadows of the surrounding buildings and the back of the building itself. Once we've both crossed over, he slips around the side, away from the front entrance and towards a second, back door.

He pulls a card from inside his uniform, runs it across the scanner on the door and waits for the click of it unlocking. I release a relieved breath as he pushes it open and it gives beneath the pressure, sliding inwards so we can slip inside.

This side of the building is unlit, but I can see well enough to make out the clean precision of the laboratory. I cross the room to the door on the other side, which is wide open, when Kole makes a sudden move towards me. He pulls me backwards and against his chest, clamping a hand over my mouth as his back hits the wall, pulling us away from the door. I can feel his thundering heart against my back. An Officer walks past the door slowly, patrolling the halls.

So it's not empty after all.

A few seconds pass, and Kole pulls me around the corner, glancing down the hall after the Officer, who's already gone.

As quietly as we can, we creep down the hall. Each door has a panel beside it, with a name printed on it.

32N Vaccine

899 Vaccine

Ti7 Cure

YSc Vaccine

'Quincy,' Kole whispers from up ahead, gesturing for me to follow him. He points to the door—

YD Antidote

He must be privy to at least some of the information regarding the search for the antidote, because he seems sure of himself as he moves towards the door.

I glance down the hall behind me as he pulls a handgun from his waistband, slowly easing the door open. Once inside he looks around the room, gun held in front of him, but it's empty.

'Okay, this is your chance,' he says. 'If it exists, it's here.' He starts searching the room, pulling cabinet doors open, searching bottles, label after label, and I start sifting through the piles of paper left on the first table.

A minute later I find a tightly packed stack of papers, and I call Kole over.

'Help me look through these,' I say, shoving a pile into his hands. 'What are they?'

'Notes,' I mumble, pushing my hair behind my ears as I scan pages. 'About the illness, I think.'

I skip to the last page, let my eyes glide across the words printed on the page.

'XV2/62,' I say, dropping the papers. Fridges line the back wall, full with hundreds of vials. 'XV2/62,' I mutter to myself, over and over again.

One entire refrigerator is labelled XV2, and I start scanning the shelves. I skip to the lowest shelf, half-full, and grab the row of vials farthest to the right.

My fingers tremble as they brush against the vials, each label the same, and my stomach drops.

Failed, failed, failed.

'Kole,' I whisper, and his head snaps up from where he's searching through more notes, but I can tell by the look on his face that he's seeing the exact same thing that I am.

'They're all failed,' I say, and my throat is starting to close. It's a death sentence. My eyes go back to the labels, and that's all I can see now.

A death sentence.

'Quincy—' Kole starts, but he's cut off abruptly by the sound of an alarm screaming around us.

I jump to my feet immediately, adrenaline spiking. 'They've found us.'

22

He grabs my hand and sprints towards the front entrance, but they're already closing in. Kole turns on his heel and runs back for the door we came through.

The second he turns around, we hear a loud crash from that direction.

They're inside.

'There's another exit!' Kole calls over the wailing of the sirens. '*Think!*' He squeezes his eyes shut, trying to drown out the noise long enough to mentally map out the building.

'Upstairs!' I yell. I can see Officers bursting through the front entrance already, so without giving Kole a chance to respond I pull him with me down the hall, around a corner and up a flight of stairs. 'There's a fire escape here somewhere!'

There has to be. I saw one outside.

We burst through the first door we see, and it's windowless, so we split up and start searching the rooms.

'HERE!' I shout. My blood is rushing so fast in my ears that I can barely hear them, but the distinct sounds of boots in the stairwell is unmistakable.

Kole is beside me in an instant, helping me hoist the window open. He urges me on and I slip through as fast as I can, landing on the fire escape outside with a thud.

'*Come on come on come on.*' I slam the window shut behind us the second he's out, and we race down the fire escape and out onto the path, breaking into a sprint just as a group of Officers appears out of nowhere and yells for us to stop.

I push my legs as fast as they will go beneath me as we slip between buildings, running along quiet streets like wraiths as we try to shake the Officers' trail. Kole catches my hand and pulls me along, forcing me to go faster, faster, faster, faster until I feel like my legs are going to give out beneath me, like my lungs can't pull in another breath.

Suddenly, Kole yanks us to the right, into a small space between two buildings, pushing me behind him as he slips deeper and deeper, away from the main street and the Officers chasing us. He turns around, gesturing for me to stay low and be quiet, and I press my hands over my mouth, trying to muffle my ragged breathing.

We wait. Hearts pounding like jackhammers in our chests, we wait as we hear the Officers getting closer and closer. If they catch us, we've cornered ourselves. There's no way out.

The footsteps get louder and louder until finally they're racing past us, radios crackling on and off as Officers shout messages into them, trying to figure out who saw us last.

Kole's head hits the concrete wall as they leave, his shoulders dropping in relief. We stand in the alley, breathing heavily, until the Officers are far enough away that we can't hear them anymore.

Kole reaches his hand out for mine, and for a second I hesitate.

'Please,' he begs. 'I don't want to lose you.'

There are too many meanings there, layer upon layer upon layer, but right now, I don't want to lose him either, so I slip my hand into his, and we run.

23

There's only one place left for us to go now. We are being hunted; we're prey. So we go where the hunted go – back to the Outer Sector.

There's another entrance into the Outer Sector, east of the main one, and that's where Kole leads me. It's used primarily for supplies and isn't heavily guarded.

Kole convinces the two guards left watching the gate to let us through immediately. The alert hasn't reached this gate yet – maybe they didn't even think we'd try to pass through the Sector wall – and after all, he's Kole Johnson.

We pause for a second on the other side of the wall, frozen.

It's anarchy.

I don't realise it straight away, but I can hear it from far off, a jumble of shouts and screams and sirens wailing. Kole tightens his grip on my hand as we work our way deeper, the crowd thickening, and I begin to realise what the riot really means.

The crowd jostles us violently, pushing us back and forth as we stumble through the streets. We shouldn't have come out here. The air smells like burning, and I can't stop glancing back at the Sector Wall behind us.

'Quincy!' Kole yells over the sound of the crowd, pulling me forward as a group of masked people scream by us. '*Focus!*'

Focus. I can barely breathe. The smell of smoke is thick in the air, and I'm struggling to keep track of Kole in front of me. I try to focus on his back, just try to keep my feet moving beneath me.

We swing down an alleyway and a gang turns a corner and almost lands on top of us. They're swinging tyre irons, looking for trouble, but before they can get a good look at us we're running in the opposite direction.

I speed up, grabbing Kole's hand and pulling him down a small gap between two buildings.

'What are you doing?'

'Trust me,' I say, stepping ahead of him at the end of the first building and pulling him left.

We turn left again, our hearts in our throats, and loop around the surrounding buildings, adding three blocks to our journey. We're half a block away when I see another group walking down the otherwise empty alley.

We stop dead, and I'm about to turn on my heel and run for it, but before I can turn there's a grip on my wrist and I'm yanked backwards violently. I slam into someone, breath knocked out of my lungs, and suddenly there's an arm around me and a knife against my cheek.

My eyes find Kole's where he stands with his hands in the air.

'Don't touch her,' he says, his voice steady. 'She's not an Officer.'

'Not an Officer? Last time I checked, people who aren't Officers don't go around wearing blue uniforms.'

I can feel the man's heartbeat at my back, rapid and frenzied and panicked, even though he's the one with the knife.

Kole takes a slow step forward, his hands bobbing in the air over his head, and the man takes an identical step backwards, dragging me with him.

'You don't know what you're talking about,' Kole murmurs, and he sounds so perfectly calm, but my palms are slick with sweat and everything in me is screaming for me to run, to try and make a break for it, even though I know it will get me killed.

The man takes another step backwards, but when he hits the wall he stops, tightening his grip on me.

'Don't come any closer,' he spits, but Kole never stops moving forward. My throat feels tight, and I want to tell him to stop, but I can't draw attention to myself.

'I'll kill her,' he says, but Kole's already in front of him. He presses the knife deeper into my cheek, forcing a gasp from my lungs as I feel the blade bite into my skin.

'No you won't,' Kole says, and so quickly I can't even see it happening clearly, he catches the guy by the wrist, pulls the knife from my face and twists the blade from his hand.

I spring away from both of them, leaning down to catch my breath as the man scrambles to his feet, backing up slightly. When Kole doesn't make an immediate move towards him he takes off down the alley, disappearing within seconds.

Kole is in front of me immediately, forcing me to stand up so he can look at me. I glance over his shoulder repeatedly as he pushes my hair out of my face to see the wound.

I want to lie down on the floor and just *breathe* for a second, but at that moment we both hear a shout from somewhere nearby, and Kole looks at me.

'We need to get out of here,' he mutters. 'Now.'

I nod, and we're running.

24

Kole bangs on the door, glancing behind him repeatedly as he waits for a response. He pushes me closer to the door so he's between me and the view of the streets and pounds on the door with his fist again.

'Goddammit, Nails,' he growls, rattling the door handle. When there's no still no response a minute later, I see worry cloud his eyes.

'Step back,' he says, pushing me backwards with his arm extended, before crashing his shoulder into the door.

I glance down to the streets behind us, but there's no one around. Kole throws his shoulder into the door once more and it bursts in. He slams it behind us, creating a makeshift barricade with a couch that must have been dumped up here after it wore out.

'It's empty.' I can't help but whisper, even though the place seems to be completely desolate. Plaster crumbles off the ceiling from the force that the door was closed with, causing me to jump as it hits the ground.

'They must be downstairs,' Kole insists, shaking his head and making his way to the door across the room, pulling it open and heading down the narrow, rickety staircase.

But I already know he's wrong. The minute I stepped inside, I knew it was empty. There's a difference between a place that holds life and one that doesn't, and it doesn't have anything to do with noise or movement.

There's no heartbeat in this place, and I can feel it in my bones.

I follow Kole downstairs anyway, because I want to get away, to get as far from the streets and the prying eyes and the threat of Oasis as I can.

I find him standing in the middle of the floor, staring blankly at the empty room.

'They're gone,' he says, whether to me or to himself, I can't tell. He starts walking around the room slowly, running his fingers along shelves and walls and the back of the couch. 'They had time to pack,' he whispers, and I can see the relief in his shoulders, but I stay where I am, rooted to the ground.

Time to pack meant that they left of their own accord. They were running from someone or something, but they weren't slaughtered on sight, and I guess that's reason enough to be relieved.

He goes to search the rest of the room, but I can't follow him. Adrenaline is slowly draining from my body, my energy along with it, and I drop my head into my hands as I collapse onto the couch.

I try to piece together some kind of plan, some kind of next step, but every time I do it falls apart. There are too many threads, too many intertwined lives, and if I pull on the wrong string, I could kill people, kill people I care about, kill people I love.

When did this happen? I rub my eyes so hard I can feel the pressure building in my head. When did I begin caring about people this much? Loving people this much? Wasn't there a reason that I didn't do that before?

I can't remember the reason – I just know that it doesn't matter anymore. There are people I need safe, and I don't know how to do that, and that's all I can think about.

'Hey,' Kole says, whisper quiet. I feel the couch dip beside me as he sits down, reaching out to push a strand of hair away from my cut cheek as I blink my eyes open. 'Are you okay?'

'I don't know,' I say, squeezing my eyes closed again. 'I don't know anything anymore.'

I press my knuckles to my temples, trying to press back the headache that I can feel building.

'Ask it,' Kole says, and when I look up, he is tense all over again.

'Ask what?'

'Ask whatever it is that's in your head right now. I already know what it is.'

'Kole—'

'Just ask.'

I don't want to. I wish I could lie to him, but I know that I can't. I wish I could lie to myself, pretend it's not nagging at the back of my brain, but I can't.

'What set off the alarms?'

'I don't know,' he says. 'They must have been waiting for us.'

My voice is small, and I feel like I'm betraying myself with the next words out of my mouth.

'Who told them we were going to be there?'

Kole looks pained, his eyes darkening.

'I need to know,' I croak, and I wish there weren't tears forming in my eyes. I wish my heart felt less like it was exploding. I wish he would just look at me. 'I want to trust you again.'

I want to be shouting. I want to be furious. With him, with this situation, with Oasis. But I'm just scared. Scared that Oasis will take this from me too.

He looks down, at his feet, at the ground, away from me. And I think I've pushed too hard. I think I've shown too many scars, shown him all the places where I revert to that scared, betrayed little girl too quickly.

The places where I need proof to trust him, even though all I want is to trust him just because I *do*.

'I was terrified,' he says, so, so softly.

'What?' I breathe.

'I was *terrified*. I didn't sleep. I couldn't sleep. Not knowing if you were okay, if you were safe. I had to find you and I didn't really care how I did it. But I didn't know where you were. I could guess, and I did, but I turned out to be wrong over and over again. And I knew he would tell me, if I came back. I knew he wanted me more than he wanted you, and that was a trade I was more than willing to make.'

My heart is a kick drum, and his eyes hold constellations of pain I don't deserve. 'You went back because of me?' He barely nods, but I don't need him to. I already know it's true.

'Kole.' My voice is a crackle and a sob and the sound of the edge of the cliff crumbling beneath my feet. What am I supposed to say? I can't say anything. There aren't words that wouldn't sound insignificant now. But I can't help asking the next question that forms itself straight away, even though it feels like an insult.

'Why didn't you tell me, before now?'

'I don't know.' He looks down at his hands, like he's the one who's ashamed. 'When you thought …' He takes a shaky breath. 'I didn't expect you to assume that I had betrayed you. I didn't know what to do. And I knew that if I said anything to you, and you believed me, you'd end up trying to get me out with you, and you'd get yourself killed.'

It makes sense. Everything clicks together quickly, falling into place. The piece of the puzzle that was missing. Why on earth would Oasis Officers yank us from the Colosseum only to release us? I've been asking myself that question ever since that day. Now it all makes sense. He was there for me, even if I couldn't see him.

It had never occurred to me that the reason they did that was because Johnson told them to. Because Kole sacrificed himself so that Johnson would let me go.

And I didn't trust him. I couldn't trust him. After years of fighting and pain and sacrifice so that he could escape his father and Oasis and the life that was forced on him, he went back. Went back and sold himself to the devil.

For me.

All along the things that made me stop trusting him were the very things he was doing to keep me safe.

I don't even realise I've broken down until Kole's gentle fingers turn my face towards him, a thumb tracing under my eye and brushing away the tears.

When I look up his eyes are alight, and I know what he's going to say before he says it, but I don't want him to. Because he's too good. He's too much *better* than everything in this world.

'I didn't say all that to make you feel guilty,' he says. 'I just need you to know. I never, ever betrayed you. I would never do that.'

My head drops forward, and he's sitting so close that forward means in to him, close to him, my head against his chest. I can't look at him. I can't let him look at me.

I don't know why I'm shocked. This is what Oasis does. It makes you doubt everything you shouldn't. Trust everything you shouldn't. It twists the world inside out until you can't tell if the thoughts in your head even belong to you anymore.

'I'm sorry,' I croak. And I am. The kind of sorry that makes you breathless. The kind of sorry that pulls guilt from your mind and makes it a tangible thing. An unimaginably cruel weight that you have to carry. And you can't even be angry.

You put it there yourself.

'It's not your fault,' he whispers, but there's too much pain in those four words. I put that pain there too.

'Yes it is. I should have trusted you.'

He pulls me tighter to him, and for a moment I go still.

'The reason you're still alive is the same reason you didn't trust me, so don't be sorry. You're cautious, and it keeps you alive. That's all that matters. I just need you to be okay.'

'I trust you,' I say, wrapping my arms around his waist. 'More than anyone else in the world, I trust you. But this place ...' I shudder involuntarily, '... it *twists* people. And now you're here, in the middle of it. I don't want it to twist you.'

'I'll be okay. I've been here before, and I'm still me.'

This close, he still smells like the Outside. He still smells like trees, like the Kole from six months ago. The one who taught me to shoot and kissed me in dark halls. Maybe it's just in my head. Maybe to me he smells like the Kole I know because he still is. Quiet, late-night talking and warm tea Kole. But I don't really care. I just care that he's here. That he's real. That he's safe.

I care that, for a few minutes, we both are.

25

We talk. I can't remember how many times in the last few months I've wished that he was in front of me, so I could just talk to him. And now he is, dark eyes watching me intently, and I want to tell him everything, but it's too soon.

I tell him where I was. That after that place they put me into the Colosseum, that Clarke was with me, that we survived until he got us out. I tell him about finding Noah and Genesis and about coming back to Oasis.

I don't tell him what happened in that place before the Colosseum. I don't tell him the things that happened while I was there, the things I did to stay alive. And he doesn't ask. He's too smart not to know that the gaps in my story are intentional, and I see the understanding flitting across his face as I awkwardly stumble over my words in an attempt to escape ugly memories.

He doesn't ask because he knows I can't answer him. Not now. Not yet. That's for another night, when the world is closer to being safe, if we ever get that far.

But he does ask about the rebels. About Mark and Walter, and those are unavoidable answers. And I feel like a girl with a knife when I tell him what happened. Tell him about Walter, tell him about Mark.

But we keep talking. Try to stitch wounds with words as best we can. And I don't know when I start to fall asleep, but I wake up suddenly, and when I look around Kole is gone.

He returns only seconds later with a blanket in his arms, and he looks shocked to see me awake. He shakes his head, walks over, covers me with the blanket. And then he hesitates, and like he realises he can't stop himself, he leans down and presses a kiss to my forehead, his arm reaching out to steady himself against the back of the couch.

I go still, and he lingers, and I'm afraid that if I move, I'll frighten him, that he'll stop.

'Can I stay?' he asks, quietly, carefully, still holding tight. 'I'm not ready to go yet.'

'Of course,' I say, and it sounds too relieved. Too vulnerable. 'Stay with me,' I whisper, and it's happening again. The falling apart and together, piece by piece by piece, and I'm worried he's getting too close to the place where I can't pull back anymore, where the pieces of me and the pieces of him become the same thing.

He settles back onto the couch and pulls me against him, and I release a long breath as I melt against him.

It's only moments like this that I feel like I can see him properly. Think of him properly. When the light has been drained from the sky and the darkness wraps around us. In these moments, the in-between moments, where we are neither adults nor children, victims nor soldiers, these are the moments when I love him the most. The moments where I know with an assuredness that comes from my absolute centre that this one thing, in the midst of a hundred thousand broken, moulded, *different* things, that this one thing hasn't been touched by it, by *them*. For once we're simple, just a boy and girl who fell together.

I press my forehead into his shoulder and I pretend, something I haven't done in a long time. I pretend that the world outside Nails's door doesn't exist. I pretend that if it did, it would be a world of serene mundanity, of simple things and simple loves. I pretend that loving Kole is as simple as breathing air, and that doing so brings no danger to either of us.

I tuck myself into him, like I can fold away, and I take his hand, run my fingers along the ridges of it. And I pretend that I can say it. I pretend that I can whisper those three words into his ear, and that he will smile, because it's not the first time he's heard me say it, and he knows it won't be the last. I pretend that loving him doesn't make me feel guilty. I pretend that there isn't a voice in the back of my head saying that loving him means caring about two people, and that I swore Sophia would always come first. I pretend that the rules of survival I made up in my years at the Dorms don't still ring true, and that I can keep more than one person safe at a time.

I pretend that I live in a world where loving him and keeping her safe aren't mutually exclusive, where I can love them both and know that I'll have one thousand tomorrows to love them.

And at some point, pretending turns into dreaming, and I fall asleep with his steady heartbeat at my ear, his fingers running through my hair slowly. And I pretend that if I wanted to, I could stop loving him.

26

When I wake up, for a few moments I'm confused, blinking sleep from my eyes as I look around the small, empty room.

I look up as the door is pushed open slowly, and Kole walks in.

'Oh,' he whispers, as if I'm still asleep and he's trying not to wake me. He shakes his head. 'Hi.'

His gaze falls onto the cut beside my eye, and he crouches down in front of me to take a better look.

'We need to clean that,' he says. 'It might need stitches.'

'Ugh,' I groan, dropping my head back, but I can feel the pain searing along my face now that the adrenaline has worn off. 'Can't I just take a shower?' I ask. I'm desperate to shower, actually. I can still feel hands pinning me and knives against my skin, like a ghost of them is still lingering on me. I need to get it *off*.

Kole touches his fingertips against the end of the cut, the side closest to my eye, his touch featherlight against my skin. His face is screwed up in concentration as he examines it.

'If that gets infected, your eye will swell up and it'll scar,' he says. I sigh, and the sides of his mouth curl up in an almost smile. 'I just want to be sure.'

He disappears off for a few minutes after that, giving me time to change into grey slacks and a T-shirt that someone, probably Kerrin, left behind. When he gets back he drops a homemade first-aid kit on the floor and kneels beside it.

'Nails always hid a spare kit under the floorboards in the backroom,' he says. 'They must have forgotten it.'

There's a small towel and a basin of water with a chip out of the side, a bottle of water and a small box. He gestures for me sit beside him and I do, crossing my legs and picking up the water bottle. I'm so thirsty.

He wets the cloth as I screw off the lid of the bottle and take a long swig.

Then my lungs are on fire.

I fall forward, coughing, as it burns a trail from my mouth to my stomach, trying to heave in a breath around the burning.

And Kole is laughing.

'What the *hell* is that?' I splutter, shoving the cap on and thrusting it back into Kole's hands, who's still laughing as I try to breathe.

'Vodka,' he says, nodding at me like I'm an idiot.

'Alcohol?' I wheeze. He nods, but he still won't stop laughing, so I punch him in the shoulder.

'Good?' he asks.

I give him a dirty look and he just laughs harder, and if I wasn't so relieved to hear that laugh, I might actually be mad at him.

Eventually he settles down long enough to wring out the cloth and touch it against the corner of the wound. I grit my teeth, and his eyes find mine.

'Does that hurt?'

'No,' I grunt. Yes.

He smiles, pressing a little harder as he continues to clean it.

'Kole?'

'Yeah?'

'When you were Inside, with Johnson, what did you think about?'

'What do you mean?' he asks, his eyes too intent on cleaning the wound.

'When I was in the Colosseum, there were things I held on to. Things that I was so desperate to come back to, they kept me alive. I want to know what you held on to.'

He pours some of the alcohol onto the cloth and presses it against my cheek. I hiss, pulling away from it automatically, but Kole places his hand at the back of my neck to hold me in place.

His eyes are boring into my face and the cloth and the wound and anywhere anywhere anywhere that isn't my eyes. But his hand is warm, and it steadies me, and somehow I can't feel the pain of the alcohol anymore.

'At night,' he says quietly, 'I used to lock myself into my room, and just sit in the middle of the floor and try to remember every stupid thing that I could.' He pulls the cloth away from my face, dropping it back into the basin, and dresses the wound carefully, his fingers deft and light against my face. 'Like the sound of Jay's boots on the gravel. The way that Lacey used to sing before Rob died. Walter's stupid jokes, and the way Mark used to look at him with so much pride. The smell of soup.' He laughs at himself as his hand drops from my face and he begins packing away the first-aid supplies. 'I used to try to remember exactly what the soup smelled like. It felt monotonous at the time, but it smelled like heaven the second it was taken from me. Remember when I took you out into the forest before the attack?' he asks, standing up.

I nod, pushing myself up off the floor after him.

'You had this expression on your face, this fierceness. You told me Aaron spent years trying to convince you that you weren't as strong as you are, but the minute you were faced with a challenge, that expression was sharp as a whip. That's what I held onto.' He smiles down at his hands, as if he's making fun of himself. 'Soup and songs and fierce expressions. That's what got me through.'

I kiss him.

I can't help myself. There's a tightness in my chest, like the best kind of agony, and it only releases when I'm this close to him. He freezes for the shortest second before he responds, his hand coming up and cupping the good side of my face as he guides the kiss deeper.

It feels new and familiar all at once, and I realise that the only memory I had of him kissing me didn't do it any justice. The memory wore out as I replayed it over and over, and lost all of the most important details.

I forgot how fast my heart gets, how it beats through my chest like it's trying to get his attention. I forgot that everywhere his skin meets mine feels like it's being lit up, like it's being woken up.

I forgot that for a few seconds, when he's this close, I forget everything else.

Kole pulls away a fraction, looking directly at me as his palm brushes against the side of my face. He looks like he's going to say something, and whatever it is I want to hear it. I want to hear it more than anything, but before he has the chance he goes completely still, and I feel him tense.

'What?' I whisper. 'What's wrong?'

His eyes snap to the door behind us and I pull back, turning to see what he's looking at, but there's nothing there.

'Do you hear that?' he asks, and we both go still, holding our breath as we listen.

And I hear it then, like a faraway banging sound. It takes me a second to realise why that sound is familiar, until I lock eyes with Kole and we both figure it out at the same time.

'Someone's trying to get in,' I breathe, and fear thrills through me, dragging every nerve to attention.

Kole puts his finger against his lips to quiet me. He pulls his gun from where he stashed it in the corner and I follow him into the hall.

We crawl up the stairs at a maddening pace, but we can't give away that we're inside. When Kole makes it to the door he gestures for me to stand on the other side.

It won't give me more than a few seconds, but even then, I don't want it. I don't want him on that side and me on this side, but I can't argue with him now. It will just put us both in danger.

He holds his fingers to his lips again, reminding me to stay quiet as his eyes focus, resting the barrel of the gun against the frame and placing his hand on the doorknob.

Then he suddenly flings the door open, dropping his aim. A second later, two figures stumble through off the balcony, and then they're standing right here in Nails's upper room with us.

Clarke and Wilke.

27

'What are you doing here?' I ask, and it sounds like the words are punched from my gut.

Clarke looks as if she's been pulled apart at the seams and Wilke stands behind her, looking shellshocked.

He keeps glancing back at the door like he's afraid what's out there will follow him in here.

'Quincy,' she says, and her voice cracks. 'They took Jay.'

'What? *Who?* Who took him? Are they on to us?'

She shakes her head. 'They took him to the quarantine zone.'

'That's where our footage came from.' Wilke speaks up, sounding choked. 'No one gets out of there. It's where they're taking people to die.'

My heart stops. 'No.' The word is barely out of my mouth before I feel my throat closing up as terror claws at my chest.

Tears leap to her eyes, and that, more than anything, makes my stomach twist. I have never seen Clarke cry. Not once, in the whole time I've known her.

I glance over at Kole, and then at Wilke. He's not supposed to be here. He's supposed to be back in Genesis, back with Silas and Sophi and the rebels.

'What's going on?'

'Silas,' Wilke says. 'He's in Oasis.'

'*Why?* If he didn't come with us the first time, why would he—'

'He brought me here with him. He's set up a meeting with Johnson.'

'Why?' I ask, an unsteady feeling settling over my skin. 'What's going on?'

'Quincy, Silas was the one who released the disease.'

My heart thuds—

Once.

Twice.

Three times, and my breath shudders out of me.

'How?'

'I don't know,' he admits, and he looks helpless. 'He must have been planning this for months. I didn't know, I swear I didn't know.'

I blink, trying to comprehend what he's telling me.

'Why?' Kole asks, cutting into the conversation. He lays a hand on my shoulder, checking if I'm okay without looking at me. 'Why is he doing this?'

'I don't know the details, but he said that he had to do it. That there was no way we would ever defeat Oasis if we didn't weaken it. Now he's meeting with Johnson to discuss a treaty – the antidote in exchange for peace – but he's lying. He's going to kill Johnson.'

'He told you this?' Kole demands.

Wilke shakes his head. 'I overheard him. He brought a small team of us with him to Oasis. He said he needed me to cut off the power to the Towers while they were working on the treaty, so Johnson's men couldn't communicate. He said it was so he could ensure Johnson wouldn't turn on him, but he was lying.'

Wilke's getting more and more distraught the more he talks.

'What did he have you do, Wilke?' My voice is gentle, at odds with my pounding heart.

'I set it up, what he asked. So when they have their meeting, the power in Oasis will die for an hour. But it wasn't so they couldn't communicate. It was so the scanners wouldn't go off when they bring the bombs in.'

There's a deadly silence as everyone realises what that means.

Wilke looks at us with the wild stare of a condemned man. 'He's going to bomb the Founding Towers.'

28

'Silas is the one with the resources. He's the one who's been building this rebellion,' Wilke says.

We're back in the common room, and Kole and Wilke are arguing back and forth.

'But no one knows what he's been planning. And no one wants to walk from one dictatorship to another; they won't fight for him if they know what he's doing,' Kole points out.

'But how are we supposed to let them know? It's not like we can go knocking on doors. There are riots in the streets,' Clarke counters.

'No,' I say, shaking my head. 'We can't, but we can use the broadcasters.' Wilke's head snaps up. I look at him. 'Can you hack the broadcasts, Wilke? Can we get a message out through the screens?'

I can see the gears turning inside his head as he drags his bag off his shoulder and pulls a laptop from within it.

'If they haven't updated the mainframe since the last time I hacked the system, then it shouldn't take too long,' he says, sitting down on the floor and opening the computer.

'When was the last time you hacked the system?'

'Two, three weeks ago?' he says distractedly, his attention already being absorbed by the screen in front of him. 'When I get this set up, we're going to have to be quick about it though. I won't be able to hold the connection for more than one or two minutes. You better be ready with whatever you're going to say.'

'Whatever *I'm* going to say?' I shift uncomfortably on my knees beside Wilke. 'What about Kole? Why can't he do it?'

'Because they hate him,' Wilke says, glancing up at Kole, who is standing, arms crossed, by the door. 'He's a symbol for everything they hate. And he's been working directly against them over the past few days to *stop* the rebellion. They'll think it's a ruse.'

I grit my teeth. 'Fine.'

'All you need to tell them is the truth,' Kole says, appearing behind me. 'Tell them the truth and give them the power to take back their lives.'

'When the power dies, the gates will open,' Wilke says. 'So that the riots would flood into Oasis. It was part of Silas's plan anyway.'

'And now it's part of ours.' Kole nods, and I force myself to nod back at him.

Wilke turns the screen towards me.

'We're live in ten.'

'Seconds?' My voice is high-pitched.

He nods from behind the computer, the light flashing three times before the small camera on the laptop turns on.

I feel heat spreading outwards from my chest to the very tips of my fingers, and I dig my nails into my palms to focus myself as I stare straight into the lens.

'My name is Quincy Emerson,' I say, and my voice sounds stronger than it feels. 'I am a Dormant, an Oasis escapee and a rebel. Tonight, the Oasis President and the head of the infamous rebel alliance known as Genesis will be signing a treaty. In return for the antidote, Johnson has promised to grant them peace, as long as their rebellion ends now. But Silas, Genesis's leader, isn't planning on surrendering the rebellion. He was the one who released the disease, and he's the one who wants to take Oasis for himself. Tonight he's going to kill the

President and burn down the Founding Towers so he can gain power. He does this because he is under the illusion that the power lies in Oasis. President Johnson has governed Oasis thus far because he was under the illusion that the power lies in Oasis.

'That is a dangerous lie, and one that we have believed for too long. *We* are the ones with the power. Oasis relies on our fear to keep it safe. I say we stop protecting Oasis and start protecting our future.

'In one hour the power will be cut, and the gates will open. It's our last chance to reclaim Oasis for ourselves. I'd prefer to die trying to be free than live another day in this cage. One hour,' I say, one more time, and then the computer cuts out, and the camera light flashes off as my last word cuts off.

It's done.

29

'I hate this,' Clarke growls.

We're sitting in the common room and everyone is on edge. Clarke sits on the couch across from me, and she won't stop tapping her foot. Kole paces in the corner of the room with his head down, tension in every movement. I'm not much better, grinding my teeth as I try not to snap in frustration.

'There's nothing else we can do,' I tell her. 'We have to wait.'

'I hate waiting.'

'Well, what else are we supposed to do? If the power doesn't go out, the gates won't open. And if the gates don't open, we won't be able to get enough people inside to stand a chance against Oasis's forces.'

'It'll go out,' Wilke says, and it's the most sure he's sounded all night. 'I was the one who set it up. It'll go out.'

If the power does go out, Wilke will stay behind. Our best chance of deactivating the bombs is Wilke, since he thinks he can connect to them remotely. Deactivating them is a different story, but by the time that's an issue, we'll hopefully have the buildings evacuated.

Kole's pacing seems to be becoming more and more agitated, until I finally walk over to him, stopping his path.

'Are you okay?' I say quietly.

'There's just too much,' he says, shaking his head. 'There's too much that could go wrong.'

'We don't have any other option. This is our last chance. Our only chance.'

'I know that.' He chews his lip, his eyes unfocused as he watches the room around us. 'I just wish there was a way that I could stop it ending like this.'

'Like what?'

'In more blood. These people – they've spent their entire lives in fear and pain. And now we're asking them to start a war they shouldn't have to fight.'

'You'd be surprised by what people are willing to do when they're desperate,' I say. 'And we're not forcing them to do anything. If they do start this war, it will be for themselves. For a lot of them, it will be the first thing they've ever done to take back that control.'

He nods, once, solemnly, his eyes dark.

'One more stand,' I whisper. 'And then it ends. One way or another.'

Kole opens his mouth to say something, but before he has the chance, Wilke comes through the door, looking panicked.

'It's time,' he says. 'The power's been shut off.'

30

It begins, at once the slowest and fastest thing I've ever witnessed, and it feels too familiar. It feels like I've done this before, like watching myself fall in reverse. I have a gun and I have the heart in my chest and little else. The gates slide open as the power goes out across Oasis, and we march into our deaths, or the beginning of our lives.

When it starts, I can't tell which.

The streets are flooded with Outer Sector civilians. They've spent days rioting unsuccessfully, but when they're finally given a real chance to fight back, they're ready.

They don't know me. As we wade through the crowd towards the Sector Walls, I am not once recognised. I wade through a sea of people, and they are *my* people; as vicious and vengeful as they are, they are my mirrors. They reflect the pulsing thing in my chest, like power and will and the refusal to let this end without a victory. We demand it in the way we hold our shoulders and lock our jaws, demand it of this world that we've never asked anything of before.

But they're not alone. Kole is behind me as my eyes land on the Sector Gate, and I can feel my blood boil with the same rage that I feel in the air around me.

I'm ready. We're ready. The Gates scream open, loud as the screams around me, and it begins.

31

We are met by a thousand Officers. That's what it feels like when I'm pressed forward into a wall of blue-clad bodies, and maybe that's what it is. Uniformly blue and hard-faced, they're ready for us, and they start firing the second we storm through those gates.

'GET DOWN!' Kole yells in my ear, and I crouch low as the Dormants swarm the Officers, and people are falling and folding in on themselves, the sound of screams mixing with the sound of gunfire as I run left, away from the thick of the battle.

I take aim, release a shot at an Officer, watch her fall.

Focus! I scream in my head, as I take down one, two, three more Officers, watch time slow as an Outer Sector rebel is shot three times in the chest.

Kole grabs my arm, pulls me away from the fray and towards the cover of the first line of houses, Clarke close behind us.

The Dormants press forward and outward, attempting to wrap around the army of Officers in front of them, but the Officers are pushing back just as hard. I watch the Officers split the Dormants down the centre, but even then they don't back down. They keep pushing, forward and forward and forward, until they are shot down.

And they are shot down. Dozens of Dormants fall, but the Officers are falling just as fast.

Kole pushes me forward, knocking me back into reality. This was the plan. To get to the Celian City and find Silas before he has a chance to set off the bombs, but as I watch the rebels force themselves forwards, the first line of Oasis defence falling back as they are overtaken, I want to be *there*.

I know what I have to do, but leaving now feels like a betrayal, like weakness, like cowardice.

'Quincy,' Clarke growls. 'We have bigger things to worry about.'

I shake my head violently, catching a better grip of my gun. She's right.

We run through the streets of the Inner Sector, which are still coldly empty, but I can't help but notice twitching curtains as people look at us with terrified eyes. To them, we're the enemy. We're the thing they've been taught to fear. Because that's the only power Oasis ever had. The more it turned us against each other, the more power it had. Otherwise, it was just a wall, just a city, just a failed idea.

As we approach the Celian City, we slow down, every inch of my skin prickling with tension as we advance on the entrance. Officers line the City wall, and I know the second we see them that there's no chance that we'll be able to take them down.

Kole leads us away from the gates, looping back towards the Inner Sector. He slips down streets until we loop around to the other side of the wall, where we came through only hours ago. Kole motions for us to be quiet, and we skim along the side of the wall until we reach the gates.

He holds up three fingers.

Two fingers.

One, and we slip around the side. There are only four Officers stationed there, and Kole and Clarke have taken shots before I can even take aim. Kole kicks the guns away from their hands, their bodies splayed out in front of them.

We don't have time to think before we're running through the streets of the Celian City. We loop around the outskirts of the City, getting as far from the Officers lined up at the main entrance as we can before circling back, towards the Justice Tower.

We're almost at the underground drop-off before Kole sees them, positioned either side of the entrance. He pushes me left, out of shot, and Clarke takes out one before the other one disappears behind a wall.

'Stay down,' Kole growls in my ear, pressing me towards a warehouse.

Clarke moves clockwise around to the other side, gun propped against her shoulder as she disappears out of sight. A moment later I hear the pop of a gunshot, and my heart skips a beat.

I push out of my crouch and run towards the entrance, following Clarke. I try to steady my breathing when I see her, to keep moving ahead.

I can't get distracted.

Speeding up, we run through the tunnel connecting the Inner Sector to the Justice Tower. We turn left and run up the emergency staircase, the sound of our boots against the stairs pounding along with my heartbeat as we push through and into the empty Officers' Quarters.

Kole jabs the elevator button to get us out of the underground Officer station, but it doesn't respond.

'The power is out,' I remind him, pushing through the doors by the elevator that lead to the stairs.

Clarke is already running ahead of us, up the stairs and into the entrance room. This time, though, it's completely empty, as desolate as the Inner Sector. It's as if everyone just disappeared in the middle of their day.

'They're hiding,' Clarke says. 'Cowards.'

We run to the stairs, which are the opposite side from the elevator bank, and we follow Clarke up. Flight after flight after flight after flight. The steps move under my feet so fast that they begin to blend together, and as we reach the thirtieth floor, I can barely stop myself from tripping on every step.

Kole holds up a hand, and we all freeze in the staircase.

'They're coming,' he says. He glances around for a second, as if to orient himself. 'Go. I'll hold them back.'

'No.' I shake my head. 'Not on your own.'

'You did this for me before. Let me do it for you now.'

I can hear them coming up the stairs, at least six sets of boots, and my heart sinks.

'Okay. But don't die,' I say. 'Don't you dare die.'

He flashes a smile, and then pushes me away from him and up the stairs. Clarke grabs me by the arm, and we tear into a sprint.

I don't look back.

Ten floors higher up, I stop in the middle of a reception hall, my heart pounding painfully in my chest. I can hear a voice shouting, and I start kicking in doors.

The fifth door I kick in reveals Johnson and Silas, standing across from each other with guns raised.

Clarke moves faster than I do, and before I even have a chance to process what I'm seeing, Clarke is launching herself across the room at Johnson.

The next few seconds pass in snapshots. Clarke is in front of Johnson's face before he can turn on her, and she's twisting his gun from his hand, but he reacts too quickly, and he's caught her by the throat, ripped her gun from her fingers, pressed it to her temple.

She struggles against him, and he presses the gun into her harder.

'Stop moving,' he growls.

My gun is aimed at him, and so is Silas's, but he's using Clarke to shield himself, and he's backing into the corner.

'Just shoot him,' Clarke spits, and she means it. She doesn't care if she dies, as long as he does too.

'Shut up, Clarke.' I take another step into the room, and another. My eyes flit to Silas, only for a second, because I think he isn't the real threat here.

Until I see the look on his face.

'Silas. Don't move.'

His eyes don't leave Johnson, not for a second.

'It's been more than ten years,' he mutters, and I can't tell if he's talking to me or Johnson or himself. 'I've waited, and I've planned, and I've worked, and you're finally here. Right where I want you.'

'Silas, *I swear to God*—' My heart is beating a thousand miles an hour and I keep advancing, but I don't know who I should be aiming at. My gun moves between Johnson and Silas as Johnson's hold on Clarke tightens.

'Stop moving or I shoot her,' Johnson growls, and this is an entirely different side of him. This is the Officer side, the trained side. The killer side.

I stop dead, but Silas doesn't even flinch. It's like he can't hear us at all.

'Miss Emerson,' he says, recognising my existence for the first time since I stepped in the room. 'Sacrifices have to be made.'

The words aren't out of his mouth before I'm jumping towards him, and I can see the two paths diverge in my head, one where I wrestle the gun from his hands, and one where I'm too late, but the sound of gunshots is already ringing in my ears and Johnson falls to the ground—

And so does Clarke.

That's all I see. The falling and the folding all over again, and it's like it's going in slow motion except one second she was okay and the next there's blood.

'Clarke!' The scream is torn from me, and I'm in front of her and I don't know how I got here, but Johnson isn't moving and neither is she, other than the blood pouring from her chest.

I can't see where it's coming from. I can't see the wound because there's so much blood, because he just unloaded half a magazine into them and it's everywhere, the blood is everywhere.

'It's done.' Silas's voice sounds like relief behind me, and my gun is in my hand again and I'm swinging towards him.

'What did you do?' I roar, and anger and pain aren't even different things anymore, they're the same emotion and it's flowing out of me, it's become me, I'm overwhelmed by it.

'I did what had to be done.' He looks grave now, but it's fake. It's so fake. This is what all of this is to him, like dress-up.

I raise the gun to take aim at his head, and my hand is shaking so badly I can't aim, but I'll shoot him, I'll shoot him even if it takes me a thousand bullets.

'You won't kill me.' He sighs, too calm. 'You can't.'

'You murdered her.'

'She died for Genesis!'

'She died for your *greed*!'

'You know as well as I do that this has to end tonight. One life for thousands. I *saved* Oasis.'

'You didn't save anything. You're just like him. You're just like Johnson.' I'm babbling, heart racing, my vision struggling to stay in focus. 'You killed thousands of Pures just so you could weaken Oasis, just so you could take it for yourself! You're just like him!'

'I'm nothing like him!' he yells, and I can tell I've hit a nerve – I've cut it open. 'None of this would have been possible without me. *None of it.*'

'Shut up,' I growl, and my hands aren't shaking anymore. I walk towards him and I can see the fear in his eyes because he knows, he knows that I'm going to kill him. 'Shut up. *Shut up.*'

'There's a bomb,' he says, his eyes wide. There's something layered behind the fear in his eyes. Something bright and smug. Glee.

I stare at him. Say nothing.

'You think I wouldn't have a back-up plan? You think I wouldn't know it would come to this? You're an idiot,' he spits. 'I rigged the whole place to blow if I don't deactivate it within the next hour.'

'We know about the bombs,' I hiss. 'The buildings are being evacuated as we speak. In a couple of minutes it's just going to be you and me.'

He only stills for a moment before he starts laughing. 'You're bluffing,' he says. 'But it's not going to work.' He tries to move past me, as if I'll just let him go, as if I won't even attempt to stop him.

'Don't move,' I say, gripping my gun.

He looks at me impatiently. 'This isn't a game, Miss Emerson.'

'You're the one who doesn't understand that this isn't a game, Silas.' I move towards him, and he doesn't even blink. Just keeps watching me with those flat grey eyes. 'You're playing with people's lives.'

'I'm not *playing*. I'm doing what needs to be done. That's what leaders have to do.'

'Leader?' I laugh. 'Of what? Genesis? Oasis? What do you even want anymore? Do you really think that they'll accept you when they know what you've done?'

He shakes his head. 'They don't need to know. I sacrificed what was necessary to bring us forward. Into the future, Miss Emerson. And if you think that you or one of your rag-tag rebels would be able to do so in my place, you couldn't be more wrong. I'm the only one—'

'You're the one who kills innocents, who released a disease onto the Pures!'

'And I'm the one with the antidote. They'll be cured and we'll move forward.'

'Not with you,' I say, shaking my head, my voice trembling as I raise the gun higher, pointing at his forehead, holding it steady.

'You won't be able to live with yourself if you do this,' he says, and he's still too calm. He's still not afraid. 'I'm the only one who can fix Oasis. You know that, I know that. You make this mistake, and it'll haunt you for the rest of your life.'

'*Shut up.*' My heart is pounding so fast in my chest I can feel it in my fingertips, and my hands, steady only a moment ago, are trembling.

One moment he's perfectly still, and the next his hand shoots out, reaching for the gun.

And I pull.

The trigger.

Back.

It takes a split second. A decision forced and made and completed. A life there and then gone.

My heart is staccato. Beating and breaking and broken all at once, time, yet again, bending for pain. I fall to my knees beside his body, a silver gun and a pool of blood and an ink-black sky. He's frozen in surprise – eyes wide, mouth open. And I have to believe that I did the right thing. I did do the right thing.

Either way, it's over.

EPILOGUE

There are things in life you won't ever recover from. Sometimes that's the way it's supposed to be.

I pause for a second in the middle of a corridor, on my way to his room.

It's been four days since the gates between the Inner and Outer Sector were thrown open and the Founding Towers overtaken. Four days since I shot Silas.

Four days since Clarke died.

You'd think that that would be the end of it, somehow. I wonder when that naivety will end. When I'll stop imagining ways to fix the world in one fell swoop.

The first thing, once the adrenaline of victory subsided, was the disease. People were still dying, whether we had won against Oasis or not.

Silas wasn't lying, at least not about the antidote. After the bombs were deactivated and the Celian City overtaken, Genesis came out of the woodwork, antidote held like a peace flag. It was administered as quickly as a torn city can do anything.

The riots, as well, did not come and go without damage, and suddenly that damage fell onto our shoulders.

Oasis belongs to us now, and that means its wounds belong to us too.

Most of the Officers submitted to the change in power the moment word spread of Johnson's death. The rest were locked up along with the Genesis recruits who helped Silas orchestrate the release of the disease, awaiting their trial.

Now we're trying to return the city to calm and find what we need before we take what we want. Housing for families who've lived in squalor all their lives. Food for the hungry. Medical attention for the injured and sick. At the end of the day, we've turned hundreds of thousands of people's lives upside-down, and maybe that's for the good, but it's our responsibility now, and it wasn't before.

The wall will come down, later, when our resources aren't being pumped into keeping everyone alive until we regain our equilibrium. I still don't sleep, but it's for better reasons. I work eighteen-hour days. It's worth it.

I shake my head. The lack of sleep is making me prone to these moments, losing myself in hallways and on staircases, halfway between sleep and memory.

I push his door open. When I can't sleep, this is where I go.

He lies, propped up on pillows in a hospital room, tubes attached to his wrist and neck. He's asleep. I sit down in the chair beside him, taking his hand into mine. His fingers twitch, and he groans.

'Who's there?' He tries to sit up, but I push him gently back down.

'It's me, Jay. It's Quincy.'

'Oh,' he says, relaxing slightly. 'What time is it?' He sounds groggy from sleep.

'I don't know.' I laugh. It's ridiculous how often I've been saying that these days. 'Two in the morning? Three? I can't keep track.'

'Where are they? Where's Kole? Where's Clarke?'

My heart twists when he says that. It twists and twists and twists until I swear it'll stop beating entirely, but it doesn't.

Stubbornly, stubbornly, it keeps going.

He goes completely still, and then he sinks back into his cushions, remembering. He does this sometimes, when he's so drugged and tired that he can't tell reality from a dream, then from now.

'Why aren't you asleep?' he grunts after a few minutes.

'Because I'm not tired.'

'I am,' he says. 'I'm always tired. Whatever crap they're feeding me through these …' his other hand grasps across the sheets until he finds the tubes, '… I can't stay awake anymore.'

'You're awake now.' I try to smile, so he'll hear it in my voice, but it ends up sounding shaky with tears.

I wish I wasn't crying. I wish I didn't cry every time I came here.

He turns his head towards me, as if he can see through bandaged eyes. As if he could see at all, even if the bandages were gone.

'Yeah,' he says, 'cause you bloody woke me.'

I laugh then, a real, genuine laugh, and his smile comes back. Sly, but not quite the knife smile I'd got so used to.

'The kid back yet?' he asks, and I go quiet.

'No,' I whisper. I sent a team out to the bunker to bring back the rest of the Genesis recruits, Sophi included, but they're not back yet. I didn't go with them.

Jay sighs.

'They'll be back soon,' I say.

He snorts, but I can tell he's slipping back to sleep.

'What?'

'That's what you say every day,' he murmurs, and then he is really asleep again.

I stay with him for two more hours. There isn't anything better for me to be doing. I wander around his room, straightening things that don't need to be straightened, filling up the glass by his bed with more water.

I pick up the notes at the foot of his bed, flicking through them, though I already know what they say. The disease had already wreaked havoc on his body, and while the antidote killed it before it could kill him, it didn't fix it. Both eyes blinded and pure black, like giant irises. His internal organs were affected, but they hope to be able to mostly reverse the effects. Paralysed from the waist down.

Lucky to be alive.

Lucky to be alive.

I know Jay is lucky to be alive. I'm deliriously grateful that he is, but some part of my brain can't understand it, how arbitrary it is. The Infected lives and the Pure dies.

There, and then not.

I make my way out of the hospital, down the packed hallways, through the front door and out into the Inner Sector. I must have been there longer than I thought; the sky is beginning to turn the first pink of sunrise.

I'm still surprised when I go outside, how it looks so similar and so different at the same time. The damage in the Inner Sector is slowly being repaired, but it's not that that makes it different. It's something beneath that, something beneath the skin of Oasis that can never go back to the way it was.

We're different now than we were before that day, and that's not something we can change.

Clarke was buried yesterday, and I was the only one there. I stood above her as they lowered her body, and I wanted it to stop. It felt like a nightmare, and I wanted it to stop. I wanted to stop it so I could breathe, so I could figure out a way to fix it.

Her family weren't there when she was buried. No one she knew was there. No one but me, and it wasn't enough. The whole world should have fallen apart when she died, but it didn't. I did, but that wasn't enough either.

It takes me over an hour to make it all the way from Jay's hospital to the Outer Sector and then all the way to the Dorms. It's strange, to just walk through from one Sector to another, without any security. I guess they're not really sectors at all anymore.

I wander through the halls of the Dorms like a ghost. It's odd the way these walls feel around me now, after everything that has happened. Like they lost all their meaning and gained it back again, but in a different way.

During the riots there was a fire set in the cafeteria, so the entire room is gutted, but the rest of the building is structurally sound. It'll take a lot of work to make it a place that people will ever want to actually be in, but somehow I can't stop myself from wanting it, wanting this.

I'm coming down the stairs when I feel my heart stutter in my chest, tears springing to my eyes.

Sophi.

She stands in the middle of the room, turning in a slow circle as she takes in the building. My hand is over my mouth as I approach her, my heart pounding in my ears.

Thump.

Thump.

Thump.

'Hey,' I say, stopping right in front of her.

She turns to me, and her eyes widen. 'Quincy,' she murmurs, and she almost looks relieved. 'You're okay.'

I kneel down in front of her, and I keep hearing Clarke's words in my head, but I can't help the tears that spring to my eyes.

'*You're* okay.'

'I'm fine,' she says, shaking her head like she's trying to reassure me. 'I'm fine.'

My head shoots up when I feel a shadow falling across us, and I look up slowly.

Kole.

Sophi and Kole came straight here after they returned to Oasis, and they're exhausted. I want to bring them both to the closest medical centre, have them checked up, make sure they're okay. But for now I don't want either of them out of my sight, and we end up sitting on the floor of the Dorms.

There are blankets that I've stored here for the nights I end up spending here accidentally, and when Sophi begins to look sleepy, I get them for her so she can rest.

Kole says she barely slept the whole way from the bunker. She falls asleep almost immediately now, curled up against the wall.

She's not the only one who's returning to this place.

When I glance up from watching Sophi sleep, Kole is looking at me with a strange expression on his face.

'What?'

'What are you thinking about?' he deflects.

I glance around the room. It's empty and bare and after I removed every piece of furniture from the entire building, to anyone else's eyes, it would look desolate.

'It's just strange,' I say softly. 'Being back here after all this time.'

'How?' He knows how. He's been through this. Seen his house, seen the Celian City since the riots. He knows how everything looks different now, how Oasis stopped being Oasis the second the Towers were overtaken.

But he's pushing for something, looking for information of some kind. He pulls his knees up to his chest as he watches me intently.

'I thought when all of this was over, I'd want to leave,' I say, drawing shapes in the concrete dust on the ground. 'I thought I'd run as far as I could get, and I'd never come back. But now that it's actually over – I can't leave.'

'Why?' The light that's streaming in the window behind him catches the fine dust that swirls around the room, making it look like the air is sparkling as he watches me.

'I don't know why.' I look back down at the concrete floor so I don't have to meet his eyes.

'Are you sure about that?' he says. 'Cause I think you do know.'

'Yeah,' I whisper. 'Maybe I do.'

'And?'

'I've lived here since I was seven years old. I belong to this place, and I guess I want it to belong to me too. When I was a younger, it was awful. It was the most terrifying place I could imagine. And I wasn't the weak one. I wasn't the one who got picked on or beaten. I was strong. They were afraid of me, and I was afraid of them, and we were all afraid of ourselves.'

I glance up to see his reaction, but there isn't any. He's just watching me with those warm, dark eyes, like he's soaking up all the bad things so I don't have to carry them around anymore.

My exhale sounds like something falling.

'When I escaped Oasis, I had to leave the old me behind. I had to change, to become a different person, because the old me wouldn't have been able to leave. But when I came back – it was like *I* had left, but she's still here. The memory of that me, of that seven-year-old kid dumped in the middle of nowhere with no family and no friends and no idea what she has just been landed with, she got left behind. And I need to make it up to her.'

He presses his lips to my forehead, just above my eyes, and my breath is caught somewhere between my heart and my mouth as I draw him down to kiss me properly.

And he presses close to me, and I press closer. I press closer and closer and closer and I'm not sure if I'll ever get close enough. He pushes my hair back from my face, his fingers winding through my hair as he finds the spot at the back of my head, releasing the pressure.

'I don't think I know how to breathe anymore,' he says as he pulls away, and then laughs, and I want to pull the sound around me.

'I don't think I know how to do anything anymore.'

'Anything but this,' he says, and he kisses me again.

And this. This is the wonderful thing. This is the place between sunsets and sunrises, the place I'm not supposed to love as much as I do. I place my hands on his back, feeling the muscles contract and release as he presses his lips to mine, and he tastes dizzy and heady and fresh, like the hard bite of morning frost when you're not really awake and the world is everything around you all at once.

'I love you,' I say, between breaths. I say it because I have to. Because I can't not say it. Because not saying it has become more painful than the idea of him not saying it back.

But the thing about loving someone is that it's all the soft places. Love is the throat and the wrist and gut. It's the place where the knife can make the deepest cut. And being in love with someone is having a space between your ribs where the knife can get in. But telling someone you love them is showing them where that space is, pressing the knife in their hand to your side, and saying, *I trust you.*

And I do. I do and I do and I do infinitely.

Kole stares at me, he stares and stares and stares until I don't know if he'll ever say anything at all.

'I fell in love with you in that kitchen,' he whispers. 'With a chipped tea cup in my hands and a knife in my back pocket. That's when I fell in love with you.'

I press closer to him, and he tucks me under his arm. Another good, warm, safe thing in this place. I'll fill it with this, fill this cold building with these moments until it's overflowing. I'll fill the halls with laughter until the walls forget what screams sound like.

'So we rebuild the Dorms,' he says, as we stretch this moment out into infinity. He smiles around the desolate room. He can already see it like I see it, in the future, where it looks like something beautiful. 'And then what?'

'Then,' I whisper, and I kiss him, because I can, until it breaks off with a smile. 'Then we rebuild the world.'